'I am afraid I may have damaged your reputation, Miss Wythenshawe,' Mr Blackwood said bluntly.

'Because you kissed me?'

He squeezed her fingers. 'Just being alone here with me is enough to compromise you.'

'I am not known here, sir. Neither are you. Who are they likely to tell?'

'A few judicious coins in the right hands might secure the silence of anyone at this inn. Are you willing to trust that no one will find out about our being here together?'

She gave him a little smile. 'What is the alternative, Mr Blackwood?'

He shrugged.

'That we marry, I suppose.'

AUTHOR NOTE

I live in the north of England, high on the Pennines, in an area of outstanding natural beauty. When I am out walking it is not uncommon to come across huge stone blocks tumbled amongst the trees in the bottom of some remote wooded valley—the remains of an early spinning mill. These mills were built more than two hundred years ago, when the industrial revolution was just beginning and water was needed to power the new machines used to spin wool, linen and cotton.

Inventions like the spinning mule and Arkwright's water frame meant that people could spin better, faster, and produce more yarn than ever before to supply a growing market. The entrepreneurs who built and managed the mills were adventurers, working at the forefront of technology—and the innovations were as startling and exciting as anything to come out of Silicon Valley.

These new industrialists were hailed as heroes, adventurers, and I have long wanted to write about them. Daniel Blackwood is my first hero from this new breed of tough, resourceful industrialists. London Society of the 1780s doesn't quite know what to make of this fiercely independent self-made man—and neither does my heroine, Kitty. I had great fun putting these two together and creating the battle of wills that ensued before they realised they were made for one another—I hope you enjoy their journey.

Kitty and Daniel's story led me to some of the darker aspects of late-eighteenth-century society. The Abolition movement was gaining pace, with Anti-Slavery Societies being set up around the United Kingdom. There was certainly one in Sheffield at the time of my book, and 8,000 people signed a petition from the people of Sheffield to Parliament in 1793, calling for an end to the Slave Trade. However, to the best of my knowledge there was never a West Riding Anti-Slavery Society—an invention of my own for the purposes of the plot.

This was also an age when children were often exploited, but some mill owners were against this—for example Robert Owen, who built the New Lanark Mills in Scotland, introduced the revolutionary idea that children should not be allowed to work in the mills before the age of ten. For the sake of historical accuracy I could not remove children altogether from Daniel's mills, but as a forward-thinking employer he does have schools and nursery buildings for the children of his workers and the apprentices.

Kitty and Daniel are a forward-thinking couple, and have very liberal views, but they are based on real characters—people who really did strive to improve the lot of the factory workers, and who fought for the abolition of the slave trade even though it was a risk to their own livelihood. The real heroes of the time.

TO CATCH A HUSBAND...

Sarah Mallory

First published in Great Britain 2011
by Mills & Boon, an imprint of Harlequin (UK) Limited,
Eton House, 18-24 Paradise Road, Richmond, Surrey TW9 1SR

© Sarah Mallory 2011

ISBN: 978 0 263 21829 9

Harlequin (UK) policy is to use papers that are natural, renewable and recyclable products and made from wood grown in sustainable forests. The logging and manufacturing process conform to the legal environmental regulations of the country of origin.

Printed and bound in Great Britain
by CPI Antony Rowe, Chippenham, Wiltshire

Sarah Mallory was born in Bristol, and now lives in an old farmhouse on the edge of the Pennines with her husband and family. She left grammar school at sixteen, to work in companies as varied as stockbrokers, marine engineers, insurance brokers, biscuit manufacturers and even a quarrying company. Her first book was published shortly after the birth of her daughter. She has published more than a dozen books under the pen-name of Melinda Hammond, winning the Reviewers' Choice Award in 2005 from Singletitles.com for *Dance for a Diamond* and the Historical Novel Society's Editors' Choice in November 2006 for *Gentlemen in Question*.

Previous novels by the same author:

THE WICKED BARON
MORE THAN A GOVERNESS
  (part of *On Mothering Sunday*)
WICKED CAPTAIN, WAYWARD WIFE
THE EARL'S RUNAWAY BRIDE
DISGRACE AND DESIRE

To Doris Sweet

Chapter One

'I am off to London, to seek my fortune!'

Kitty Wythenshawe glanced up hopefully at the young farm-hand driving the gig. He did not look overly impressed with her announcement, but perhaps that was because he had known her for years and had always thought of her as the seamstress's daughter—which, of course, she was—but now she was off to stay with her godmother. And her godmother was *A Lady!* Lady Leaconham, to be exact.

'Well, Joshua?' she demanded. 'Are you not pleased for me?'

The lad moved the straw he was chewing from one side of his mouth to the other.

'Nowt to do wi' me.'

Kitty sighed but did not allow her companion's indifference to damp her spirits. The overnight rain had given way to a beautiful spring morning, the sun had driven off the early mist from the moors and she could see the lapwings circling lazily over a distant field. It was as if Nature itself was smiling upon her adventure. Kitty glanced down at her olive-green walking dress with the yellow leaf motif embroidered down the front and around the hem. Mama and Aunt Jane had worked so hard for this occasion. She had never before had so many new clothes at one time.

'Dunno what tha wants wi' goin' t' Lunnon,' remarked Joshua, suddenly becoming loquacious.

'I have to find a husband,' said Kitty, clasping her hands together in a sudden moment of anxiety. If only she could marry well then she could provide for Aunt Jane and Mama. They were both widows, eking out their meagre savings with a little dressmaking. Their home was a little cramped, to be sure, but Kitty had grown used to that. However, she was painfully aware that Mama and Aunt Jane were growing older and the cold, damp cottage was not so comfortable in winter, when the water would seep up through the earth floor and Mama's joints would become stiff and painful, and Aunt Jane's cough always became much worse. They were the daughters of a gentleman and this was not what they had been born to. Kitty knew it was her duty to improve their fortunes and if she had to sacrifice herself at the Matrimonial Altar then she would do it—not that it seemed to Kitty much of a sacrifice to marry a rich man: it was all very well to read novels where the heroine gave up everything to follow her heart, but Mama had married for love and Kitty did not think that she was particularly happy, living in such straitened circumstances. Indeed, had she and Aunt Jane not scrimped and saved every spare penny to give Kitty this one chance to go to London expressly for the purpose of achieving a good marriage?

Letitia Leaconham had been a close childhood friend of Mama's and had gone on to make a brilliant marriage, while Mama had defied her family and married Walter Wythenshawe for love. He had been in possession of a moderate income, but he had not prospered, and as Mama was wont to point out at times of stress, strict principles and enlightened views were all very well but they do not pay the bills. Upon Papa's death there had been any number of accounts to be settled and so it had come to pass that Kitty and her mama had moved into the tiny cottage in Fallridge with Aunt Jane, the widow of an impecunious curate. Since then Mama had spent every penny she could spare upon Kitty's education in the belief that if only she could be launched into Society she would make a good marriage. After all, her birth was impeccable, even if she had no dowry. As Aunt Jane said, Kitty was their *Last Hope;* if she could only find a rich husband then they could all be comfortable.

'I'd marry thee.'

This utterance put an end to Kitty's ponderings.

'I beg your pardon?'

'I said I'd marry thee,' repeated Joshua. 'If tha needs a man.'

'Oh, Joshua, that is very kind of you!' Kitty put a hand on his rough sleeve. 'Indeed it is very generous, but you see, if I am to support Mama and Aunt Jane, that they may live out their years comfortably and without more suffering, I need to marry someone… someone…'

'A lord,' said Joshua, spitting out his straw. 'Some 'un richer nor me. Aye, well, me mam's set her heart on my marrying Lizzie Greenwood, since she will inherit the farm from her faither, so I suppose it wouldn't do fer me to be marryin' a lass with nowt to 'er name.'

For a few moments Kitty's sunny mood clouded: it was very lowering to think even Joshua considered her a poor prospect for marriage. Her spirits soon recovered, however. She was a gentlewoman by birth, and as Papa had always told her, it was a person's actions that were important. So Kitty pulled herself up and said graciously, 'No, but thank you for the offer. And it is very good of you to drive me to Halifax, and so kind of your father to let us use the gig. I am to meet with Mr and Mrs Midgley at the Crown. You may not know them; Mr Midgley is a cloth merchant, which is how Mama became acquainted with the family, for she often buys cloth from him. They are taking their samples to London, you see, and have agreed to take me with them, which was very fortunate, because otherwise Mama would have been obliged to send me on the stage and hire a maid to go with me. So you see everything has worked out very well.'

She ended on a cheerful note with a sunny smile for Joshua but he was not attending. He was staring ahead of him and frowning.

'Well?' said Kitty. 'What is it?'

Joshua scratched his head.

'I ain't right sure which road we wants.'

Kitty followed his stare. They were dropping down from the hills and she could see the junction in the distance, a large, open space where several highways converged.

'The road to Halifax will be the main route,' suggested Kitty, but even as she said it she realised that this did not help. All the roads leading away from them were in good order and wide enough for two carts to pass.

'Da said to keep goin' downhill 'til we get to Halifax.'

'That is all very well,' retorted Kitty, beginning to lose patience, 'but there are at least three of those roads leading downhill. Think, Joshua. Can you not remember which one you take?'

'Ah, well, I've never bin this road afore,' he confessed. 'Uncle Jed allus makes this run.'

Kitty closed her lips to prevent herself making a hasty exclamation. It would help no one and might upset her companion, who, after all, was going to considerable trouble for her. As they descended to the crossroads she spotted a large black horse standing at the side of the lane. At first she thought the animal unattended, but as they approached a man stepped into view. His serviceable buckskins and brown riding jacket were liberally spattered with mud and he was hatless, his black hair unconfined and hanging wild and disordered to his shoulders. He did not look around as they approached, but was concentrating upon securing the straps of his saddle.

'That fellow might know which is the correct road,' said Kitty. 'You should ask him.'

Joshua looked at the bedraggled stranger and pulled a face. 'Nay. No need for that.'

'To be sure he looks very rough, but he might know the way.'

'Tha can't be certain o' that.'

'Well, it would do no harm to ask,' said Kitty, trying to hide her impatience.

Joshua ignored her. When she realised that he had no intention of asking for directions she decided she would have to act. As they drew abreast of the man she leaned over the side of the gig and called out to him.

'I say, my man—yes, you: which one of these roads leads to Halifax?'

She was not used to accosting strangers, and a mixture of nerves and irritation at her companion's stubbornness made her tone much sharper than usual. The man turned slowly and looked up at her from beneath heavy dark brows. Kitty found herself facing the blackest, fiercest stare she had ever encountered.

It was as much as Kitty could do not to recoil from the stranger's angry glare. With some alarm she realised that Joshua no longer intended to drive past. He brought the gig to a halt and the man walked over to stand before them, looking very much as if he would drag her from the gig at any moment. Swallowing hard, she sat up straight, determined not to show fear. She said haughtily, 'Did you understand me, fellow?'

Those piercing black eyes held hers for a moment, then they swept over her, from the crown of her bergère bonnet down to the nankeen half-boots peeping out from under the hem of her walking dress. Kitty had the unsettling feeling that he could see right through her clothing to the flesh beneath. She felt thoroughly exposed and her cheeks flamed. She snapped her head up and stared straight ahead.

'Drive on, Joshua.'

The stranger's long arm shot out and one big hand caught the pony's bridle.

'Nay,' he said in a slow, deep drawl. 'First tha needs to know t'road.'

Kitty shot a furious look at him.

'Then perhaps you would be good enough to tell us!'

'I'll tell thee nowt afore I hears a civil word from yer ladyship.'

Joshua shifted uncomfortably beside her. Kitty wondered that he did not stand up to the stranger, but a moment's consideration told her that her companion, a stocky youth of sixteen, was no match for the tall, broad-shouldered stranger some ten years his senior. The man stood at their pony's head, one hand gripping the leather cheek-piece while the other stroked the animal's neck with slow, reassuring movements. The pony, traitor that he was, turned his head and rubbed against the stranger's arm.

Kitty realised that, however angry the man might be with her, he was in control of himself and the situation. They could not move on until he allowed it.

She ran her tongue over her dry lips.

'I beg your pardon,' she said politely. 'Pray be good enough to direct us to the Halifax road.'

Silence.

It dragged on for a full minute. Kitty gave the stranger a challenging look but he did not move, merely stared back at her with his unfathomable black gaze. He looked as hard and immobile as the rocky granite outcrops that littered the moors.

Joshua rubbed his nose. A bullock cart lumbered up to the junction and turned along one of the lanes but still the stranger held Kitty's eyes. Then, just when she was wondering if Joshua would dare to use the shotgun that she knew lay beneath the seat, the man stepped back.

'That's thy road.' He pointed to the lane where the bullock cart was disappearing around a bend. 'Just follow yon wagon t'bottom of t'hill.'

With a slight nod of acknowledgement Joshua flicked the reins and they began to move.

'Thank you.'

Kitty felt obliged to utter the words as they drove away, but she kept her eyes fixed on the road ahead. From the tail of her eye she saw the man tug his forelock but there was nothing subservient about the gesture and she could not shake the horrible conviction that he was enjoying her discomfiture.

* * *

Daniel Blackwood watched the gig pull away, a deep crease in his brows. He was in the worst possible humour but he should not have taken it out on that young couple. He had been travelling since yesterday afternoon, his horse was lame and he had been obliged to spend the night on the moors. He was in a devil's own temper and it had not been improved by being addressed by an arrogant chit as if he was a lackey!

He had seen the gig approaching, but knowing the young couple could do nothing to help him he had ignored it, only to be summoned like a servant to give directions. True, the girl was young and pretty, but he was in no mood to appreciate the heart-shaped face, the large green eyes fringed with dark lashes or the dusky curls that escaped from beneath her wide-brimmed straw bonnet. He watched the gig rolling away down the hill, the little figure in her green robe and yellow bonnet sitting rigidly upright beside the boy who was driving. Probably some farmer's daughter trying to impress her swain by acting the great lady. Well, she had chosen the wrong man to try out her airs and graces!

With an angry snort he bent to pick up his greatcoat and hat from the grass verge and gathered up the reins of his horse.

'Come up, Marnie. I'll walk you to the inn and Fletcher can keep you there until you're fit to come home.'

Kitty arrived at the Crown and was informed by the landlord that she was expected: Mr and Mrs Midgley were waiting for her in the coffee room. Kitty nodded and he directed one of his servants to carry her trunk across to the travelling carriage standing in the middle of the yard. Before stepping into the inn she turned to say goodbye to Joshua, thanking him for his trouble and pressing into his hand a sixpence which he was somewhat embarrassed to take, but she insisted. She watched him drive away in the gig, a tiny pang of homesickness mingling with the excited anticipation she felt for the journey ahead of her.

Mr and Mrs Midgley greeted her with unfeigned delight, declaring that she had not kept them waiting at all, and begging her to sit down and join them for breakfast before they set off.

'For if I am not mistaken,' said Mr Midgley, twinkling at her, 'you were up before dawn, miss, and too excited to take a bite to eat.'

'Very true,' laughed Kitty, removing her bonnet and shaking out her dark curls. 'If you are sure we have time?'

'All the time in the world, my dear,' replied Mr Midgley. 'We travel to London in easy stages. I don't mean to press the horses, for we shan't be changing them again for some while, unlike the mailcoach.'

'Nor will we be careering along at such a breakneck speed,' added Mrs Midgley, chuckling. 'So come along, my dear, sit by me and you can tell me how your dear mother does.'

Kitty readily complied. She was not well acquainted with her hosts but their warmth and kindness soon broke down any reserve and she found herself chattering away quite naturally while they breakfasted upon freshly baked bread rolls and scalding coffee.

'So you arrived in style, Miss Wythenshawe,' remarked Mrs Midgley, when they had finished their meal and Mr Midgley went off to check if their carriage was ready. 'You say the farmer's boy drove you in his gig? I have no doubt your mama was very pleased you were not obliged to travel here with the poultry for market!'

'If I had done so then my driver might have known the way,' replied Kitty with a sigh.

She decided not to recount the incident at the crossroads. The man had been odiously rude and not a little frightening, but Kitty was aware that her own conduct was not what it ought to have been. If she had not spoken in such a proud, disdainful way perhaps the whole unpleasant incident might not have occurred. She deeply regretted her own conduct but it was too late to apologise. She would learn from it and do her best to make sure she did not act in such an ill-mannered fashion again.

She gave Mrs Midgley a bright smile. 'But I am here now, and very much looking forward to our journey.'

'Bless you, my dear, then we shall be off directly,' declared Mr Midgley, coming in at that moment. 'If you would care to don your bonnets and cloaks, ladies, the berline is ready and we can be on our way! Oh, and we have a passenger for the first part of the journey: I'll just go and hurry him along.'

With that he was gone, leaving his wife to tut and direct a rueful glance at Kitty as they gathered up their belongings and headed out to the yard.

While they had been breaking their fast the clouds had gathered and now it was raining steadily, a fine, soaking drizzle. The ladies hurried across to the waiting carriage and made themselves comfortable on the forward-facing seat while they waited for Mr Midgley. He soon appeared at the door, standing back and addressing someone beyond her view.

'Get in, my boy, get in. You will find Mrs Midgley inside, and our young guest Miss Wythenshawe. This is Mr Blackwood, my love,' he called in through the open door. 'His mare is lame, so I said we would take him up as far as Hestonroyd.'

A large figure in a greatcoat and wide-brimmed hat filled the doorway, his shadow momentarily darkening the interior of the carriage, but as he sat down opposite her, Kitty bit back a gasp of dismay. It was the boorish stranger from the crossroads! He had washed his face and hands and tied back his hair, but there was no mistaking that strong jaw shadowed with its dark stubble or the coal-black eyes that now rested upon her with a look of cool disdain. Embarrassed, Kitty looked down and nervously twitched her skirts out of the way. He had such long legs that she was obliged to keep her feet tucked in to avoid dirtying her hem on his muddy boots. She knew her walking dress would not remain clean for very long, but it was new and she was determined to take care of it. She fully appreciated all the hard work Mama and Aunt Jane had put in, making all the gowns and clothes for her stay in London. She had helped, of course, but Mama had worked long into each evening, sewing by lamplight until her eyes were red and sore with strain.

'There, now, we are off at last!' declared Mr Midgley as he climbed into the carriage and they began to move. 'What a merry party we shall be.' He turned to his wife. 'Blackwood here lives at the Holme and—'

Daniel was quick to interrupt him, saying in a very broad accent, 'Nay, sir, I don't think the ladies is fetched to know about me.' He glanced at the young woman sitting opposite and added, 'They'd be more interested in frills and furbelows.'

Mrs Midgley chuckled.

'You are far too modest, Mr Blackwood. I take it you are Samuel Blackwood's son?'

'Aye, ma'am.' Daniel kept his response brief: if they knew his father they might well wonder why his son spoke in such an uneducated manner!

'We are well acquainted with your parents,' Mrs Midgley went on. 'If we had time I would suggest we call upon them when we drop you off, but Mr Midgley is determined to reach Market Harborough tonight, so we must not tarry. Do, pray, remember me to your mama.'

Dan nodded silently in response and earned a disapproving frown from Miss Wythenshawe. He returned her look with a cool one of his own and had the satisfaction of seeing her blush. As well she might, given her own behaviour towards him that morning.

He wondered if he should have hired a horse after all, but by the time he had walked Marnie to the inn the rain had set in and Mr Midgley had been most insistent. Daniel had seen the cheerful-looking gentleman with his full wig and bushy side-whiskers sheltering under the arch leading to the stableyard and he had nodded as he passed him. The man touched his hat.

'By Gad, sir, you look as if you have been through the wars!'

Daniel stopped. He looked down at his muddy clothes and gave a wry grin.

'My horse took a tumble yesterday evening and I landed in the dirt. I was unhurt but my mount was lamed, so I was obliged to spend the night on the moors.'

'And in the rain, too.' The gentleman shook his head.

Daniel shrugged.

'A little damp won't hurt me. I am even now going to find our host and hire a horse to take me back to Hestonroyd.'

The man looked up, his little bright eyes gleaming.

'Oh? Not the Holme, by any chance? Samuel Blackwood's place?'

'Why, yes, sir. I am his son.'

The gentleman gave a hearty laugh.

'Well met then, Mr Blackwood! My name is Midgley. I have known your father for many a year—a good man, and an honest businessman, too!'

'Indeed.' Daniel nodded. 'I will give him your regards, sir. Now, if you will excuse me, I must see if Fletcher can find me a horse...'

'No need, sir, no need,' cried Mr Midgley. 'I am going your way—that is my berline over there. We shall be setting off shortly—we have many miles to cover today!—but I should be delighted to take you up.'

'Indeed, sir, I would not wish to put you out...'

'Not at all, my boy, not at all. You do not want to be riding in this weather. And besides, we shall be driving through Hestonroyd and can drop you at the very gates of the Holme. Now, there is plenty of room in my carriage for another body, so let me hear no more arguments!'

Daniel hesitated, but only for a moment. His greatcoat was still wet and the idea of getting another soaking was not a tempting prospect, so he accepted Mr Midgley's offer. Now, looking across at Miss Wythenshawe's haughty profile, he thought that if he had known she was one of the party, he would have preferred to walk back to Hestonroyd in the rain rather than sit in a closed carriage with such a disagreeable wench.

Kitty stared resolutely out of the window. Heavens, she had thought Joshua taciturn, but this man had no conversation at all, except to be uncivil. Her conscience suggested that this might be her own fault. The thought made her uncomfortable, but she could not bring herself to utter an apology before Mr and Mrs Midgley: if she did that she would also be obliged to give them an explanation. She decided to put the matter from her mind and concentrate on the passing countryside.

The view could not fail to excite her. She had never been so far abroad before and as they travelled on, the harsh grandeur of the moors was left behind for a softer, greener landscape. Orderly fields stretched away on either side towards rolling, wooded hillsides. She was only a few hours from home and already everything looked strange: how much more diverting would it be in London? Mr Midgley said it would take two full days' travelling to reach the capital. A little tremor ran through her: how would she go on? She had never even been to school!

There had never been any money to send her to one of the select academies that taught young ladies how to behave. Not that her education had been lacking. Mama and Aunt Jane had seen to that. When Papa had died they had been obliged to release her governess but Mama and Aunt Jane had continued her lessons, which she had augmented by extensive reading of the books kept from her father's well-stocked library. Most had been sold to pay his debts but those suitable for a young lady's education had been retained—as well as less improving works. Mama might not wholly approve of novels, but she and Aunt Jane enjoyed listening to Kitty reading from the works of Mr Fielding or Mr Richardson while they sewed. They had managed to keep the little pianoforte for her to practise upon but there had been no money for a dancing master, so Kitty had joined the Squire's daughters for dancing lessons, repaying this kindness by helping their harassed governess with their schooling. Mama had been at great pains to teach her to be a lady. There had been extensive descriptions of life in a big house, lessons on how to address the various ranks of nobility and how to prepare tea, but Kitty suspected it would be very different practising all she had learned in London rather than in the tiny cottage in Fallridge.

She clasped her hands together. Mama had never taught her how to deal with rough, wild-looking gentlemen like the one now sitting opposite her. The only men she had met before had either been the young boys of the village or fatherly types like the Squire or Mr Midgley. In all her nineteen years she had never met anyone who had made her feel so ill at ease. She stole a glance across the carriage at Daniel Blackwood. He had removed his hat and was leaning back against the leather squabs, his eyes closed, his head moving gently with the swaying motion of the carriage. If, as Mr Midgley said, he had been travelling all night that would explain his wild, unkempt appearance. But it was clear that he did not favour a powdered wig, for he wore his own dark hair tied back at the nape of his neck and that, together with his heavy dark brows and straight nose, gave him a rather hawkish appearance. With his greatcoat hanging open she could see the broad width of his chest straining beneath his brown riding jacket and the outline of his muscled thighs encased within the buckskin breeches. He exuded strength and power. She thought back to their first meeting on the edge of the moors above Halifax: that, she realised, was the perfect setting for such a wild, vigorous creature. He was not a man to be crossed, but it occurred to her that he would be a good man to have as a friend.

At that moment Mr Blackwood opened his eyes and Kitty found herself once more staring into their coal-black depths. She had the oddest feeling that he was looking into her very soul and reading her thoughts. Blushing, she forced herself to turn away. She fixed her gaze on the window again. Really, the man was insufferable. She hoped they would be reaching Hestonroyd very soon, so that they would be free of his unsettling presence.

The carriage lurched and bumped as their route wound down through a steep wooded valley. The rain had stopped, but the leaves and the ground glistened in the watery sunlight, while tumbling streams ran down the hillside, creating frothy waterfalls between the trees. The carriage slowed and came to a stand. Mr Midgley let down the window and put out his head to direct an enquiry to his coachman. Kitty could not hear the man's reply, but it caused his master to climb out of the carriage, closely followed by Mr Blackwood. Kitty leaned across to look out of the open doorway. They had reached the valley bottom where a new cobbled road had been laid to take vehicles through the ford. Now, however, the stream was swollen by the recent rains and it rushed and tumbled across their path. Mr Midgley came back to speak to them.

'Roberts doesn't want to drive across the ford with you ladies inside,' he told them. 'He is afraid of what might happen to you if the carriage should be overturned by the fast-flowing waters. You can see that it would not be unprecedented.' He nodded towards the far bank of the stream, where the remains of a farm cart protruded from the water. 'Roberts thinks it would be safer for us to use the bridge yonder.'

He pointed upstream, where an ancient stone bridge arched across the waters. It was wide enough for a single horse, but it was clear that it would not accommodate a carriage.

'Is it quite safe?' enquired Mrs Midgley, eyeing the bridge with some misgiving.

'Oh, aye, ma'am, the bridge is sound enough,' said the coachman cheerfully. 'It's not much used now we have the new road, but the pack-horses still cross by it.'

Kitty gave a little shrug. 'And so must we, it seems. Let us go to it.'

She followed Mrs Midgley out of the carriage and the party stood and watched as the coachman slowly drove across the ford. The water surged between the horses' legs and frothed around the wheels of the carriage, splashing up over the coach body and making it sway alarmingly, but at last the berline was drawn up safely out of the water on the far side.

'Excellent,' declared Mr Midgley, 'Well done, Roberts.' He held his hand out to his wife. 'Come along then, ladies. It is our turn!'

He set off towards the little bridge. The track was wet and over-grown and the ladies were obliged to hold up their skirts to keep them out of the mud. Kitty did her best to ignore Daniel Blackwood, who fell into step beside her but did not offer her his arm. The bridge was soon reached and they paused for a moment on the apex to gaze over the low parapet at the turgid water.

'I should not like to fall in there today,' remarked Mrs Midgley. 'The rains have swollen the stream so much it is in danger of over-flowing its banks.'

'It has certainly flooded on this side,' said her husband, who had walked to the edge of the bridge and was prodding the grass with his cane. 'The ground is sodden here.'

Mrs Midgley followed her husband to where the cobbles of the bridge ended and the grassy track began.

'Well, we have to get across,' she said prosaically.

She laid her hand on her husband's arm and put one foot on the track. Immediately she sank ankle-deep into the mud.

'Oh, good heavens!' cried Mrs Midgley, picking up her skirts and stepping quickly back on to the cobbles. 'The ground is a quag-mire. We cannot walk on that!'

'I am afraid we have no choice, my dear,' cried her spouse.

They watched as he strode purposefully forwards to the carriage, his feet sinking into the ground until the mud came halfway up his top-boots. When he finally reached the road he turned and looked back rather helplessly.

'Well, what else are we to do, my love? The carriage is on this side now, so we must cross somehow.'

Daniel Blackwood stepped forward.

'Allow me, mistress.' In one easy movement he scooped Mrs Midgley into his arms and carried her across the muddy stretch, setting her gently on her feet beside her husband, where she stood, a little red-cheeked and flustered by such cavalier treatment.

'Oh, well done, my boy!' cried Mr Midgley, clapping his hands. 'Now if you will do the same by Miss Wythenshawe we will be on our way.'

Kitty's throat tightened in alarm. That big brute of a man was bearing down upon her, a look of unholy enjoyment in his eyes. She looked at the mud and wondered if she dared run through it, but the thought of ruining her new half-boots and very likely muddying both her walking dress and her petticoats was too horrific to bear. Her dark tormentor stood before her, grinning.

'Well, Miss Wythenshawe, if tha's ready?'

She bit her lip and nodded. The sensation of being swept off her feet left Kitty feeling giddy and very helpless. She was held tightly against the man's chest, her face only inches from his jaw, so close that she could see the black stubble on his cheek and smell the damp wool of his greatcoat. As he turned his feet slipped a little on the cobbles and her hands flew up around his neck. His arms tightened even more. He held her firmly but he was not crushing her, yet for some reason she found it difficult to breathe. Her heart was pounding erratically, thudding against her ribs as if trying to escape her body. She had a sudden and inexplicable desire to lean her head against the man's shoulder. She had to admit it looked very inviting, and reassuringly wide. She realised that this was a situation she had dreamed of, a chivalrous knight coming to the rescue of a beautiful maiden. Only in her dreams her hero was a fair, handsome young knight, one deserving of his reward, not a big, brutish oaf with no manners. She peeped up at the strong, rather hawkish face of her rescuer, noting the long black lashes around his eyes, his straight nose and the smooth curve of his lips. Suddenly, surprisingly, Kitty found herself wondering what it would be like to kiss him.

He glanced down at that moment and she found herself staring into those dark eyes, unable to look away. For one alarming moment she thought he had read her mind and that he would actually kiss her. She was in his arms and completely at his mercy. Her heart raced. A moment's heady excitement was followed quickly by panic. To cover her confusion she said crossly, 'Pray do not hold me so tightly. You are crushing my dress.'

He chuckled.

His amusement only served to increase her discomfiture. She said angrily, 'I vow I cannot breathe! Loosen your hold, you oaf!'

The black brows snapped together and a dangerous gleam flared in his eyes. He released his grip on her legs and she gave a little cry as her feet touched the sodden ground.

'Ee, lass, seems I lost my grip on thee.' Her tormentor still had an arm around her shoulders, hugging her to him. She managed to free one hand and brought it up to his grinning face with a slap.

'How dare you do that to a lady?'

He looked down at her, his eyes narrowing. Then, very deliberately, he let her go. She gave a shriek, her arms tightening around his neck as she tried to lift her feet from the mud. Calmly he reached up and pulled her hands away and she was obliged to stand, the cold muddy water oozing around her ankles and into her boots.

'If that wants trettin' like a lady,' he growled, 'then that mun act like one.'

And with that he turned and walked to the carriage.

Kitty lifted her sodden skirts and pulled one foot clear of the sticky, cloying mud. With slow, unsteady steps she made her way to the road, biting her lip in rage and mortification. She had been very rude, to be sure, but how dare he drop her in the water? She looked down at her feet. Her new boots were ruined and instead of a jaunty yellow decoration around the hem of her walking dress, the bottom six inches of her skirts glistened with slick brown mud.

When Kitty reached the road she was too upset to speak and after scraping the worst of the mud from her boots and stockings she climbed silently into the carriage, biting her lip while Mrs Midgley clucked and fidgeted around her like a mother hen.

Daniel looked down at his legs. His topboots were almost completely covered in mud and it had splashed up over his buckskins.

He walked to the edge of the ford to wash the worst of the dirt away before climbing back into the carriage. Mr Midgley gave the word and they set off again. The atmosphere inside the carriage was distinctly uncomfortable. Daniel looked at the young woman huddled in the corner: she was staring out of the window, her jaw set hard. He saw her blink rapidly and guessed that she was trying not to cry.

'I beg your pardon,' he said quietly. 'Miss Wythenshawe, I—'

'Now, now, my boy, you did your best,' put in Mr Midgley. 'I did not see quite what happened, as I was helping my wife into the coach, but I am sure it could not be helped. We must be thankful that one of our ladies at least was carried safely across the mud. I have no doubt Miss Wythenshawe is most grateful for your efforts, isn't that so, my dear?'

Daniel saw the little chin tremble. Miss Wythenshawe averted her face but he could not mistake the bitterness in her voice when she replied.

'Mr Blackwood's *efforts* will not be forgotten.'

'There, now, all's well, you see.' Mr Midgley beamed around the carriage. 'Once the mud has dried, we can clean it off and your boots and your gown will be as good as new!'

Daniel sat back, closing his lips against further comment. Mrs Midgley did not look convinced by her husband's cheerful assurances and as for Miss Wythenshawe, she kept her gaze fixed firmly upon the passing landscape. He leaned forwards, his hand going out to her.

'Perhaps you will allow me to—'

'Pray do not touch me!' she said icily. 'I think you have done quite enough damage today!'

Daniel drew back immediately. He had been about to offer to pay for a new gown, but it was quite clear the young woman wanted nothing further to do with him. Stifling a sigh of exasperation, Daniel turned to stare out of the window beside him, praying that his nightmare journey would soon be over.

Chapter Two

The carriage slowed to negotiate a winding village street and Daniel sat up, relieved to recognise the familiar buildings.

'Hestonroyd.' He turned to Mr Midgley. 'This will do for me, sir, if you would direct your driver to stop.'

Mr Midgley pulled the check-string and Daniel jumped down. He bowed and offered his thanks to Mr and Mrs Midgley but when he touched his hat to Miss Wythenshawe she merely hunched her shoulder and looked away. With a shrug he waited until the carriage had moved off then walked briskly along the street until he arrived at the gates to the Holme, an imposing new house set back from the road. As he strode up the drive, the front door flew open and a young lady ran out.

'Daniel, at last!'

He caught her up in his arms, swinging her around and laughing.

'Have you been looking out for me, Bella?'

He set her back on her feet.

'Since daybreak. But what *have* you been doing, brother dearest? You are covered in mud.'

He grinned.

'That is a very long story. Let us go indoors. I need to clean myself up.'

'You must be quick, then, for Mama is waiting in the drawing room for you. Papa is at the mill, but he said we were to send word as soon as you arrived.' She twinkled up at him. 'He would not say so, of course, but he has missed you, and was mightily disappointed when you did not come home last night.'

Daniel put his arm around her shoulders.

'Well, you can send him a message now to tell him I am safe, and inform Mama that I will be with her as soon as I am presentable!'

The clock in the hall had chimed two more quarters before Daniel finally made his way downstairs to the drawing room. It was a large well-proportioned chamber, comfortably furnished, everything of the finest quality, and it had a quiet elegance that Daniel found very restful. His mother was seated at her new writing desk, her dark hair neatly confined beneath a lace cap.

'Well, Mama, I am home at last.'

She looked up, a smile lighting her face.

'Daniel, my love.' She rose to greet him, hugging him tightly. She would never admit it but he suspected she had spent a restless night worrying over his safety. He held her away from him.

'You are looking very well, Mama, and that is a very fetching coat. Is it new?'

'It is a *pet-en-l'air*,' she told him, smoothing her hands over the grey velvet of the loose jacket she wore over her morning gown. 'They are not so fashionable now, I'm afraid, but just the thing for these chill spring days.' She gestured to him to sit down with her. 'Bella tells me you have had an eventful journey.'

'Yes, Marnie is lame; we took a fall coming back from Barrowford. No, no, I suffered no injury,' he added quickly when he saw the alarm in her face. 'I was obliged to leave Marnie in Halifax but was fortunate to meet Mr Midgley and his lady on their way to London and they took me up. They send their regards, Mama, but would not stop.'

'That was very kind of them, but are you sure you are not hurt? No doubt you were cutting across the moors again. I wish you had kept to the roads, my son.'

'I wish I had done so, this time,' Daniel responded with a rueful grin. 'You will say I was well served, Mama, for I had to spend the night sleeping on the heather.'

'He was covered in mud,' added Bella, following him into the room. 'Up to his knees!'

'Not from my sojourn on the moor,' Daniel was quick to reassure his mother. 'The stream was in full spate across the ford and Midgley deemed it safer for us to walk across the bridge.'

'Heavens, if it was that muddy what did poor Mrs Midgley do?' asked Bella, eyeing the scalloped hem of her own gown.

'I carried her, since her husband could not.'

'Oh, famous!' Mrs Blackwood clapped her hands, laughing. 'A veritable hero! I have no doubt the lady was very pleased to have you with them.'

'*She* was, perhaps,' remarked Daniel, his brow darkening, 'but not her companion. Too high in the step for me. A right top-lofty piece…'

'Daniel!'

'I beg your pardon, Mama, but you know how I dislike it when people put on airs that don't become them! And this young miss, hah! Far too high and mighty *she* was! She took one look at me and wrote me off as a mere nothing.'

'I have no doubt she mistook you for a common labourer if she saw you in all your dirt,' remarked Bella sagely. 'I am sure she soon realised her mistake when she knew who you were.'

'Nay,' drawled Daniel, 'I weren't about to put 'er right.'

Mrs Blackwood frowned at his sudden lapse.

'My dear, I trust you were not uncouth.'

Daniel hesitated, thinking back over the events of the morning. He had behaved very badly by Miss Wythenshawe, he knew that, but it was too late to do anything about it now. He gave his mother an apologetic smile.

'Alas, Mama, I fear I was very uncouth.'

A deep, amused voice was heard from the doorway.

'What is this? Is my son up to his tricks?'

'Papa!' With a shriek Bella flew across the room and flung herself into the arms of the gentleman who had just entered.

'Father.' Daniel rose. 'I beg your pardon, I sent a message to assure you I was safe. I did not mean you to leave the mill early—'

His father smiled across the room at him.

'It was no hardship. 'Tis a poor manager I would be if my manufactories could not function without my presence! But what has been occurring, my son, to bring that black scowl to your face?'

'A minor irritation, sir, too trivial to bore you with.'

'Good manners are never trivial, my son,' put in Mrs Blackwood, a troubled look in her eyes. 'I had hoped your education had taught you how to mix with your fellow man, from humble labourer to the highest in the land. But I know that temper of yours: you will act rashly if your will is crossed.'

'Oh?' Mr Samuel Blackwood raised his dark brows at his son. 'And who has had the temerity to cross you, my boy?'

'A young lady,' put in Bella before Daniel could reply. 'She saw Dan in all his dirt and mistook him for a rough, coarse fellow.'

'And is my son so lax in his manners that he is judged solely upon appearance?' asked Mr Blackwood gently.

A dull flush mantled Dan's cheek.

'Not generally, sir, I assure you.'

'I am very glad to hear it,' returned his father, smiling a little. 'Because your manners are going to be sorely tested, I fear.'

Daniel looked up.

'Sir?'

'Yes, my son, I have some matters of business for you to attend to.' Mr Blackwood reached into his pocket and took out his snuff box. 'I am sending you to London!'

*Dearest Mama. You will know from my previous correspon-
dence that I think Lady Leaconham the kindest, most generous godmother in the world! She delights in showering gifts
upon me and will not hear of my spending the money you
gave me upon anything other than little luxuries for myself—
pin money, she calls it—and every time I remonstrate with
her she merely laughs and says what else is she to spend her
money upon, if it is not her goddaughter?*

Kitty put down her pen. She had been in Portman Square for
four weeks now, and already Lady Leaconham had spent more
money upon her than Mama and Aunt Jane earned in a year. Letitia
Leaconham had been a widow for a long time. Her husband had
left her with a comfortable income that allowed her to hire a house
in London for several months each year and entertain her acquaintances in lavish style. She had one son, Garston, but since attaining
his majority four years ago he had set up his own bachelor establishment, leaving his mama to yawn over her morning chocolate and
bemoan the fact that she had no daughter to comfort her in her twilight years. She was therefore delighted to welcome her goddaughter into her house and even more delighted when she discovered
Kitty to be an attractive young lady with very pretty manners. She
began immediately to make plans to introduce her goddaughter to
her friends, and wrote to Mrs Wythenshawe to assure her that, despite Kitty's complete lack of fortune, she had no doubt she would
be able to secure for her a very advantageous marriage.

Since this was her sole reason for coming to London, Kitty could
only be grateful that her godmother entered so fully into her concerns and therefore she stifled her misgivings and threw herself into
her new life. Kitty had to be honest; it was not difficult to enjoy all
the amusements that London had to offer. Lady Leaconham took
her to the theatre, they attended concerts, and spent hours brows-
ing in shops that carried such a wide variety of merchandise Kitty's
eyes grew round in amazement. It was also very pleasant wearing

modish gowns and having my lady's *coiffeuse* coax her soft dark hair into fashionable ringlets. It had not taken Kitty long to realise that Lady Leaconham was a wealthy woman with very little to do, and she looked upon her goddaughter very much as a novelty, an amusement—a doll to be dressed and petted and exhibited to her friends. For the first week or so Kitty had found the experience deliciously exhilarating, but a life dedicated to nothing but pleasure was not something she could wholly approve. Her father had been a very religious man with a strong moral code. He had died before Kitty was twelve years old but by then she had been inculcated with his principles and a strong sense of social justice. She believed that the advantages of wealth and rank carried with them responsibility for those less fortunate, a belief that did not seem to be shared by many of the fashionable ladies she had met since arriving in Town. She took up her pen again.

> *Pray be assured that I carry out such errands as Godmama will allow and take her little dog for his daily exercise, but this is small recompense for her generosity.*

Kitty paused. She did not think Mama would quite approve of the number of times Lady Leaconham had taken her shopping, positively showering her with purchases until Kitty's room was overflowing with hats, bonnets, cloaks, pelisses, dancing slippers and half-boots as well as more day dresses, morning and evening gowns and walking dresses than Kitty could ever imagine having time to wear. She broke off from her reverie as the door opened and Lady Leaconham came in.

'Ah, so there you are, Kitty my love,' she greeted her with a smile as she drew off her gloves. 'Now, what are you about, here all alone in the morning room?'

'I am writing to Mama. I beg your pardon, Godmama: is there something you would like me to do for you?'

'No, no, child, you work far too hard as it is—no one should be writing letters so early in the day!'

Kitty laughed.

'This is not *work,* Godmama!'

'Perhaps not for you,' returned my lady, casting a dubious eye at the sheet of paper with its closely written lines. 'I have noticed that you like to read a great deal, too.' She looked at Kitty, a slight frown creasing her brow. 'My dear, I do hope you are not *bookish,* and pray tell me you do not wish me to get you an invitation to my neighbour Mrs Montagu's blue-stocking parties! Nothing would be more fatal to your chances of making a good match, you know.'

Kitty hastily disclaimed and Lady Leaconham gave a very visible sigh of relief.

'Very well, my love, put away your letter now, if you please: you may finish it later. I have just come from Bond Street where I saw the prettiest pair of sandals! I just had to buy them for you. I thought they would go very well with your yellow muslin. I had Meakin put them in your room so perhaps you would run upstairs and try them on. I am expecting my sister Lady Harworth to call shortly and thought you might like to change your gown for her visit.' Kitty looked down at her closed robe: it was one of the gowns Mama had made for her. As if reading her thoughts, Lady Leaconham said quickly, 'I know how hard your dear mama and your aunt worked, making all those lovely gowns for you, and while they are perfectly suitable for quiet days at home, I do believe you should wear something a little more…stylish when we are entertaining guests such as Lady Harworth. And I do so want you to make a good impression upon her.'

'Oh, why should that be, Godmama?'

'Well, she is very well connected, and she has a daughter only a year or so older than you; I should like her to think you a fitting companion. Also…' My lady slipped off her pelisse and gave her attention to laying it carefully over the arm of the sofa. 'Also, she has a son, and Lord Harworth is unmarried.'

Kitty was not deceived by her airy tone.

'Surely you do not think a *lord* would look at me, Godmama.'

'I do not see why not,' returned Lady Leaconham. 'Now that Meakin has cut your hair and dressed it a little more stylishly, you look exceedingly pretty, and your manners are very good, so I have no doubt that if you exert yourself a little you could make yourself very agreeable—you must not talk about your family, of course.'

'Oh, must I not?'

'No, my dear. It is not the thing in Town to chatter on about people known only to oneself.' My lady clasped her hands together, her pale eyes taking on a dreamy look. 'Only think how pleased your mama would be with both of us if we were to catch you a lord!'

Kitty did not think it worth trying to reply, so she obediently slipped away to her room to change into her new gown of lemon-coloured muslin with the blue sash and to put on the soft yellow kid sandals that her godmother had purchased for her. When she returned to the morning room some twenty minutes later she found her godmother sitting with her visitors.

'Ah, my dear, come in.' Lady Leaconham drew her forwards. 'Clara, may I present my goddaughter Katherine to you?'

'Why, she is quite charming,' cooed Lady Harworth as Kitty dropped into a deep curtsy. 'And how old are you, child?'

'Not yet twenty, ma'am.'

'Oh, how wonderful. You must talk to Ann, my daughter. She is only a little older than you. She will attain her majority in June. I have no doubt you will have much in common.'

The fair-haired young lady sitting beside Lady Harworth rose to her feet, smiling.

'Mama says that of every young lady we meet. But in your case I think she may be correct.' Ann Harworth took Kitty's arm and led her away to the other side of the room. 'There is a liveliness about your countenance that I like very much.'

Kitty blushed and laughed.

'Thank you, Miss Harworth, I hope I do not disappoint you.'

'I am sure you will not. You come from Yorkshire, you said? We have estates there, or rather my brother does, which is the same thing. Come, sit here in the window with me and tell me how you like London!'

Kitty happily obliged and after a half-hour's lively discussion was pleased when Miss Harworth declared that she had found a friend.

'I am so glad to have discovered someone with a wit to match my own. And someone who knows their own mind, and is not afraid to say so, Miss Wythenshawe.'

'Am I so unusual, then?' asked Kitty, her eyes twinkling. 'I must learn to guard my tongue if I am not to be labelled an oddity.'

'No, no, you must say exactly what you mean. I always do. We are holding a ball on Friday and—Mama, have you invited my aunt?'

'Manners, my love.' Lady Harworth frowned at her daughter's impetuous interruption. 'As a matter of fact we were just discussing it, as well as the little party we will be holding next month to mark your birthday, Ann.'

'So your son will be there on Friday?' enquired Lady Leaconham, flicking a small, triumphant glance towards Kitty.

'I would not consider such an event without his being there,' replied Lady Harworth. 'It is his house now, after all, and while he says I must continue to treat everything as my own until such time as he takes a wife, it is so very difficult, for I no longer feel like the true mistress now I am a widow. But you must understand that, dear sister, since you are in very much the same position.'

'Well, Garston is somewhat younger than his cousin, Clara, and he is content to leave everything as it was when his dear father was alive,' replied Lady Leaconham.

Kitty heard the faint note of dissatisfaction in her voice and closed her lips tightly to prevent herself from expressing her own opinion. She had not yet met Lord Leaconham but she could not help thinking that at five-and-twenty, her godmother's only son was more than old enough to be taking responsibility for his inheritance.

'But you will come?' Ann implored her. 'Do say you will, *dear* Aunt!'

'Lady Leaconham has agreed to attend, and to bring Miss Wythenshawe with her,' replied Lady Harworth, a touch of impatience creeping into her well-modulated tones. 'Now, pray you go away with your new friend and talk quietly so that your aunt and I may enjoy a little conversation.'

Ann turned to address Lady Leaconham.

'Perhaps Miss Wythenshawe and I could take your dear little dog for a walk, Aunt.'

'But Kitty took him out this morning.'

'I am sure he would enjoy another airing,' Ann persisted. 'It is such a lovely day. I am sure the fresh air would do us good.'

'Oh, do let them go out, sister,' begged Lady Harworth. 'My maid is sitting in the hall with nothing to do, so she may accompany them.'

In the face of such enthusiasm Lady Leaconham capitulated. Ten minutes later the girls were stepping out into Portman Square with the little Scottish terrier trotting merrily along beside them on his silken leash.

Ann gave a noisy sigh and slipped her arm through Kitty's.

'It is so good to be on our own, where we may say what we please. Oh, you need not worry about Norris,' she added, as Kitty glanced back towards the maid following silently behind them. 'She has been with us for ever and is *very* discreet. And I am so pleased that you will be coming on Friday.'

'It will be my very first ball,' Kitty admitted.

Ann gave a little squeak of excitement.

'How wonderful! I shall be able to introduce you to everyone! How long will you be staying in Town?'

'I do not know…as long as Lady Leaconham is pleased to have me with her.'

'I hope it is for ever!' cried Ann. They had reached the gate in the low railing that surrounded the gardens and she stopped. 'This is very pretty, but shall we go instead to Hyde Park? There will be so many more interesting people there.'

Kitty hesitated. 'I do not think...'

'Oh, do say yes,' Ann squeezed her arm. 'We have only to slip across Oxford Street to get there.'

'I do not know London as well as you, Miss Harworth, but I do not think one can *slip across* such a busy thoroughfare.'

'No, but there are crossing sweepers, and we have Norris, so there can be no objection. Oh, do say yes, Miss Wythenshawe!'

Kitty was not proof against her new friend's entreaties. They left the square, safely negotiated the traffic of Oxford Street and soon found themselves in the relative peace of the great park. Although it was not the fashionable hour there was a considerable crowd and several carriages to be seen, but once they had crossed the broad carriageway and walked some distance from the gates they found themselves alone. Kitty released the little dog and watched him running happily amongst the bushes.

'Oh, this is infinitely better than a dusty street,' declared Ann.

Kitty turned her face up to the sun, so much warmer here than in her native Yorkshire.

'I have to agree, Miss Harworth.'

'Let us be done with this formality. You must call me Ann and I shall call you Katherine.'

'Kitty, if you please—apart from when Godmama introduces me to new acquaintances the only time I am called Katherine is when I am in disgrace.'

'Very well, then, Kitty! And since we are now such good friends, you can tell me if you have a beau.'

'Goodness me, no,' replied Kitty, laughing and blushing at the same time.

'What, is there no gentleman waiting back in Yorkshire for you?'

Kitty shook her head. 'There were no gentlemen in Fallridge. None that Mama approved,' she added, thinking back to the occasions when she had seen the carriages driving up to the King's Arms for the monthly assembly.

'Farmers and tradesmen,' her mother had said, dismissively. 'Very good people, I am sure, but not suitable companions for *you,* my love.'

'Were you very lonely?' asked Ann.

Kitty looked up quickly, and Ann smiled at her.

'You looked so wistful that I thought, perhaps...'

'Yes, I *was* lonely,' Kitty confessed. 'I should have liked to go to school—'

'Oh, I went to school,' broke in Ann, pulling a face. 'It was the most horrid experience and of very little use, for apart from learning to dance what do I need with history, or the use of globes, or even to speak French, when we are forever at war with that frightful country?'

'But surely you made friends there?'

'Well, of course, although most of them are married now. Or betrothed.' She flicked a glance at Kitty. 'I am considered quite old to be still unwed, you know. Poor Mama is beginning to despair.'

'And do you not wish to marry?

'Oh, yes,' replied Ann casually, 'eventually I suppose I must accept someone. Poor Mama is even more desperate for Bertram to wed, because he is nearly forty and Mama says we must have an heir. As for me, I am enjoying myself far too much flirting with all the gentlemen of my acquaintance! Do you like flirting, Kitty?'

'I do not think I have ever tried it.'

Her frank reply brought Ann's astonished gaze upon her.

'Never?'

'No, never. I know so few gentlemen, you see. The Squire and Reverend Denny are the only gentlemen who called upon Mama, and they are both very old.'

'But surely you must have come into contact with younger gentlemen?' said Ann, appalled.

Kitty considered for a moment.

'Well, there is Joshua, of course: he is the local farmer's son who drove me to Halifax.'

'No, a farmer's boy does not count,' declared Ann firmly. 'But you must know others. *Think,* Kitty.'

Kitty tried to think, but the only other man who came into her mind was the fierce-eyed Mr Blackwood, and he had not even liked her. At last she shook her head, saying ruefully, 'I fear I am not the sort of girl that gentlemen like to flirt with.'

'Gentlemen will flirt with any female,' Ann retorted. 'It is quite clear to me that you have lived far too sheltered a life, Miss Kitty Wythenshawe, so we must do what we can to make it more exciting!'

Kitty laughed at her. 'I shall be delighted if you can do so! For now, though, we had best return to Portman Square before Godmother thinks we have been kidnapped!'

Kitty called the little dog to her and fastened him on the leash, then the two young ladies set off to retrace their steps in perfect harmony. When they reached the edge of the park Kitty noticed something white fluttering against the trunk of one of the trees. As they drew closer it became clear it was a printed sheet, secured to the trunk with a nail.

'It will be a handbill,' said Ann, when Kitty directed her attention to the paper. 'Perhaps there is a new play at Drury Lane!' She stepped closer, peering up at the words. 'No, it is one of Mr Clarkson's meetings.'

'Thomas Clarkson the abolitionist?'

'You have heard of him?'

'Why, yes,' said Kitty, coming forwards to stare at the paper. 'He travels the country with his talks on how badly the slaves are treated. I have never attended a meeting, however. I have only read reports.'

'Then perhaps we should go to this one,' said Ann slowly. 'It is at the Red Lion in Lombard Street—in the City, where the banks are.' She turned to Kitty, her eyes shining. 'Shall we go? We have a week to concoct a story that will please Mama and Aunt Leaconham. We will take a hackney carriage to the City. It will be so exciting.'

'Now, that's enough, miss,' said Norris, stepping up. 'You know her ladyship will never allow it.'

'She will not know,' replied Ann. 'Not a word of this to anyone, Norris, or I shall have you turned off for insolence.'

The maid snorted loudly. 'I should like to see you try that, miss. What, when her ladyship knows just what a handful you are?'

'You are right, of course, and I should never let you leave me, *dear* Norris!' Ann put her arms about the older woman and hugged her ruthlessly. 'But I am quite determined to go to this meeting, so you must come with us, Norris, to make sure we are safe!'

Kitty could not but admire her tactics. The maid argued for a few moments, but soon gave in to Ann's cajoling, saying bitterly that if she refused then her mistress was quite capable of sneaking off alone and unprotected.

'And what her ladyship would have to say about that, I don't know,' she ended, shaking her head.

'No more do I, Norris,' chuckled Ann, turning to take Kitty's arm again. 'Come along then, we had best make haste back to Portman Square or Mama will be demanding to know just what you were about to let us tarry so long in the gardens!'

They set off, Ann taking no notice of the maid's outraged mutterings. Instead she began to describe for Kitty the gown she would wear to the forthcoming ball. As they prepared to cross Oxford Street Kitty found her attention caught by someone standing on the far side. There was something familiar about the tall, commanding figure encased in a close-fitting coat of dark superfine wool and nankeen knee-breeches. As they approached the gentleman turned and with dismay Kitty recognised the dark, aquiline countenance of Mr Daniel Blackwood. He was deep in conversation with another gentleman and Kitty lowered her gaze, hoping they would be able to walk by unnoticed, but her companion broke off from her talk of shell-pink satins with old rose ribbons and scalloped hems to give a delighted cry.

'Bertram! Oh, by all that is famous, what luck is this! Kitty—it is my brother!'

With a sinking heart Kitty watched the gentleman standing with Daniel Blackwood turn towards them. She was struck immediately by the similarity between brother and sister, both fair-haired and grey-eyed, although Lord Harworth was much older and his countenance was the more serious of the two.

Introductions could not be avoided. She allowed Ann to present her to Lord Harworth but all the time she was aware of Daniel's dark, piercing gaze fixed upon her. When at last Lord Harworth drew his companion forward she raised her eyes, opening her mouth, ready to admit they had already met, but Daniel was there before her.

'Miss Wythenshawe and I are already acquainted.' He spoke calmly, with no hint of the broad Yorkshire accent she had expected. Stunned, she could only watch as he reached out for her hand and lifted her fingers to his lips with all the practised ease of a gentleman. 'So we meet again, ma'am.'

Kitty tried to think of something to say, but was distracted by the shrill barking of her canine companion. She looked down to see that the little dog was greeting Daniel like a long-lost friend, jumping up and emitting a series of ecstatic yelps.

Kitty jerked on the lead, saying sharply, 'Down, Titan!'

Daniel raised an enquiring eyebrow. *'Titan?'*

Kitty bridled. 'Be careful,' she said in a voice of rigid self-control. 'He bites.'

Daniel looked down and uttered one quiet command. 'Sit.'

To her surprise Titan sat down immediately, obviously recognising a voice of authority.

'Oh, how sweet,' declared Ann. 'He likes you, Mr Blackwood.'

'Yes, he does,' Daniel responded. He bent to scratch Titan's ears. 'Very intelligent animals, dogs. They have an instinct for a fellow's true character, while humans are so often misled by appearances.' He straightened. 'Would you not agree, Miss Wythenshawe?'

The wicked glint in his black eyes made her seethe inwardly. She put up her chin and gave him back look for look.

'I have always maintained that *actions* are the real mark of a gentleman, Mr Blackwood.'

He bowed. 'Ah, but even a gentleman may fall from grace if the provocation is great enough,' he murmured.

Kitty glared at him, guilt and anger bringing a flush to her cheeks.

'But what are you doing here, Bertram?' Ann demanded of her brother. 'Are you on your way home from your club?'

'No, no, I have been meeting with Blackwood. He is advising me on a—ah—business venture that I am considering. When I found he was staying in Greenwich, I told him it was foolish of him to remain at the Spread Eagle when there is so much I want to discuss with him, so he has agreed to be my guest for the remainder of his stay.'

'You never told me about this, Bertram,' said Ann, smiling up at Daniel in a way that Kitty considered to be far too friendly.

'We have only this minute decided upon it,' replied her brother. 'We are on our way back to Harworth House now, to send a messenger to Greenwich with instructions for Blackwood's man to pack everything up and bring it here. But what are you doing out, Ann?' asked Lord Harworth. 'Does Mama know?'

'Oh, yes,' came the airy reply. 'She is visiting Aunt Leaconham. Aunt is Miss Wythenshawe's godmama, you know. We offered to take her dog for a walk and are on our way back to Portman Square now. Why do you not come with us? You can say hello to Aunt Leaconham and I am sure Mama would be glad of your escort back to Cavendish Square.'

'An excellent idea,' declared Lord Harworth, holding out his arm to Kitty. 'What do you say, Blackwood, will you help me escort these two young ladies to Portman Square? It is not far out of our way and there will still be plenty of time to get a message to your man and have him back here with your bags before dinner.'

Kitty's hopes rose a little when Daniel hesitated.

'Will that not be an imposition? After all, I do not know Lady Leaconham…'

'Then we shall introduce you,' cried Ann. 'I am sure she will be pleased to meet an acquaintance of her goddaughter. Besides,' she added naughtily, as she took Daniel's arm, 'I am intrigued to know more of you, sir. Miss Wythenshawe assured me she had no personable gentlemen amongst her acquaintance.'

'Did she indeed?' Again those coal-black eyes quizzed Kitty. 'I suppose our meeting slipped her mind. It was quite a trivial event, after all.'

Trivial! Kitty's eyes blazed with fury. She had been picked up and dropped, quite callously, into cold, muddy water that had quite ruined her gown and boots and stockings. If Godmama had not been so generous she would even now be obliged to walk out in skirts stained quite six inches deep at the hem!

'You are right.' She threw the words over her shoulder as she and Lord Harworth led the way back to Portman Square. 'I had quite forgotten you, Mr Blackwood.'

Kitty turned her attention to her escort, forcing herself to converse with Lord Harworth as they made their way back to Lady Leaconham's house, but all the time part of her mind was racing with conjecture about Daniel Blackwood. Just to know he was behind her made her spine tingle, as if he might pounce upon her at any moment. What was he doing in London, and what had happened to the rough country voice he had used in Yorkshire? She thought she knew the answer to her last question and her conscience pricked her when she remembered how uncivil she had been towards him. She had assumed he was a rough labourer and he had responded in kind. She deserved that trick, she acknowledged, but she had *not* deserved his subsequent treatment of her! Her indignation grew with every step and by the time they arrived at Lady Leaconham's door Kitty was full of righteous fury. When they entered the hall she left all the explanations to Miss Harworth and stalked past the wooden-faced butler to hand Titan over to a hovering footman. By the time she turned back the rest of the party were divesting themselves of hats and surcoats. Daniel took advantage of the confusion to step up to her.

'I have long wanted to offer you an apology, Miss Wythenshawe,' he said quietly. 'My actions when we last met were inexcusable.'

'I do not want your apology!' she said in a fierce whisper, and immediately regretted her incivility.

'But I would like to make some recompense to you—I fear I ruined your gown—'

A mixture of anger and remorse combined in Kitty and she answered recklessly, 'My gown is of no consequence. I have *trunks* full of clothes, so you need concern yourself no further with me!'

With that she put her nose in the air and sailed into the morning room.

'After you, Blackwood.'

Lord Harworth was standing back, waiting for Daniel to follow the ladies.

'Thank you, I really do not—' Daniel bit off the words. He wanted to tell Harworth to go to the devil and storm out of the house, but that would be the height of incivility, and, however little Miss Wythenshawe might think of him, he had been brought up a gentleman and would act like one. Curbing his temper, he nodded and strode into the room, forcing himself to smile and say everything that was required of him, but all the time he was aware of Kitty standing in the corner, biting her lip and darting fiery looks at him from those stormy green eyes. He had offered her his apology and it had been rebuffed. He clenched his jaw, smiling with even more spurious interest at something Ann Harworth was saying. If the chit could not bring herself to act in a civilised manner than he would have to show her how it was done!

Kitty could barely suppress a sigh of relief when at last the visitors took their leave and it was the greatest trial for her to sit quietly while her godmama declared herself delighted with the success of the visit.

'And what a sly little puss you are, my love,' Lady Leaconham chuckled, tapping Kitty's knuckles playfully with her fan. 'I send you out for a little walk and you return with two eligible gentlemen in tow!'

'Mr Blackwood is not in the least eligible,' protested Kitty.

'He is my nephew's guest, is he not? To be sure a mill-owner's son is not what your mama would like for you, but he is very gentlemanlike, *and* he is related to some of the wealthiest shipping families in Liverpool.'

'It smacks of trade, Godmama.'

'It smacks of a fortune, my dear,' responded Lady Leaconham drily. 'However, I will grant you that a man like Mr Blackwood should only be considered as a last resort. Lord Harworth would be a more prestigious match for you.'

'He is indeed more what Mama had in mind,' agreed Kitty. 'But is he not a little…old, Godmama?'

'At eight-and-thirty? Not at all, my love. It makes it all the more likely that he is looking in earnest for a wife. But we must be practical. Every cap in Town will be set at such an eligible *parti*. However, not every young lady will have an invitation to the Harworth ball, so I have great hopes for Friday, my love. Great hopes indeed!'

Chapter Three

Any hopes Kitty might have had for her very first ball were eclipsed by apprehension. Mama had insisted that learning to dance was a prime requirement for every young lady but Kitty was very sure that dancing with the Squire's daughters in the privacy of Fallridge Manor was a very different matter from standing up with a gentleman in a crowded ballroom. And she would have to stand up at least once because Lord Harworth, prompted by his sister, had requested that she save a dance for him.

When Friday arrived Kitty resolved to wear the evening gown that Mama had made for her rather than any of the dresses purchased by Lady Leaconham. Politely but firmly she rejected her godmother's suggestions of the pink sarcenet or the blue spider gauze and insisted on wearing the simple white crape gown ornamented with silver embroidery to the sleeves and hem. Aunt Jane had embroidered a silk shawl to match and she had a pair of white satin dancing slippers to complete the ensemble. Kitty was quite satisfied with the result, but she was more than a little nervous when she joined her godmother in the drawing room

'Well, Godmama, what do you think?'

She spread her skirts and gave a little twirl before fixing her anxious gaze upon Lady Leaconham.

'To be sure it is a much simpler design than the evening gowns I had made for you,' said my lady, studying her closely. Kitty held her breath. At length her godmother smiled. 'But is looks quite perfect upon you, my love. And no one will recognise the seamstress, you may be sure of that.' She blinked rapidly and began to hunt for her handkerchief. 'You look like an angel, my dear.'

'She does indeed!'

Kitty spun round to see a rather portly young gentleman in the doorway, regarding her through his quizzing glass.

'Garston!' Lady Leaconham flew up from her chair in a flutter of lace. 'My dear boy, when did you return to Town?'

'At noon, Mama,' replied Lord Leaconham, suffering her embrace. 'Thought I should come and tell you I was back. Didn't know you had company…'

'My love, this is my goddaughter Katherine, come to keep me company for a few weeks,' said Lady Leaconham. 'Kitty, my dear, allow me to present my son Garston to you.'

Kitty dropped into a curtsy, blushing a little as Lord Leaconham bowed over her hand.

'Delighted, Miss Wythenshawe. Proule informs me that you are about to go out, so I know that all this splendour is not in my honour.'

'We are off to Harworth House,' replied Lady Leaconham, a note of triumph creeping into her voice. 'Your cousin Ann has taken a great liking to dear Kitty. Why do you not come with us, my son? I am sure your aunt would have invited you, had she known you were back in Town.'

Lord Leaconham was still casting an admiring eye over Kitty, who found the prolonged scrutiny a little unnerving.

'I am dining with friends at my club tonight but I may well look in later.'

'Well, if you are coming, pray be in time to dance with Kitty and do not spend all your time in the supper room,' replied his mother, picking up her wrap. 'Now, we must be off. Come along, my dear, we will go downstairs to wait for the carriage.'

* * *

Lady Harworth might complain that her house was not situated on the magnificent west side of Cavendish Square but it seemed to Kitty that the whole of fashionable London was intent upon attending the ball. The square was crowded with vehicles. Coachmen and postillions traded insults while liveried footmen directed the carriages to the entrance before tenderly handing down the occupants and escorting them into the house.

Kitty followed Lady Leaconham up the wide sweeping staircase, her nervousness somewhat alleviated when she saw Ann waiting for her at the top of the stairs, a beaming smile upon her face as she held out her hand to Kitty.

'Is this not wonderful? I have never seen so many carriages in the square before. It is going to be *such* a squeeze, and Mama has hired a whole host of musicians to play for us. I cannot *wait* for the dancing to begin!'

'Well, you must contain yourself a little longer,' put in her mother, directing a smile towards Kitty. 'There are any number of people still to arrive. Now pray, Ann, allow Miss Wythenshawe to move on, that the other guests may approach.'

Kitty glanced behind her: a column of gorgeously gowned ladies and elegant gentlemen stretched all the way down the stairs. It was quite unnerving to see so many strange faces. She knew so few people, despite having been in Town for a whole month. Kitty was so daunted by this thought that when she saw Daniel Blackwood enter the house and join the line she could not suppress a smile of relief.

It was unfortunate that the gentleman should glance up at that moment, raising his brows when he saw her smiling down at him. Kitty quickly turned away, blushing furiously. What had possessed her to smile at the man? Resolutely putting this aberration aside, she followed her godmother into the ballroom, only to stop on the threshold and gaze about her in astonishment. The lofty room was ablaze with light from several glittering chandeliers. Everywhere was colourful and noisy confusion, the sounds of the musicians tuning up adding to the laughter and chatter of the guests.

'Good evening, Aunt, Miss Wythenshawe.' Lord Harworth stepped up to them and bowed. He gazed at Kitty, appreciation in his slightly protuberant grey eyes. 'I hope, Miss Wythenshawe, that you have not forgotten you have promised to dance with me later this evening?'

Kitty gave him a shy little smile. 'No, indeed, my lord.'

'Good,' responded his lordship. 'Capital. I shall look forward to it.'

'Well, that is an exciting start,' declared Lady Leaconham, as Lord Harworth moved off to greet more guests.

'It is, ma'am,' said Kitty, feeling rather overawed. 'At least I shall have one dance partner tonight, and if Lord Leaconham should turn up and dance with me as well I shall think myself very content.'

'Oh, I do not think we need to rely upon Garston tonight,' declared her godmother, her voice rich with satisfaction. 'I have already noticed several gentlemen looking at you with interest, my love. I shall introduce you to everyone I know, and with you looking so very pretty this evening I have no doubt that we shall soon find you any number of partners. And with luck a good many of them will be unmarried!' She took Kitty's arm and began to look around her. 'Now, where shall we begin?'

Between them, Lady Leaconham and Miss Harworth introduced Kitty to so many people—turbaned matrons, bewhiskered lords and eager young gentlemen—that there was no possibility of her remembering all their names, but she should not complain, for when the musicians finally began to play she had the satisfaction of walking out on to the dance floor to join the very first set. Her initial anxiety soon disappeared as she realised she was familiar with all the steps and she uttered up a silent prayer to the squire for employing such an excellent dancing master. After that first dance, she found there were a number of gentlemen eager to partner her and she began to enjoy herself. Rather to his mother's surprise, Lord Leaconham arrived in time to stand up with Kitty for a minuet and even came back later to escort the two ladies to the supper room, where he remained to entertain them until it was time to return to the dancing.

It was towards the end of the evening when Lord Harworth came to claim his dance with Kitty. He appeared to be in the very best of spirits, although she suspected that the high colour in his cheeks was partly the result of the rather potent punch being served at supper. After a particularly lively country dance he pulled her hand on to his arm.

'Well done, Miss Wythenshawe. My sister informs me this is your very first ball, but to see you dance one would never know it.'

'Thank you, my lord,' Kitty replied. 'I did not expect to enjoy myself half so much. Everyone has been most kind, especially you, sir, and your sister.'

'Phshaw!' Lord Harworth puffed out his chest. 'Think nothing of it, Miss Wythenshawe. Now, where shall I take you, who is your next dance partner?'

'Why, sir, I do not think I have one, so perhaps you could escort me back to Lady Leaconham…'

'What, no partner?' cried my lord. 'But these will be the last dances of the night. We cannot have you sitting out! I promised m'sister we would keep you amused tonight, so we must see what we can do…'

Lord Harworth raised his head and began to look about him.

Kitty disclaimed and declared herself perfectly ready to join her godmother, but her escort merely patted her hand as he raised his voice to address someone.

'Blackwood—just the man! You are not dancing?'

The press of people had prevented Kitty from spotting Daniel Blackwood, but she saw him now as he stepped towards them, unsmiling, towering over her, a dark and brooding figure in the colourful crowd.

He said briefly, 'No, my lord. I do not dance.'

'Nonsense, man, you trod a very pretty measure with Ann earlier this evening, I saw you! I have here a delightful partner for you.'

Kitty went cold.

'Believe me, my lord,' she began, 'there is no need—'

'Nonsense, you will be doing Mr Blackwood a great service,' cried Lord Harworth jovially. 'I am appalled to think he has been standing around all evening.'

'I assure you, my lord,' Daniel began, his tone clipped, 'I have partnered more than one young lady tonight—'

'Then you must dance again, sir!' Lord Harworth took Kitty's hand and held it out. 'Come along, Blackwood, take Miss Wythenshawe to the floor!'

Kitty thought she might die of embarrassment. Daniel, his face cold and shuttered, held out his arm to her and when she slipped her fingers on to his sleeve he silently led her away.

'I am sorry,' she managed, biting her lip. 'I know you want this as little as I do.'

'Society has its rules, madam, and we must both adhere to them.'

His indifferent tone had its effect in rousing Kitty's spirit. She put up her chin.

'For either of us to walk away would have given rise to conjecture.'

'Quite,' he replied. 'So let us get through this dance as best we may.'

'Certainly,' she said icily. 'After all, we need only stand up for one dance, and there is no necessity for us to speak to one another.'

However, once the music started and she put her hand into his, something very strange happened. It was as if she had danced with Daniel Blackwood many times before: their steps matched perfectly as they followed the traditional movement of the country dance and when they were required to separate their fingers seemed reluctant to part. Bemused, Kitty raised her eyes and regarded her partner, only to find him watching her with a fierce glow in his eyes that brought the colour rushing to her cheeks. She had danced with many gentlemen that evening, she had even performed a very stately minuet with one fair-haired young man reputed to be the epitome of a fashionable Adonis, yet none had had the same effect upon her. Not one of them had infused her with the soaring elation she experienced now, the feeling that she and her partner were alone in the room, the only people in the world.

The dance drew to its conclusion. He bowed, she made her curtsy, but neither made any move to leave the floor. The cry went up for the last dance and suddenly they were surrounded by even more couples, all jostling to find space. With so many dancers on the floor Kitty found herself very close to Daniel, so close that she could not move without her arm brushing his sleeve. Kitty looked up and saw the rueful smile upon his face as if he, too, realised there could be no possibility of maintaining a cool reserve once the lively music began. With a jolt of surprise Kitty realised she did not mind. Suddenly all the hurt and anger she had felt for the man melted away. He took her hands.

'Are we ready, Miss Wythenshawe?'

She found herself smiling up at him.

'Perfectly, Mr Blackwood.'

Kitty would never forget that final country dance at Harworth House. It was hot and noisy and it seemed as if all the world was crushed into the ballroom, everyone bouncing and skipping, laughing and shouting and determined to expend every last ounce of energy before they went home. Garston and Lord Harworth were on the floor, each squiring a handsome young lady, and at one point she came close to Ann dancing with the fair-haired Adonis, but Kitty hardly noticed them. All her attention was on Daniel. She no longer thought him dark and menacing. She could see beyond the rather austere cast of his countenance to the warmth in his dark eyes, the faint curve of his lips that was not quite a smile yet told her he was happy to be at her side. He was not the tallest man in the room yet to Kitty he stood head and shoulders above every other gentleman. He held her hand and led her confidently about the room, skilfully manoeuvring to put himself in the way and prevent her from being buffeted by the jostling dancers. He bore no resemblance to the boorish brute who had treated her so abominably, but instead was more like a guardian angel, strong, gentle and protective. She stole another look at him as he danced her down the line. No, *not* an angel: the strong jaw and athletic frame were more those of a warrior. A hero. By the time the music ended Kitty was the victim of such conflicting emotions that she dare not even look at her partner. She wanted to appear calm and assured, but she suddenly felt extremely shy.

Daniel was enjoying himself. It surprised him, for the stately minuets of the first part of the evening had been a lifetime away from the lively dances he had enjoyed at home and, although he had partnered one or two of the blushing young ladies Lady Harworth had brought up to him, he had found the evening a little dull. He had even considered how soon he would be able to make his excuses and retire. If Harworth had not persuaded him to stay in Cavendish Square he could have excused himself on the grounds of the long journey back to Greenwich. To leave the party and travel no further than the next floor would be the height of incivility.

He had been aware of Miss Wythenshawe from the first moment he had looked up and seen her at the top of the stairs, such a delightful smile on her face that his heart had flipped over, until he came to his senses and realised that there was no possibility that she could have directed such a smile at him, and he looked around him, trying to discover just who was the lucky recipient of her favour. He had done his best to prevent his eyes dwelling on her as she glided about the room in her sparkling white gown, her dark curls glowing in the candlelight. She had made it very plain that she despised him and thus she was not worth his notice. When Harworth had insisted he lead her on to the floor Daniel had fully intended to leave her after that first dance together, to make some excuse to quit the ballroom, but she had been so light on his arm, had danced so beautifully that he had forgotten she was the proud disdainful woman who had scorned him. He saw only an entrancing, ethereal creature that bewitched his senses. So he persuaded himself that it was only polite to remain for the last set. Harworth would expect it of him.

The final, energetic measure of the evening was much more like the assemblies he attended at Hestonroyd: too many dancers, too little space. He remembered standing up with his sister Bella, leading her through the movement of the dance and all the time trying to protect her from the other couples who were charging up and down the room. But this silver and white creature beside him was most definitely not his bouncing, boisterous sister! He was almost sorry when the music ended. He stood beside his partner as they joined in the spontaneous applause for themselves and the musicians, then he held out his arm, ready to escort her back to Lady Leaconham. Some of his good mood evaporated when he looked down at the still little figure beside him. Her lips were firmly closed and she laid only the tips of her fingers on his sleeve, as if she could not bring herself to touch him. He was disappointed at the change from his lively, sparkling dance partner. Silently he delivered her back to Lady Leaconham but in response to his parting bow her thanks to him were uttered in a cold, stilted manner and she turned away immediately. Daniel's jaw tightened. So much for enchantment!

'An excellent evening, eh, Blackwood?' Lord Harworth came up to him, his mother leaning on his arm. 'I hope you enjoyed yourself, sir. 'Twas your first ball here in Town, was it not?'

'It was, my lord.'

'I doubt you have such glittering occasions in the north, Mr Blackwood,' remarked Lady Harworth.

'Certainly we cannot boast such elevated society as one finds in Town, ma'am,' returned Daniel, 'but we have our balls and assemblies.'

'Indeed, Mama, they ain't savages,' chuckled Lord Harworth. 'And we shall soon be adding to the society, ma'am, will we not?' He turned to Daniel, smiling. 'Mama has suggested that we should open Kirkleigh Hall and take a party to Yorkshire in July. You suggested we should travel north to look at the mills and Kirkleigh is perfectly placed between Hestonroyd and Arkwright's mills at Cromford, less than a day's ride from either place. No harm in mixing a little business with pleasure, eh, Blackwood?'

'No indeed, my lord,' said Daniel. 'Although I had planned to show you more than just Cromford: if you are serious in building a mill of your own we shall not have a great deal of time for society—'

'Nonsense, sir, there is always time for society!' declared Lord Harworth. 'We shall take a little longer over the business, that is all, and I have no doubt Mama will like to entertain while we are there—even a ball, eh, Mama, now you have seen Blackwood dance? I am sure we can find you a few pretty girls to stand up with, although none to surpass your last partner.' He gave Daniel a playful dig in the ribs. 'Exceptionally pretty little thing, ain't she?'

'Miss Wythenshawe?' said Daniel coolly. 'She is far above my touch.'

'Indeed?' said Lady Harworth, suddenly showing an interest. She turned to watch Kitty as she walked out of the room. 'Letitia was not very forthcoming about her family. I believe she comes from the north, too—do you know her family, Mr Blackwood? Are they very wealthy?'

Lord Harworth laughed.

'Must be as rich as Croesus if they won't look at Blackwood, Mama. His family owns half of the West Riding!'

Daniel disclaimed, but Lady Harworth was not listening. She excused herself, saying, 'I believe my dear sister is about to leave, and I must go and say goodbye to her.'

* * *

'Well, that was a success and no mistake!' Lady Leaconham settled herself back into the corner of her carriage and gave a satisfied sigh. 'You danced every dance, and I cannot tell you how many compliments I received for you, my love! You were enchanting.'

Kitty gave a little nod but said nothing. She knew that at least one person was less than delighted with her. She had been quite dismayed by her behaviour towards Daniel Blackwood at the end of the evening, when she had suddenly been overcome with nerves. She had intended to be charmingly grateful for his standing up with her, yet when she spoke she had been cool to the point of rudeness. Even now she was embarrassed to think of it.

So she would not, she decided quickly. She would concentrate instead upon what her godmother was saying.

'Yes, Kitty dear, I could see from the first that Lady Harworth was disposed to like you. I was afraid she might think you a little *too* pretty, but with your dark hair you are such a contrast to Ann's fair beauty that you complement one another perfectly! And nothing could have exceeded Clara's affability, when she came up to us just as we were leaving. She hinted at many more invitations this summer.'

'How delightful for you, Godmama.'

'For *me?* Kitty, you little goose, the invitations will be for you, too.'

'But I have already been with you for a whole month, ma'am. I thought I should be thinking of returning home very soon...'

'Nonsense,' retorted her godmother briskly. 'A month is nothing, and if my niece has taken to you then nothing could be better than for the two of you to be seen together—so much more attractive than to be always accompanied by a matron!' Lady Leaconham paused while she smoothed the wrinkles from her long gloves. 'My sister can seem a little...cold to those she thinks beneath her notice, but I know she takes her responsibilities very seriously. I have no doubt she would like to see Bertram settled and raising a hopeful family, but Ann must be causing her some anxiety, to be nearing one-and-twenty and still unmarried! So I can quite see why Clara is happy to promote your friendship with her daughter. Two such pretty young ladies out on the Town together will be sure to attract any number of gentlemen.' Lady Leaconham reached out and placed a hand on Kitty's knee, saying urgently, 'Think of it, my dear: if we can secure a gentleman of good birth with even a modest fortune, the settlements will allow your mama and her sister to give up their sewing and live in the manner more suitable to their stations!'

'Yes, I suppose so,' said Kitty, brightening. 'And you think it is possible, Godmama?'

'I think it very likely,' returned Lady Leaconham, leaning back in her corner. 'You charmed a number of gentlemen this evening, even my nephew. What a great thing it would be if he were to offer for you.'

'Lord Harworth? Oh, no, ma'am, surely not. He was merely being kind to me, because I am your goddaughter.'

'He showed you a great deal of attention, my love. But perhaps you are right: we must not be too ambitious for you. But neither must we settle for anything less than your equal in birth—whoever we choose for you *must* be a gentleman!'

From the number of callers at Portman Square over the next few days it did indeed appear that Kitty had made a good impression at her very first ball, as her godmother was quick to explain to Ann when she came to see Kitty.

'I am delighted to hear it,' declared Ann, smiling. 'I have never known Mama to be so taken with any of my friends before.' She added, when Lady Leaconham had left the two young ladies alone, 'Was it not the most wonderful ball? I was engaged for every dance, and whenever I looked across you were always dancing, too!'

'Yes, I was very fortunate. I had not looked for such attention.'

'And you even persuaded dour Mr Blackwood to stand up with you.'

'Why do you call him dour?' asked Kitty, intrigued in spite of herself.

Ann wrinkled her nose. 'Well, he is perfectly *polite,*' she said slowly, 'but he is so very quiet, and only seems to want to talk business with Bertram.' Her eyes twinkled and she added ruefully, 'He makes no attempt to flirt with me. In fact, he makes no attempt to engage my attention at all! I am most impressed that he danced with you.'

'That was your brother's doing.' Kitty felt the colour rising to her cheeks. 'I think, since he is staying in your house, he could hardly refuse to dance with me when Lord Harworth suggested it.'

'Yes, that will be it.' Ann nodded. 'They have become wondrous great friends. My brother wrote to old Mr Blackwood when he first conceived the idea of building a mill and they were corresponding for several months before Mr Daniel Blackwood came to London. Bertram says that with the exception of Mr Arkwright, no one knows more about mills and manufacturing than the Blackwoods. But this is very boring talk! Let us discuss instead the Abolition meeting tomorrow evening. Have you given any thought to how we shall get there?'

'I confess I have not,' admitted Kitty. 'Perhaps we should not go, if your mama disapproves…'

'Mama disapproves of everything except achieving a great match for Bertram and the same for me,' declared Ann. 'I am determined to go. It is quite the fashion now, you know, to support the abolition of the slave trade.'

'My family have been fighting against slavery since before I was born,' replied Kitty. 'My father was vehemently opposed to it, and my mother still does what she can—we do not buy sugar from the West Indian plantations, you know.' She wanted to add that Mama could not afford to buy very much sugar at all, but remembered her godmother's warning that she should not chatter on about her family. Ann was regarding her with admiration.

'How good you are! I have no idea whether Bertram has any

slaves, but I am even more determined that we shall go to the meeting tomorrow. Now all you need do is to tell Aunt Leaconham that I am taking you to join us for dinner tomorrow and that we will not be returning until late. What time shall I call for you?'

'It cannot be too early,' replied Kitty. 'I have an engagement tomorrow. With Lord Leaconham. He is going to take me driving in the park.'

She ended a little hesitantly. Garston had issued the invitation and Kitty had accepted quite happily without reference to her godmother, but when Lady Leaconham heard of her plans she had looked a little shocked.

'I am sorry, Godmama,' Kitty had said, anxious and bemused. 'I thought there could be no harm in going out with Lord Leaconham in an open carriage.'

'No, of course not. It is just that…' Lady Leaconham bit her lip and gazed at Kitty, a shadow of unease in her eyes. 'It is just…I do not want you to develop a *tendre* for Garston, my dear. I had planned on finding him, um…'

'You want him to take a rich wife,' Kitty finished for her. She had been in Town long enough to know that every man and woman of marriageable age was intent upon making a brilliant match. 'Yes, I quite see that, Godmama, and you need have no fear: I am sure Lord Leaconham only offered to take me out in order to please you.'

'I expect you are right,' said Lady Leaconham, much relieved, 'and it will give you the opportunity to be seen in the park at the fashionable hour.'

So Lady Leaconham gave the outing her blessing.

Kitty set off with Lord Leaconham, knowing that her godmother would be far more disapproving of her engagement with Ann Harworth, if ever she learned the truth of it.

It was a beautiful summer's day and much as Kitty wanted to turn her face up to the skies and feel the sun's warmth on her skin, she knew that this would be frowned upon. Instead she unfurled her parasol, looking around her with interest as Lord Leaconham drove his phaeton through the busy London streets. Her initial apprehension at riding so high above the ground soon disappeared and she relaxed, looking forward to her excursion.

'Heavens, how crowded it is,' she remarked, as they turned in through the park gates. 'I thought it busy enough when Miss Harworth and I brought Titan here for a walk one morning.'

'Oh, I have seen it ten times worse than this,' cried Garston, gaily flourishing his whip. 'I have been here when we have been forced to crawl along at a snail's pace because there is so much traffic. But it is not yet five o'clock. We are early. I have no doubt it will fill up later.'

Kitty heard this with dismay. She had been expecting the great park to offer some peace and solitude after the hustle and bustle of the busy streets but all she could see was a host of fashionably dressed people riding, driving or walking, everyone intent on seeing and being seen.

Their own progress was slow for the park was full of Garston's friends, some of whom she knew, but many she did not, so that each stop necessitated explanations and a few moments' conversation.

'Well, Miss Wythenshawe, are you enjoying yourself?' Lord Leaconham enquired as they moved off from yet another introduction.

'Why, yes, my lord. Very much. Although I am afraid that with so many of your acquaintances here today we shall not complete even one circuit of the park.'

He laughed. 'What a jokesmith you are, Miss Wythenshawe! One does not come to Hyde Park for the drive! No, no: when I go to White's this evening I shall be complimented on the fine new rig I was driving this afternoon, and of course upon my charming companion. To be seen here will bring you to the attention of a great number of useful people, I assure you.'

She did not know what to reply; she was not at all sure she wanted to be brought to anyone's attention.

Kitty was beginning to wonder if she would be back in Portman Square before Ann called for her when she suddenly heard her escort give a low whistle.

'By heaven, that is a most beautiful piece of horseflesh.'

Kitty looked up to see two riders approaching and had no difficulty in recognising the creature that had drawn Garston's admiration—a sleek black horse with a deep chest, refined head and a bold eye. The animal seemed well aware that it was a handsome beast for it carried itself proudly, almost as proudly as the straight-backed gentleman in the saddle: Daniel Blackwood. He was accompanied by Lord Harworth but to Kitty's mind neither the older man's bearing nor his glossy bay hack could compare with the dark grandeur of Daniel and his mare. But Kitty remembered seeing the very same horse and rider when they had looked much less grand, covered in mud in a lane above Halifax. Once again the mortification of that encounter overwhelmed her and she hoped fervently that the two riders might not see them in the crowd, but Lord Leaconham pulled up the team, waving his whip to attract their attention. She smothered her dismay as the gentlemen drew rein and turned their mounts towards the phaeton.

Lord Harworth greeted Kitty in his usual friendly way but his companion gave only a slight nod of recognition.

'Blackwood, ain't it? We met at the ball the other night. By Jove, that's a fine horse you have there, sir,' declared Garston. 'Broad chest, good sloping shoulders, intelligent eye—magnificent!'

Daniel acknowledged the compliment with a nod.

'Thank you. She's Yorkshire bred, of course.'

'Of course.' Garston laughed. 'We've a few good hunters at Leaconham but nothing as fine as that.' He cocked an eyebrow at Daniel. 'How much d'you want for her? She looks up to my weight. Yes, I'd like to buy that mare.'

Daniel's dark brows rose.

'What, when you haven't seen her put through her paces?'

'No need, Blackwood. I can tell just by looking that she is a good all-round mount, certainly at home here in Town, but I have no doubt she comes into her own in the hunting field. Well, Blackwood, what d'you say? Name your price, sir!'

'Thank you, my lord, but no. Marnie has been with me for so long I believe she will see her days out in my company.'

'As you wish,' replied Garston, shrugging. 'But I'm not beat yet. Mayhap you will give me a chance to win her from you one night, when we've had a few glasses of wine together. Now what d'ye say to that, sir, eh?'

Kitty saw the faint hint of contempt creep into Daniel's dark eyes.

'I never gamble—'

'Never gamble?' cried Garston, 'why, man, you will be telling me you don't like cock-fighting next!'

'As a matter of fact, I don't,' Daniel replied curtly. 'But I was going to say that I never gamble with what is important to me.'

'Ha, very wise,' agreed Lord Harworth. 'That's a lesson we could all learn, eh, Leaconham? But we are holding you up, sir, and we should not keep the horses standing. Nor should we keep a lady here in this heat. You will want to get on, Miss Wythenshawe.' He smiled at Kitty. 'Has that madcap sister of mine acquainted you with her latest scheme?' Kitty's eyes widened. Had Ann told her brother of their visit to Lombard Street that evening? She was about to speak when Lord Harworth continued, saying jovially, 'A picnic! My mother has a small property a little way out of town, on the Cambridge road. She rarely uses it but the grounds are very pretty and Ann has decided we should dine there, *al fresco*.'

'Miss Harworth has said nothing to me, my lord,' replied Kitty, thanking Providence she had not mentioned the Abolition meeting.

'Well, depend upon it she will. I have no doubt that she is even now plaguing my mother to write the invitations.' He touched his hat. 'Good day to you, Miss Wythenshawe. Leaconham.'

As the gentlemen moved off, Garston turned in his seat to watch them.

'Do you know, I was not that enamoured of Blackwood when I first met him. Far too serious for me, and he drinks hardly any-thing—Bertram tells me he never goes beyond the third bottle. Not the sort to go out on a spree! But having seen his horse, damn me, I think he can't be such a bad fellow after all! I can even for-give him for not liking to gamble! Seems to be great friends with Harworth.'

'I believe Mr Blackwood is a manufacturer,' said Kitty carefully.

'Ah, that might explain his gloomy looks,' nodded Garston, set-ting his team in motion. 'Not brought up to enjoy himself, or to ap-preciate the finer things in life.'

'He is a very good dancer,' she responded, determined to be fair.

'Ah, well, that might give him an advantage with the ladies, but a man without a taste for gambling, or cock-fighting, well—'

He broke off as he negotiated the busy road leading out of the park and Kitty was pleased to let the subject drop. She had come perilously close to defending Daniel Blackwood, and that would never do!

There was little time for conversation when she returned to Portman Square. By the time she had changed her gown and tidied her hair, Lord Harworth's carriage was at the door. She had told her godmother that Ann had invited her to dine since her mother and brother were to be out that evening. This was perfectly true, but what she did not explain was that they would be having a very hurried dinner before setting out for Lombard Street.

During her short time in London Kitty had never been further east than St Paul's, but now they were venturing deep into the City and she felt a little apprehensive as their hired cab trundled over the cobbles in the narrow streets.

'Is this not exciting?' exclaimed Ann, her eyes shining. 'I have never been to a public meeting before!'

'I am not sure that your mama or your brother would approve,' murmured Kitty, regarding the garishly painted inn where the carriage had drawn up.

'No, that is why I suggested we should be veiled,' Ann replied, unabashed. 'And why I did not want to use one of our own carriages with the crest upon the door.' She laughed. 'Do not look so anxious, dear Kitty. We shall be perfectly safe for we have Norris with us, do we not?'

Kitty nodded, trying to look more cheerful, but a quick glance at Ann's maid sitting silent and tight-lipped in the corner was far from reassuring. However, when they had pulled their veils down over their faces and descended from the cab Kitty was heartened to see that the people making their way up the stairs to the meeting room looked most respectable. It was, after all, early evening, she told herself. They would be safely back in Cavendish Square before the long summer's day had drawn to a close.

Kitty would have preferred to slip on to one of the benches at the back of the room but Ann had spotted empty chairs much nearer to the dais where the speaker would be standing and was already making her way towards them, so Kitty had no alternative but to follow. At the front of the room a tall gentleman with a shock of red hair was opening up a large trunk in the centre of the dais and she heard someone address him as Mr Clarkson. Kitty regarded him with interest, for she had read a great deal about the fiery speaker who travelled all over the country promoting the abolition movement with evangelical zeal. He was very pale and there were dark circles beneath his eyes: she suspected he was worn down by the arduous task he had set himself.

'Oh, goodness,' hissed Ann suddenly. 'Look who has walked in! You see how wise we were to disguise ourselves.'

Kitty turned to see Daniel Blackwood striding towards the front of the room. As he approached, Mr Clarkson looked up and greeted him with every appearance of delight.

'Well, of all people I did not expect to see Mr Blackwood here,' Ann whispered. 'Bertram told me he is connected to one of the foremost shipping families in Liverpool, and they derive a great part of their fortune from slaves, you know. However, he does seem to be on the best of terms with our speaker.'

There was no opportunity for Kitty to reply because at that moment a large bewhiskered gentleman banged on the table to bring the meeting to order. From behind the safety of her veil Kitty allowed her eyes to follow Daniel as he retreated to a chair at one side of the room. The audience hushed as Mr Clarkson began to address the crowd.

Kitty had not known what to expect from the meeting: she had read in the newspapers about the Abolition meetings held in Manchester and Leeds, but when Mr Clarkson began to explain about the horrific conditions endured by the slaves during their long sea voyage from Africa to the West Indies she found her indignation growing, and when he reached into the trunk and took out the thumbscrews, shackles and branding irons that he had collected during his investigations into the cruelty of the trade, she felt physically sick. Kitty was not alone in her sentiments: murmurs of outrage ran around the room during the meeting and she heard cries of anguish from some of the other ladies present. She was so incensed that when the meeting ended she ignored Ann's whispered protests and joined the queue of people waiting to sign their name to a petition that would be presented to Parliament.

'What is the point in our coming here so secretly if you are going to declare yourself?' demanded Ann, standing beside her.

'I do not think my name will stand out amongst the hundreds already written on the paper,' she replied as she took up the pen.

'Besides, I want to show that I am opposed to such cruel practices. My father certainly would have approved of my actions. There…it is done.'

Ann grasped her arm. 'Very well, now let us get out of here before we are discovered.'

They were forced to walk in line between the rows of empty chairs that stood between them and the door. Ann led the way and Kitty followed, head bowed, lost in her own thoughts. Suddenly she realised that her friend had stopped and she looked up to find Daniel Blackwood blocking their way. He towered over them, unsmiling, as he inclined his head.

'Miss Harworth, Miss Wythenshawe.'

'M-Mr Blackwood, what a pleasant surprise!' replied Ann, quick to recover her composure. 'If we had known you were coming here—'

He interrupted her, saying drily, 'You would not ask me to believe that Lord Harworth knows you are here unattended.'

'Well, no,' confessed Ann, while Kitty stood silently behind her. 'However, we were determined to come, and it is *such* a worthy cause!'

'It is, of course,' he responded gravely. 'But you will notice that all the other ladies here are accompanied by a gentleman. If you will give me a moment, I shall escort you home.'

His tone brooked no argument and he went off to take his leave of Thomas Clarkson. Ann turned to Kitty.

'Well, it was unfortunate that he recognised us, but I think we may yet persuade him not to give us away.' She added philosophically, 'And if Mama does learn of our coming here, at least she will be comforted to know that we had Mr Blackwood's escort.'

By the time they left the meeting room the crowd had disappeared and it was a matter of moments to find a cab to take them back to Cavendish Square. They were still settling themselves into the worn leather seats when Ann threw back her veil and demanded to be told how Mr Blackwood had recognised them.

'I made sure with our cloaks and veils no one would know us,' she added.

'As a guest in your house you should expect me to recognise your maid, Miss Harworth,' he replied with the glimmer of a smile. 'And since I was in the room when you asked your brother to send the carriage for Miss Wythenshawe, I deduced that she was your companion.'

Kitty put up her veil: there seemed little point now in disguise.

'And did Lord Harworth know that you were attending the meeting this evening, Mr Blackwood?' she asked him.

Daniel's dark brows went up.

'I had made no firm plans before Lord Harworth went out this evening so no, he did not. But even if I had told him it would make no odds; Lord Harworth is not my guardian, after all.'

'No, but there will be no need to tell him you saw us, will there, sir?' said Ann, giving him a coaxing smile. 'After all, no harm has been done.'

'No harm this time, but such meetings can turn ugly. We were fortunate that the slave-traders did not send in a mob to break up the meeting, as I have heard they are wont to do. But in any case I would never advise you to travel into the City unescorted, Miss Harworth. These streets can be very dangerous: there is more to be lost than your reputations, you know.'

Kitty knew he was speaking the truth. They had been foolish to take such a risk. With her impeccable lineage and large fortune, Ann might be regarded as high-spirited or eccentric if their escapade was made public. For Kitty, however, the consequences could be disastrous. As her godmother constantly reminded her, if she wished to make a good marriage she would need to protect her reputation.

At that moment Daniel's gaze shifted to her face. The harsh features relaxed slightly and again Kitty saw the smile lurking in his eyes.

'I will not lie, Miss Harworth, but I shall not say anything about this evening, unless I am taxed directly.'

'Oh, thank you, sir! Kitty, are we not greatly indebted to Mr Blackwood? And you must be sure to accompany us on our picnic, sir. I shall insist that Bertram brings you along. We shall be as merry as grigs!'

Perhaps it was because her own mind was still struggling over the plight of the slaves that Kitty thought she saw a shadow cross Daniel's face when Ann spoke with such frivolity. Ann was chattering on about her plans for the forthcoming picnic, but when she drew a breath Kitty said quickly, 'May I ask how you know Mr Clarkson, sir?'

'Cambridge,' said Daniel. 'We were there together when he won the Latin Essay contest.'

'And were you both concerned for the plight of the slaves then?' asked Ann.

Daniel shook his head.

'I doubt if either of us gave it a thought at that time. Clarkson started looking into the subject of slavery to write his essay.' He shrugged. 'We were not close friends: when we left Cambridge, I went back to Yorkshire to join my father running the family business. But it seems that Clarkson could not forget what he had learned about the slave trade. Instead of going around the world as he had intended he came to London and has been working with the Society for the Abolition of the Slave Trade ever since, travelling the country setting up sub-committees and organising petitions. I have followed his career from the reports I have read, but have not seen him for years. Then I heard of the meeting this evening, and as I was not engaged elsewhere I thought I would look in.'

'But does not the Abolition run contrary to your own family interests, sir?' asked Kitty. 'I understand you have connections with shipping...'

'Not at all,' he replied coolly. 'My concern is manufacturing. It is true the cost of cotton may rise if slavery is abolished, but we will weather that storm, I am sure. Those members of the family more closely connected with the slave trade must look to their own consciences.'

'Let us pray that they do, sir.'

Kitty's earnest response brought his hard eyes upon her.

'And what is your interest in this matter, Miss Wythenshawe?'

She met his gaze without flinching.

'Hardship and suffering such as we have heard about tonight should be the interest of every Christian, Mr Blackwood!'

'It *should* be, Miss Wythenshawe,' he agreed, 'but so many prefer to turn a blind eye and enjoy a life of ease and enjoyment.'

She bristled at that.

'My father was a great supporter of the Abolition. He died when I was a child but I hope I have not lost sight of his principles.'

'Well, I will insist we no longer purchase sugar from the West Indies,' declared Ann. 'I shall tell Aunt Leaconham to do the same. Only...what of my sorbets and sweetmeats?' She looked up at Daniel. 'Oh, dear, shall I be obliged to give them up completely?'

Her look of dismay was so comical that both Daniel and Kitty laughed.

'There are other sources of sugar, Miss Harworth,' Daniel told her, 'but they may not be quite so plentiful, or so cheap. You may still have your sorbets and sweetmeats, but fewer of them.'

It was agreed they should take Kitty to Portman Square before Daniel escorted Ann and her maid back to Harworth House.

'There is no point in your coming back with me just to go home again,' reasoned Ann.

The carriage rolled up to the door of Lady Leaconham's house and Daniel jumped down, ready to hand Kitty out of the carriage.

'Now remember, Kitty, tell no one where we have been tonight!' Ann warned her, but Kitty hardly heard the words. She was very conscious of her hand lying snug in Daniel's strong grip as he helped her to alight and she was not a little alarmed at the effect his proximity was having upon her breathing.

'Well, Miss Wythenshawe, will your conscience allow you to lie?'

She saw the gleam of amusement in his eyes. There was no animosity there, no attempt to belittle her. She ventured a small smile.

'I shall do my best to avoid the subject.' She added, as he had done, 'Unless I am taxed directly!'

He executed a little bow and squeezed her fingers. Kitty dropped a curtsy. Peeping up at him, she found he was smiling down at her and she was unable to tear her eyes away. She wanted to speak, but words would not come to her. The breath caught in her throat: some silent message was passing between them. She could not comprehend it, but it left her excited, exhilarated and frightened, all at the same time. Her pulse was galloping, thudding through her body. Did he feel it, too?

'Kitty, make sure you tell Aunt Leaconham to look out for Mama's letter, inviting you both to our picnic.' Ann's voice from the carriage recalled Kitty's wandering senses. With a final, tremulous smile she pulled her fingers free and hurried indoors, hoping the servants would not notice her burning cheeks.

Daniel climbed back into the carriage. He was only dimly aware of Ann chattering away to her maid in the corner. In his mind he was going over again the recent exchange with Kitty. So there was another side to the proud and disdainful Miss Wythenshawe. She appeared to be deeply affected by what she had heard at the meeting. Not that there was anything so unusual there, for Clarkson was a great orator and could soften the hardest heart, but what she had told him of her father hinted at deep-seated liberal opinions, something he had not even guessed at.

There had also been a moment of shared humour. Daniel flexed his fingers, feeling again the shock of excitement he had experienced when he had taken her hand. His reaction unsettled him, the more so because it was very rare for him not to be fully in control of any situation. Silently he stared out of the window: he was intrigued to learn more of Miss Kitty Wythenshawe.

Chapter Four

Two days later Lady Harworth's letter was delivered to Portman Square, inviting Lady Leaconham and her goddaughter to join her picnic party at Wormley.

'Well, this is excellent,' she told Kitty as she perused the note with a smile of satisfaction. 'My dear Clara has never invited me to one of her *al fresco* parties before, even though we are sisters!'

Lady Leaconham's pleasure at the forthcoming trip was somewhat dimmed when she discovered that her son had no intention of accompanying them. Lord Leaconham was dining at Portman Square when his mother mentioned the forthcoming picnic.

'Devil a bit, Mama,' protested Garston, looking pained. 'I'm engaged to join a party of friends for a beefsteak dinner at Chipping Barnet.'

'But surely, escorting Kitty and myself to Wormley Hall should take precedence? Lady Harworth's hospitality will not be stinting, I am sure.'

Lord Leaconham pulled a face.

'Perhaps not, but she will not be serving beefsteak and oysters, now will she? And I can't say I want to wander about the gardens all day before dining *al fresco* on cold meats, Mama. Not my style at all.'

Regarding Lord Leaconham's substantial figure, Kitty considered that wandering around a garden might be more beneficial to the young man than sitting indoors drinking porter and eating beefsteak, but she held her peace.

However, Lady Leaconham was not to be put off. She continued to refer to the picnic throughout the evening.

'But my love, surely you do not want your mama driving out of town without a gentleman's escort? Why, it is not done.' Lady Leaconham resorted to her finest weapon, her handkerchief. She flicked it out and dabbed at her eyes. 'I should never be allowed to travel unescorted if your father was alive.'

'Very well, I will tell you what I shall do,' said Garston, exasperated. 'I will come with you as far as Barnet—it is on the way, after all.'

'On the way?' retorted my lady, in a far from lachrymose tone. 'What nonsense is this? We will be taking the Cambridge road!'

'Well, if you take the Great North Road instead you could drop me at the Rising Sun. After that it would not take you long to cross Enfield Chase to pick up the Kentish Lane. There, what do you say to that?'

It was not ideal; Lady Leaconham would much have preferred to have her son's company for the whole day, but he was not to be moved so she had to be satisfied.

'After all,' she said to Kitty once Garston had left them, 'my son is a dear, dear boy but he is so very much like his father: not *stubborn* exactly, but a man of fixed views, and once he has made up his mind, there is no changing it.'

Kitty did not see Ann again before the picnic, and since she heard nothing more about their outing to Lombard Street she hoped their attendance at the Abolition meeting had gone unnoticed. Although she was relieved at this, Kitty was nevertheless anxious to support the cause, but apart from persuading her godmother to refrain from buying sugar imported from the slave plantations there was little she could do as a single young lady. Judicious enquiries of her godmother elicited the information that the Leaconham fortune came from estates in England and Ireland and although an earlier Lord Leaconham had dabbled in investments in the West Indies these had not been a success and the link had been broken. A suggestion to Lord Leaconham that he should raise the matter in the House brought the daunting response that he had not yet taken his seat, being far too busy. However, the subject raised a dilemma for Kitty and when she next sat down to write to her mother she voiced her concern that since so many of the families in Town had connections with the slave trade she could not, as Papa's Daughter, consider an alliance with any of them. Not that she had as yet received any offers, she hurried to point out. Her mother's response was typically pragmatic: much as she applauded her daughter's liberal views, Kitty must do and say *nothing* to discourage any advantageous offer, but to remember that as the wife of a rich man she would be much better placed to influence both her husband and the debate.

Lady Leaconham said much the same thing and, while she agreed that they would no longer use cane sugar from the West Indies, she begged Kitty not to voice her opinions in public.

'It is a very worthy cause, I am sure, and I have read that Mr Wilberforce is very eloquent on the subject, but it is not something to be discussed in my drawing room.'

'I beg your pardon, Godmama,' replied Kitty, anger bringing a warm flush to her cheek, 'but it should be discussed in *every* drawing room!'

'Well, perhaps when you are with your close friends,' conceded Lady Leaconham, 'but it makes people uncomfortable to think about it, and that will make them shy away from you. My dear, the reason for you being here is to find you a husband, and we shall not do that if you do not *conform*. And while we are talking of such things, perhaps I should just drop you a word of warning.' Lady Leaconham began to fidget and pluck at the skirts of her gown. 'I have been very careful not to be too explicit about your circumstances.'

'My…circumstances, Godmama?'

'The fact that you have no fortune, my dear. It is nothing to be ashamed of, and you have such pretty manners that people cannot fail to like you, but we do not want to prejudice anyone against you.'

'Are you saying that people will not wish to be acquainted with me if they know I am *poor?*' said Kitty baldly.

'My dear, there is no need to be quite so blunt,' protested Lady Leaconham. 'All I ask is that you refrain from discouraging eligible gentlemen by being too truthful—about your country upbringing, for example—or expressing your more…liberal views.'

Kitty bit her lip. She very much wanted to say that she did not want a husband if he did not share her opinions, but then she had a vision of poor Mama and Aunt Jane, sitting in their cold little cottage, struggling to set their stitches in the failing light and unable to afford to buy good candles and coal from their meagre income. They had scrimped and saved, forgoing all luxuries to send her to London. The more she thought about it the more she realised that, having spent their savings on this trip, Mama and Aunt Jane were now in a very perilous position, for if they could no longer make a living from their sewing then they would have nothing at all to live on. Fearful visions of them being thrown onto the streets began to haunt her. She must not let them down. Kitty fought down a sigh: her resolution to marry well had not seemed quite so problematic when she had been in Yorkshire.

Kitty saw that Lady Leaconham was regarding her anxiously and she gave her a reassuring smile. 'Very well, Godmama, I promise you I shall try to avoid saying anything that would make you uncomfortable. I will do my best to do my duty.'

Lady Leaconham gave a very audible sigh. She smiled and patted Kitty's cheek.

'There. I knew you were a good girl! Oh, and I almost forgot to tell you that your new walking dress has arrived.'

'Another dress? Oh, ma'am, you are spoiling me!'

'Nonsense. We were agreed that you should have a new one, were we not? After all, you walk out every morning when you take Titan for his exercise.'

Kitty laughed.

'No one sees me at that time in the morning, Godmama!'

'Nevertheless you cannot have too many walking dresses. And when I was with Madame Sophie last week I saw the most beautiful sprigged muslin that I knew would look lovely on you. It is for our picnic tomorrow. I want you to look your best for Lord Harworth.'

'But I am sure Lord Harworth has no interest in me, except as his sister's friend.'

'Perhaps not, but there is no harm in your looking your best for the picnic,' responded Lady Leaconham. 'And since you will be together for most of the day tomorrow, it would do no harm to make yourself agreeable to him, now would it? After all, he is by far the most eligible bachelor we know, and even if he is only a baron think how happy your mama would be if you were to become Lady Harworth!'

With her godmother's words ringing in her ears, Kitty rose the next day and made her preparations for the picnic. She dressed carefully in the new gown of pale primrose, its bodice embroidered with tiny flowers in a deeper lemon, and she allowed Meakin to style her hair so that her glossy dark curls would peep out beneath the shady brim of her villager straw hat. When a servant scratched upon the door to tell her Lord Leaconham had arrived and that Lady Leaconham was waiting for her in the morning room, she took a final look in the mirror, picked up her parasol and hurried downstairs.

'My dear, you look charmingly,' smiled Lady Leaconham as she entered the morning room. 'Well, Garston, what do you think of my protégé now?'

'By Jove, Mama, she's a veritable diamond!' declared Lord Leaconham. 'Been thinkin' so for a while now.' He raised his quizzing glass to stare at Kitty, who wished she had draped a neckerchief around the low neckline of her gown.

'Yes, well I am hoping we can fix Lord Harworth's interest,' put in Lady Leaconham, adding pointedly, 'It is not so important for *him* to find a rich wife.'

'Dash it, Mama, he is not that much wealthier than me!' muttered Garston but his mother was not listening.

She swept up, put her arm through Kitty's and carried her towards the door. 'The carriage is here—shall we go?'

In recognition of the sunny weather, Lady Leaconham had elected to travel in the open landau, and once the busy streets were left behind Kitty had to admit that it was very pleasant to be bowling along with the sun shining down upon them. There was just enough breeze to make it necessary for her to pull her Norwich shawl about her shoulders, which had the added advantage of screening her décolletage from Lord Leaconham's admiring gaze. She was not sorry when at last they reached the steep hill leading to Chipping Barnet, where they were to part company with the young lord and she had the impression that her godmother, too, was relieved he was not now accompanying them further. Lady Leaconham had taken the precaution of hiring outriders, two liveried servants on horseback who would accompany them to Wormley and as they drove away from Barnet she now declared herself perfectly satisfied with their escort.

'And who knows,' she ended with a hopeful little smile, 'you are looking so pretty today, my dear Kitty, that Lord Harworth might decide to accompany us on our homeward journey!'

Kitty said nothing. She could not recall Lord Harworth paying her any particular attention, and she hoped for nothing more from the day than a pleasant time spent in congenial company. The image of Daniel Blackwood flashed into her mind and in an unguarded moment she hoped he would be there. She quickly stifled the thought: she had come to London to find and marry a gentleman, not a blunt Yorkshire manufacturer!

Wormley Hall was a beautiful old manor house set in large grounds that had been landscaped some fifty years ago. The trees had matured, the gravel paths and artificial lakes were somewhat overgrown and the whole now possessed the beautiful, slightly neglected air that was fashionably romantic. Several carriages were drawn up on the drive when they arrived and it was not long before Kitty was being introduced to Lady Harworth's guests, those considered worthy of sharing the treat of an *al fresco* dinner. Several young people were present and Ann soon carried Kitty away to join them.

'I am so glad you could come,' she declared, linking arms with Kitty. 'I do so love to eat out of doors. We are going to dine down there.' She waved her arm in the direction of the lake, where a dozen or so servants were following a lumbering wagon to the far bank. 'But before we walk there Mama wants to show everyone the formal gardens.' Ann giggled, then lowered her voice. 'Mr Grant has written an ode that he is going to read to us.'

Kitty followed her glance towards a very thin young man with a mop of brown hair. He was even now poring over a notebook.

'Do not expect too much, Miss Wythenshawe,' laughed another member of the party, a stocky young man with a florid complexion. 'Julian's poems are never very good.'

'Y-you w-will eat your w-w-w-words one day, Ashley,' retorted Mr Grant, pushing his hair out of his eyes. 'Just w-w-wait until my work is published!'

Laughing and chattering, the group of young people followed their elders round the house to the south front, where the formal gardens stretched before them. They gathered round while young

Mr Grant read them his 'Ode to a Fallen Rose' and applauded politely, then Lady Harworth conducted them around the gardens, pointing out the new plants and marble statues that had recently been introduced.

'I wonder that you will take so much time over these gardens, Mama, when you never stay here,' said Ann, smothering a yawn.

'One never knows what might happen,' replied Lady Harworth, leading them back towards the house. 'I am minded to live here, should Bertram take a wife.'

Lady Leaconham was looking about her anxiously. She waited for Ann to come up to her and said casually, 'Ann, dear, is your brother not joining us today?'

'Oh, Bertram is around somewhere…yes, here he is now.'

Kitty found herself smiling at her godmother's look of relief when Lord Harworth emerged from the house, Mr Blackwood walking beside him.

'My apologies that I was not here to greet you, ma'am,' said Lord Harworth, bowing over his aunt's hand. 'Blackwood and I were looking at the new range we have installed in the kitchen—the latest thing, you know, enclosed firebox, bigger hot-water tank…'

'Oh, Bertram, our guests are not interested in that,' protested Ann.

'Not yet, perhaps,' put in Daniel. 'It may not be so necessary on a warm day like today, but imagine yourself coming in after a day's hunting, muddy and dirty and wanting a bath before going down to dinner. By keeping a small fire in the range there will always be hot water for you.'

He was smiling directly at Kitty, who found herself wanting to smile back until Lady Harworth's voice cut across the moment.

'Very interesting to *you,* I am sure, Mr Blackwood, since you understand these things and are always talking to my son about spinning jennies and water frames, but I do not think our guests wish to concern themselves with the domestic arrangements of the house, what do you say, Miss Wythenshawe?'

Everyone's attention turned to Kitty. Her godmother was watching her and she read the appeal in her eyes—she must not appear provincial. She thought of her mother and her aunt in their cottage in Fallridge, cooking on the little hob-grate with only a maidservant to help them.

'You must excuse me,' she said quietly, 'I know nothing of cooks and kitchens.'

'That is not to say she is not an excellent housekeeper,' Lady Leaconham rushed in, giving a nervous laugh. 'But I doubt my goddaughter has ever had the need to venture into a kitchen. Am I correct, Kitty?'

'No, I have not.'

'Then Miss Wythenshawe is very fortunate,' murmured Daniel.

His smile had disappeared and Kitty wanted to protest, to explain that it was not because she had an army of servants at her beck and call that she had never entered the kitchen of a grand house, but Lord Harworth was turning towards her, offering her his arm.

'I think we should be making our way to the lake. May I escort you, Miss Wythenshawe?'

Kitty did not need the little nudge in the back from Lady Leaconham to remind her of her duty, but she did try to smile a little more warmly at Lord Harworth as she tucked her fingers into the crook of his arm and walked off. She would not think of Daniel and his black looks, nor the fact that when she had put her hand on Daniel's arm at the recent ball she had felt a little buzz of excitement run through her body. She could remember even now the feel of the hard sinews beneath his sleeve, the coiled energy of the man in the solid muscle. Lord Harworth's arm merely felt...solid.

The party making its way around the lake to the picnic site was a very jolly one, with plenty of chatter and laughter and Kitty did her best to join in, responding in kind to her escort's jovial remarks. She tried not to think of Daniel, who was following some way behind. When they reached the designated dining area Lord Harworth excused himself and rushed off to instruct the servants on the placing of the remaining tables and Kitty was left to wait for the others to come up. Daniel and Ann were the first to arrive and as they approached she was somewhat surprised to hear Ann alluding to the Abolition meeting.

'Kitty has successfully persuaded my aunt to give up plantation sugar, but I have not been able to help at all,' Ann was saying to Daniel. 'Bertram has investments in the West Indies, you see, so it is impossible for us to purchase our sugar elsewhere. And as Bertram says, if we all stop buying sugar then the poor plantation workers will starve, and what good will that do?'

'It might force change,' Daniel replied, but Ann was not listening.

'Besides, if you consider what we use in one household,' she continued reflectively, 'it is not so very much, after all, so what good would our little protest do?' She smiled at Kitty. 'We would be inconveniencing ourselves to very little effect, do you not agree?'

Kitty hesitated; her godmother's warning was still fresh in her mind.

'I think, if there were enough *little protests,* they might have a profound effect,' she replied carefully. She excused herself and moved away, determined not to be drawn into the argument, but not before she heard Daniel's comment.

'Miss Wythenshawe does not appear quite so eager to support the movement now. Perhaps her enthusiasm has waned since the meeting.'

'We were all moved by Mr Clarkson's talk that evening,' replied Ann. 'But when the heat of the moment is passed then rational thought returns. I tried to dissuade her from signing the petition, but she was adamant she would do it...'

Kitty heard no more. She moved away quickly to join her godmother, who was being invited by Lord Harworth to sit at his table. It would do no good to assure Ann that she was as passionate as ever about the evils of slavery, and such a public declaration could only upset her godmother, so she tried to put the conversation out of her mind and concentrate upon the picnic.

The sun continued to shine and the party was in excellent spirits as the footmen served them with a delicious assortment of dishes, most impressive of which were the sorbets and chilled lemonade brought down from the house in a wagon full of ice.

'Oh, this is delightful,' cried Ann. 'I do hope the fine weather holds a little longer. Perhaps we could dine out of doors for my birthday, Mama.'

'And where would you suggest we do that, miss?' retorted her mother. 'The terrace is not wide enough and Harworth will not allow you to trample all over his flowerbeds.'

'No, indeed,' chuckled Lord Harworth. He turned to Kitty. 'You must know, Miss Wythenshawe—indeed, I am sure Ann has told you, such good friends as you have become!—that my sister has persuaded me to hold a little dance for her birthday before we go north for the summer. I hope you will be able to come?'

'Oh, I—um—'

'Of course we shall, Bertram dear.' Lady Leaconham smiled. 'And I am sure Leaconham will come, too.'

'But why is my nephew not here today?' demanded Lady Harworth. 'I made sure my invitation included him.'

'He is engaged to join a party of friends today, at Barnet,' explained Lady Leaconham, helping herself to another dish of sorbet.

'Barnet,' cried Lord Harworth. 'Ah, that will be at the Rising Sun, no doubt. They are famous for their dinners.'

'That is correct,' affirmed Lady Leaconham. 'We shall drive back that way and collect him on our return to Town.'

'I hope he has a good head then,' laughed Mr Ashley, sitting at a nearby table. 'I believe the wine and brandy flow pretty freely at those affairs!'

'Not sure I'd want *my* m-mother to see me after such a meal!' remarked Julian Grant.

'Heaven forbid,' muttered Mr Ashley. 'It might give you inspiration for another of your dreadful odes!'

Lady Leaconham was busy conversing with her sister and Kitty was thankful she did not hear this interchange.

'Tell me, Miss Wythenshawe…' Lord Harworth turned to address her '…how does this compare with your life in the north?'

'It is very…different, my lord,' she replied.

'A little warmer, I don't doubt,' he chuckled. 'My mother always bemoans the fact that when we are at Kirkleigh the weather is rarely conducive to dining out of doors. So how do you amuse yourself at home? Balls, assemblies…'

Kitty was at a loss to know how to reply and was thankful when her godmother came to her aid.

'My dear Kitty has lived very retired, my lord. Her mother is a widow now, of course, but Mr Wythenshawe was a man of *very* strict principles. Not,' she added hastily, 'that he had any objection to parties, but only in *select* company.'

'And are you well acquainted with Mr Blackwood's family?' enquired Ann.

'Not at all,' Kitty replied hastily.

'Oh?' Ann looked up, surprised. 'But when we met him in Oxford Street you said—'

'Yes, but we do not move in the same circles.'

Kitty hoped in vain that her words had not carried across the table to Daniel. She saw his dark frown descend.

'I told you, my lord,' he said, 'Miss Wythenshawe is far above my touch.'

The icy words coincided with a small cloud crossing in front of the sun and a sudden, uneasy hush fell over the company. It lasted only a couple of seconds, but Kitty was mortified.

'No, no, I never meant—'

Her anguished protest was no more than a whisper and it was

lost as Lady Harworth rose from the table, signalling the end of the meal. There was a sudden flurry of activity as everyone followed suit and Kitty looked towards Daniel, hoping she might be able to apologise and explain herself, but he was already moving away, giving his arm to a dashing young matron.

'Miss Wythenshawe?' Lord Harworth was holding his arm out to her. 'Shall we walk?'

Silently she put her fingers on his arm, responding mechanically to his remarks while inwardly berating herself. It was so difficult! In trying to please her godmother and conceal her impoverished circumstances she appeared proud and conceited. Suddenly she could restrain herself no longer; she burst out, 'My lord, when I spoke just now, about my family in the north, I fear I offended Mr Blackwood—'

'Blackwood, offended?' exclaimed Lord Harworth. 'No, no, I am sure he is not. After all there is no denying that he is a manufacturer and while you might bump into him at Harrogate, perhaps, it is not surprising that you have not met him at any of the grander houses. Not but that the situation might change in the future,' he added and when Kitty looked an enquiry he tapped his nose. 'Meetings in Whitehall, m'dear! Can't say more, but let us just say that I am not averse to furthering my acquaintance with the Blackwood family.

'Now, Miss Wythenshawe, if we take this path you will find we have a very good view of the house across the lake…well, what do you think of that? Magnificent, eh?'

Kitty duly admired the view, but even while she was conversing with her escort she was thinking of Daniel. She must talk to him. Despite their past differences and the fact that he had treated her abominably, her conscience would not allow her to rest until she had explained herself. However, Lord Harworth and his guests were in no hurry to conclude their rambles through the woods and it was a good hour before the party gathered again at the house and carriages were summoned. Kitty spotted Daniel standing by himself and resolutely made her way across to him, steeling herself for her apology. She needed all her nerve to keep going, for the look he bestowed upon her when he saw her approaching was not at all encouraging. Kitty squared her shoulders, bracing herself to meet his harsh stare.

'Mr Blackwood, if I may have a word with you.' He regarded her with eyes as hard as stone. She took a breath. 'I w-wanted to beg your pardon. I think my words earlier might have been misconstrued.'

'Oh, I understood you perfectly, Miss Wythenshawe.'

'No! I never meant to imply that my family was above yours,' she told him earnestly. 'I know nothing of your circumstances.'

'That much is very true!'

'And you know nothing about me!' she retorted. 'I am sorry for it if I appear to you to be bent upon nothing but pleasure.'

His lip curled.

'Why should you be any different from all the other fashionable young females in Town? And do not think that your attendance at Clarkson's meeting gives you any reason to feel especially self-righteous: I am well aware that it is currently a fashionable cause.'

Kitty's cheeks flamed. She said angrily, 'Not for me!'

She saw the disbelief in his eyes and was surprised at how much his contempt stung her. She hated arguments and wanted desperately to turn and walk away: after all, what did it matter what he thought of her? But she found it *did* matter. She forced herself to speak.

'My father died ten years ago, Mr Blackwood, when I was but a child, yet I remember his liberal views, and his correspondence with like-minded acquaintances on the subject of slavery. A number of pamphlets on the subject remain amongst my father's papers. I have always considered the plight of those less fortunate than ourselves to be of the utmost concern.'

Kitty held her ground, steadily meeting his dark, unfathomable gaze. At last he said coldly, 'Then perhaps you should be committing your energies to the cause of abolition, madam, rather than looking out for a rich husband!'

Daniel turned on his heel and strode away. Hell and damnation, could he never meet the woman without quarrelling? She had come to him to apologise for her ill-chosen remarks. He should have received her apology with a dignified silence. After all, he was used to being snubbed by those who considered themselves to be his superiors, regardless of the fact that they had little to their name except a title. Their ancient houses were for the most part crumbling and impoverished. He had thought himself above such considerations, proud of his heritage, knowing that his father had earned his money with honest toil and now held the welfare of hundreds, if not thousands, in his hands: spinners, weavers, carders, combers and silverers—the list of those involved in the manufacture of cloth was endless. As he himself became more involved then the responsibility fell upon his shoulders, too.

He strode through the ornamental gardens and on around the side of the house, and as he worked off his anger in exertion, he found himself considering the situation more rationally. He stopped, his head coming up as the realisation hit him. It was not Miss Wythenshawe's comments that had angered him, but seeing her hanging on Harworth's arm. By God, he was jealous!

Daniel began to walk again, more slowly this time, while he tried to understand this new emotion. Damnation, Miss Katherine Wythenshawe had got under his skin. She was nothing like the ripe beauties who had caught his eye when he had first come to Town, women with whom it was possible to pass an enjoyable hour or so, but who were then so easy to forget. No. Katherine—Kitty—was proud, self-opinionated and extremely annoying, but one could not forget her!

He had reached the stable block by this time. Through the arch he could see the yard was full of activity as the teams of horses were brought out from the stables and harnessed to the respective carriages, each one under the watchful eye of the coachman. It had been agreed that Daniel would accompany Lord Harworth and his party back to Town later, when the rest of the guests had departed, so he saw no reason to add to the workload of the grooms by demanding his horse should be saddled up immediately. He perched himself on a mounting block just outside the entrance to the yard, intending to regain his composure in this shady spot before rejoining the main party. The noise from the stables spilled out of the yard and the clatter of hooves echoing under the arch told him that the first of the carriages was about to leave. He turned to watch Lady Leaconham's coachman overseeing the stable boys as they pulled up and secured the hoods of the landau, while the two outriders stood to one side, drawing on their gloves. None of them noticed Daniel, sitting still and silent in the shadow of the wall.

'So we're to pick up his lordship at the Rising Sun,' said one of the outriders.

The other gave a short laugh.

'That's what 'er ladyship thinks.' He turned to spit on the ground. 'I'd wager he's caught a fox by now!'

'The mistress won't like that,' growled the coachman. 'She told him to be ready to come home at six o'clock.'

'Aye, she might've *told* 'im but he'll have been drinking since she set 'im down. And let's be honest, his lordship ain't one to hold his drink well.'

The coachman chuckled.

'There'll be fireworks at Barnet, then,' he said, climbing up onto the box. 'Come on, lads, mount up, else 'er ladyship will be after your hides, too!'

Daniel sat back against the wall and watched the carriage drive past him, the two outriders trotting smartly along behind. He remembered the chit's look of horror when he had climbed into Mr Midgley's carriage in all his dirt. A grin tugged at his mouth: how much more uncomfortable would she feel making the journey back to Town in the company of the drunken Lord Leaconham!

Chapter Five

The drive back to Chipping Barnet was accomplished in good time, with Lady Leaconham expressing herself highly satisfied with the day.

'To dine *al fresco* with the Harworths is an honour not afforded to everyone,' she told Kitty. 'And that my nephew should choose to spend so much time with you is very encouraging. I was pleased to see you making yourself so agreeable to him.'

'I hope I did not seem too forward, Godmama,' replied Kitty, alarmed. 'I had no thought other than to be polite. I would not like Lord Harworth to think I was encouraging his advances…'

'That is exactly what you were doing, you silly puss,' chuckled Lady Leaconham. 'I admit when you first came to me I had no thought of aiming so high for you. I had hoped to find you a gentleman of comfortable means, but a *baron,* and my own nephew at that—well!'

She subsided into her corner, engrossed in her own happy thoughts and leaving Kitty prey to much more disturbing reflections. There was no doubt she was enjoying her time in London, although she missed Mama and Aunt Jane. She found the society diverting, but although she knew her mother had sent her to Town in the hope that she would find a husband, the idea of spending more than a day in the company of any of the gentlemen she had met, even Lord

Harworth, filled her with dismay. Sadly she had discovered that most of the eligible gentlemen were empty-headed and so full of their own conceit that she found them positively disagreeable after a half-hour's conversation. Others, like Lord Harworth, were perfectly agreeable but, she was ashamed to admit it, rather *dull*.

The thought flashed into her mind that Daniel Blackwood was neither dull nor empty-headed. He was infuriating, of course, and arrogant, and outspoken, but one could never accuse him of being boring.

The carriage began to slow and Kitty saw that they had arrived at the Rising Sun. The shadows were already lengthening in the cobbled yard as they drove in. The landlord came bustling out to greet them, grinning broadly and wiping his hands on his apron as he addressed them through the open carriage window.

'Good day to you, ma'am—and you, miss! 'Tis very busy here today, but I am sure we can find you a room…'

The man's genial smile disappeared when Lady Leaconham demanded to see her son.

'L-Lord Leaconham, m'lady? He's one of those who came for the beefsteak dinner in the upstairs dining room, I believe. I am afraid they are not yet concluded.'

He cast a glance upwards, where sounds of raucous merriment could be heard coming from an open window on the first floor.

'Then you will inform him I am here!' commanded my lady.

'Aye, ma'am.' He flicked his head and a young boy scampered away into the inn. 'Will you not come in and take some refreshment, madam…?'

'No, I want to collect my son and go home.'

'Well, ma'am, you see…' The landlord shifted uncomfortably.

Lady Leaconham waved to him to open the door and she alighted from the carriage, Kitty following close behind her.

'What is the matter with you—he is here, is he not?' demanded Lady Leaconham.

'Aye, he's here. That is—'

'Well, let us to him!'

Lady Leaconham swept towards the inn, the landlord hurrying after her, but before they had gone more than a few steps Garston appeared in the doorway, looking flushed and bleary-eyed.

'Oh, so it *is* you, m'm.' He placed one hand on the doorframe to steady himself. 'Wasn't expectin' you yet.'

'I think you have lost track of the time, my son,' replied Lady Leaconham. 'Come along now, fetch your things and let us be off. I want to reach Portman Square well before dark.'

'Ah, well, that's the thing,' replied Garston, enunciating his words with enormous care. 'Not sure I'm up to travellin' at the moment.' He gave his mother a smile of great sweetness. 'Excuse me, Mama. Rather fancy I'm about to cast up my accounts.'

With that he swung round and vomited at the side of the doorway.

Kitty gasped, while Lady Leaconham remained rooted to the spot, staring at her son. Behind them, one of the outriders gave a short laugh.

'Told you 'e wasn't one to 'old 'is drink.'

Lady Leaconham whirled about.

'How dare you be so impertinent! You are dismissed, both of you!'

'But, Godmama, we need their escort—'

'I will not tolerate insolence!' retorted Lady Leaconham, white with fury. 'How dare they suggest my son is...is inebriated! Go, I say! You will be gone from my service by the morning—and leave your livery behind you, or I shall have you arrested for robbery!'

In dismay Kitty watched the two outriders clatter out of the yard. Lady Leaconham took a few steps towards Garston, who was still leaning against the wall, groaning. Tentatively she put her hand out to him.

'Come along, my son, get into the carriage and let us be gone from this place. What were your friends about, could they not see you are unwell? Come, my love, let me help you.'

'Don't think…anyone…can…' muttered Garston.

He turned, leaning his back against the wall as his legs crumpled under him and he slid to the floor, unconscious. Lady Leaconham gave a little scream.

'Oh, good heavens—oh, my poor boy! Quickly, someone, run and fetch a doctor!'

The landlord stepped forwards, shaking his head.

'Nay, my lady, I'm sure if we was to get him upstairs and into a bed—'

'No, no, fetch a doctor! Oh, I shall go distracted,' cried Lady Leaconham, reaching out to grip Kitty's arm. 'Quickly, child, where is my vinaigrette? I fear I am going to faint.'

'Now that won't help anyone, madam,' said a deep, calm voice behind them.

Kitty looked round to see Daniel Blackwood jumping down from his horse.

'And the landlord's right,' he continued bluntly. 'Leaconham is drunk: best to take him upstairs and let him sleep it off.' He signalled to the coachman and footman, who ran forward to pick up Garston and carry him inside.

Kitty felt Lady Leaconham sag against her, but even as she struggled to support her, Daniel stepped up to take the matron's free arm.

'Come, ma'am,' he said. 'Allow us to escort you inside.'

The landlord led them to a small parlour where Kitty and Daniel half-carried Lady Leaconham across the room to a cushioned armchair beside the empty fireplace.

'Have a bottle of wine brought in,' ordered Daniel. He glanced at Kitty. 'Will you look after Lady Leaconham while I go upstairs and see what I can do for her son?'

Kitty nodded and as he strode away she searched in her godmother's reticule for her smelling salts.

* * *

By the time Daniel returned Lady Leaconham had recovered a little and was sipping at a glass of wine.

'How is Leaconham?' she asked him anxiously.

'Sleeping,' he said shortly. 'He is unlikely to stir before the morning.'

'Then perhaps we should go home, Godmama,' suggested Kitty. 'There is still time to reach Town before dark.'

'And leave my son here, alone?' declared my lady, setting her glass down with a snap. 'Never. The poor boy has obviously eaten something that disagreed with him. Did he not say he would be dining on oysters? I have no doubt that was it. I make it a rule never to touch shellfish.'

As Daniel opened his mouth to reply Kitty met his eyes and gave a tiny shake of her head. He shrugged.

'Whatever the cause,' he said, 'Lord Leaconham is in no condition to travel today. The inn is very busy.' Loud voices and a burst of raucous laughter from the room above added weight to his words. He continued, 'You are best to go home, ma'am. The landlord here can be trusted to look after Leaconham.'

But Lady Leaconham merely shook her head and dabbed at her eyes with the wisp of lace that was her handkerchief.

'I do not think I could travel another yard tonight,' she said querulously. 'Seeing Garston in such distress has completely destroyed my nerves. Kitty, my dear, go and find the landlord. Tell him we need rooms for the night.'

'But, ma'am, it is not far to Town,' protested Kitty, 'I am sure you would be more comfortable in your own bed.'

'You forget, Katherine my dear,' said my lady in reproachful tones, 'that we have no outriders to escort us, and the sun is already setting.'

'I would be very happy to escort you to Town, madam,' put in Daniel, stepping forwards.

'That is very kind of you, Mr Blackwood,' came the gracious

reply, 'but I cannot contemplate leaving my poor boy here alone. What if he should wake in the night, calling for his mama?'

Kitty saw Daniel's lips twitch and she said, trying to keep the laughter out of her own voice, 'My dear ma'am, Garston is five-and-twenty. He has had his own establishment for years now.'

'That is not the point,' returned my lady in dignified accents. 'I am still his mama, and I am the person he needs when he is ill.'

'He is not ill, ma'am, he is dead drunk!' retorted Daniel with brutal frankness.

Lady Leaconham gave a little shudder and collapsed back in the chair. Kitty stepped up and took her hands, chafing them gently between her own.

'Now look what you have done!' She cast an angry glance towards Daniel. 'How can you be so unfeeling?'

'Well, you know I am an insensitive, uncouth, northern fellow!'

'And you can stop that nonsense this minute,' she told him crossly. 'I know very well it is all play-acting designed to annoy me.'

He laughed suddenly.

'So it is, Miss Wythenshawe. Very well, tell me what I can do to help.'

'Bespeak rooms for us, if you please, and ask the coachman to stable the horses. If Lady Leaconham is determined to stay, then we must do so, I think.'

He disappeared, coming back a few moments later to inform her that a room was being prepared.

'I hope you will not object, but they are very busy tonight so I have arranged for you to share a room. I thought you would prefer that to having separate rooms at opposite ends of the building, which is all they have free.'

'Yes, thank you, sir. That is very satisfactory is it not, Godmama?' Kitty looked to Lady Leaconham, who was leaning back in her chair, her vinaigrette clutched in one hand.

'And is my room near my son?' asked the widow in a faint voice.

'I am afraid not, but I have directed the landlord to have someone sitting up with him tonight.' said Daniel. 'There is a very small chamber available next to Lord Leaconham, so I have taken that for myself. If he wakes in the night and—er—calls for you, ma'am, I will be able to send word.'

Kitty frowned.

'That is very good of you sir, but I am sure there is no need for you to stay—'

'Oh, but there is,' Lady Leaconham interrupted her. 'Surely you would not expect Mr Blackwood to abandon us in this horrid place when my son is too weak to act as our protector? As for Garston...' She hesitated, a look of distaste crossing her face. 'I shall wait until the morning and then if I think it necessary I shall summon a doctor. I am in your debt, Mr Blackwood, and gladly accept your protection for myself and my goddaughter. I am very grateful.'

'Think nothing of it, my lady. They have tea here, so I have ordered them to send in the Black Bohea, to restore your nerves.'

'Now that *is* kind of you, Mr Blackwood,' murmured Kitty, allowing herself to smile at him for the first time.

'It is my mother's remedy for most ills,' he told her, with the flash of a smile.

The sudden transformation in his dark features momentarily robbed Kitty of her breath, and she was relieved that the maid came in with the tea tray at that moment and she could give her attention to the ritual of making tea for them all.

The hour was quite advanced when Lady Leaconham put down her cup and declared she would retire. She struggled to her feet.

'Kitty my dear, give me your arm. We will ask the landlord to direct us to our bedchamber.'

Daniel opened the door for them.

'Would you like me to have a little supper sent up to you, my lady?'

Kitty felt her godmother shudder as though even the thought of food made her feel unwell. Daniel observed it, too, and inclined his head.

'Very well, ma'am, but do not forget that this parlour is at your disposal until the morrow, should you wish to make use of it.'

Murmuring her thanks, Kitty accompanied her godmother to the chamber allocated to them. It was a large room overlooking the street, where Lady Leaconham declared that there was so much noise she would not get a wink of sleep.

'I have no nightgown,' she complained tearfully. 'And no maid. Who is to undress me and look after my clothes? I would not trust them to a common inn servant!'

'Oh, dear, if we had thought of that earlier we might have sent to Portman Square for Meakin to come here and to bring you a change of clothes,' said Kitty, dismayed. 'We are not so very far from home, after all.' She summoned up a smile. 'No matter, Godmama, I will look after you. I shall help you out of your gown and you may sleep in your shift.' She added cheerfully, 'This is a very respectable inn, ma'am. Look, the sheets are clean and they have even used the warming pan in the bed.'

An hour later Lady Leaconham was sleeping peacefully. Kitty had helped her to undress, carefully folding her gown and placing it with her stays, petticoats, shoes and stockings in readiness for the morning. She pinched out the candles and moved the solitary lamp so that the light did not fall directly upon her godmother's face. However, Kitty herself was reluctant to go to bed. It was not late, the summer twilight was still evident outside the window and she was aware of a gnawing hunger. She would not risk disturbing her godmother by ordering a meal to be sent up to the room, so she decided to go in search of food.

The inn was quieter now, the noisy diners had left or retired to their beds to sleep off their potations and there was no one on the stairs as she made her way down to the ground floor.

She found the little parlour illuminated by candles on the mantelpiece and a branched candlestick on the table, where Daniel was sitting before a mouth-watering array of dishes. He rose as she entered the room.

'Miss Wythenshawe!'

'I came in search of supper...'

He pulled up a chair.

'There is more than sufficient here for the both of us, if you would care to join me. Sit down and I will send for another plate and glass.'

In two strides he was at the door, calling for the waiter. She heard the rumble of voices in the passage before Daniel returned.

'Our host has promised to lay a cover for you immediately. It should not take more than a few minutes.'

'I am interrupting your meal...'

'Not at all,' he said politely. 'I have only just begun and will now wait until you can join me. Will you not sit down?'

Kitty moved over to the chair he was holding for her and sat down with a quiet word of thanks. Daniel resumed his own seat and silence filled the room.

At last Kitty said, 'You have not told us, sir, why you were travelling this way. This is not on your route back to Town.'

He looked down at the table, intent upon straightening his knife and fork.

'I overheard your coachman talking. It seemed pretty clear that he did not think Leaconham would be fit to travel: I thought you might need assistance.'

The entry of a serving maid caused a diversion and they watched silently while she laid another place at the table. When they were alone again Daniel poured Kitty a glass of wine.

'Will you take a little of the lamb?' he asked her. 'It is very good. You will note I have not ordered the oysters.'

Kitty chuckled.

'We both know they were not the cause of Lord Leaconham's malaise.' She sighed. 'Poor Garston. Poor Godmama! I doubt she has seen her son in that condition before.' He made no reply. Kitty put down her glass. 'I know you think him weak and foolish. After all he knew we were coming back this way to collect him, but have you no compassion at all? No, obviously not.' She bit her lip, then said with difficulty, 'I beg your pardon, that is unjust. You have shown great kindness in following us to this place.'

He looked across the table and held her gaze.

'My opinion of Leaconham is not high. The man may go out and drink himself into oblivion every night for all I care, but to do so knowing that he was needed to escort two ladies back to Town, I find that foolish and irresponsible.'

'You are right, of course. Which makes it all the more generous of you to look after us.'

'I am not doing this for Leaconham, nor for your godmother.'

Kitty caught her breath, wondering if she had misunderstood him.

'I do not deserve that you should be so kind to me,' she said in a low voice. 'Every time we meet I am impolite to you.'

The corners of his mouth lifted a fraction.

'You certainly like to remind me of my place.'

There was a heartbeat's pause before she spoke again.

'I made an assumption about you on that first morning we met. I was wrong. I beg your pardon.'

'And I beg *your* pardon for reacting as I did,' he said. 'Will you cry friends with me now?'

Kitty looked up to respond and found him smiling at her. Once again she was aware of her heart behaving erratically. Like a wild bird in panic, fluttering against its cage. The first time it had happened she had thought it the result of fear and alarm, because she had been trapped in his arms as he carried her through the mud. Here in this candlelit room there was no such danger.

Was there?

'F-friends?' she managed to say. 'Yes, of course.'

She lowered her eyes and fixed her attention upon her plate. Nerves had diminished her appetite, but her companion's quiet good manners did much to calm her. He wasted no time on small talk, but proved himself a considerate host, serving her himself and encouraging her to partake a little of each dish. She declined the roasted pigeon but managed to eat a little of the lamb and a few French beans, and by the time she had finished her glass of wine she was feeling much more relaxed and able to enjoy a small portion of gooseberry syllabub. She even accepted a small glass of Madeira wine.

'I hope you do not suspect me of trying to make you drunk?' said Daniel as he refilled her glass.

'No. I know you now for a gentleman.'

His brows went up, but at that moment the servant returned to clear the table, and he said merely, 'Shall we move over to the window? The armchair there will be more comfortable for you.'

Kitty hesitated. She was suddenly aware that she and Daniel were alone, and the chair he indicated was well away from the candles' golden glow.

'I should perhaps retire.'

'Are you weary?'

'No.' The blood was singing through her veins. She felt more like dancing than sleeping. 'No, not at all.'

'Then sit with me for a while. After all, your godmother has accepted my protection for you both. And you yourself said I was a gentleman.'

The glint of amusement in his eyes as he said this made Kitty laugh and did much to ease the tension. She sank down into the cushioned armchair and sipped at her wine. He carried a chair across from the table and placed it opposite her.

'I am not at all high in the instep, you know,' she said as he sat down.

'You surprise me, Miss Wythenshawe.'

'No, really. Before, I would have mistaken your tone for condemnation but now I know you are teasing me, are you not?' she looked up a trifle anxiously. 'I think I have given you a false impression, and…and would like to explain, if I may.' She wrapped her hands around her glass and braced herself for a confession, thankful for the dim light. 'You see, I am…not rich.'

She looked up, waiting for his reaction. He said mildly, 'I am not sure Harworth knows that.'

'Perhaps he is not aware of my *exact* circumstances.' She blushed. 'Godmama suggested we should not give out such information too freely. I doubt if she would approve of my telling you so much.'

'You do not need to disclose anything further, Miss Wythenshawe—'

'But I want to!' she said quickly. 'I thought it might help you to understand why, why I acted as I did. Why I was so rude to you when we first met.'

'Very well. If you wish to talk, I will listen.'

She paused, gathering her thoughts.

'I was very excited by the thought of coming to London. The gown I was wearing the day we met was a new one. It was my only walking dress. At that time I did not know Lady Leaconham, that she would buy me another gown and positively shower me with gifts and clothes. She is so very, very generous. I was nervous, you see: so eager to make a good impression when I arrived in London that I am afraid I quite forgot my manners on the journey.' She looked up suddenly and said with spirit, 'You will admit, sir, that you were extremely dirty!'

'I cannot deny it. I had spent a night on the moors, in the rain.' He spoke gravely, no hint of a smile, but she perceived the softening of his look.

'I thought you very ill mannered, and I was afraid that…contact with you would make my gown dusty.'

His lips twitched.

'I did much more than that, and I am very sorry for it.'

She waved aside his apology.

'If I had not been so uncivil to you—! I was puffed up with con-ceit, as if I had been a very fine lady, which I am not.' She settled into her chair, determined on a full confession. 'If you will allow me to explain: Mama is the widow of a gentleman, a very good man, but unfortunately a series of ill-judged investments meant that when he died suddenly, poor Mama was left with almost nothing and we were obliged to live with my aunt in Fallridge.' She held up her head and added, a hint of defiance in her voice, 'Mama and Aunt Jane earn a living with their sewing.'

'Very commendable,' remarked Daniel.

'Yes, it is,' agreed Kitty. 'Mama used all her savings to ensure that I had an excellent education and that I learned all the accom-plishments a young lady might require—dancing, singing, playing the pianoforte. I speak French excellently and know a smattering of Italian—'

He put up his hand to stem this recital.

'I have not been in Town very long, Miss Wythenshawe, but I know that many young ladies get by with far fewer accomplishments.'

'Yes, but *they* have dowries,' replied Kitty drily. 'It is much easier to find a husband if one has a fortune.'

Daniel settled himself back in his chair.

'Is that why you came to London, Miss Wythenshawe, to find a husband?'

'Yes. Mama taught me how to make my curtsy to a duke or to an earl, to hold my fan just so and how to address everyone, from a duchess to a dairymaid.' She took another sip of her wine. The sweet nutty flavour of the Madeira was very pleasant and she was beginning to feel a warm glow spreading through her. 'Everything, you see, to make me fit to marry a lord. It has been my dream since I was a very little girl.'

'I fear you are aiming at the moon, Miss Wythenshawe.'

She put up her chin.

'Perhaps, but I have been given this opportunity and I must make the most of it.'

'Of course.'

A little of her certainty drained away. She said pensively, 'I am Mama's only hope, you see. I *have* to marry well, because I need my future husband to make such settlements that Mama and Aunt Jane will be able to live out the rest of their lives in comfort. Mama said it is very important that I act like a lady, because she is very particular about the sort of husband I should have.' She saw his brows twitch together and added, 'I know, it sounds quite ridiculous, but you see, Lord Harworth has been so kind to me that Lady Leaconham is encouraged to think an alliance might be possible and she has written to Mama to say so! And he is her nephew, so she cannot think me too unsuitable, can she?'

'Is that why you went off into the woods with Harworth this afternoon?'

Kitty nodded.

'Godmama suggested I should be friendly, and it is not at all difficult, for Lord Harworth is most agreeable. He was most kind, explaining all about the park and the woods at Wormley, and the new planting he wants to do there—' She broke off as Daniel gave a shout of laughter.

'Are you telling me that he took you along that secluded path and did nothing but talk of landscaping the gardens? What a cod's head.'

'Why, yes, he—' She broke off, her eyes widening. 'Do you mean he should have *flirted* with me?'

'It's what any man would do with a pretty girl.'

'Oh…' She blushed, momentarily diverted. 'Do—do you really think I'm pretty?'

His eyes rested on her for a moment, a look in them that she could not interpret.

'As a matter of fact, I do.'

'Oh,' she said again. 'Well, perhaps he did flirt with me, and I didn't know it.' She got up and walked to the window, staring out into the yard, which despite the late hour was still bustling with activity beneath the light of a dozen flaming torches.

'What did he say to you?' he asked.

She frowned, trying to remember.

'I really cannot recall, we merely strolled along the path.'

'And did he walk very close to you?' asked Daniel.

Kitty did not need to turn her head to know that Daniel was standing behind her; his body was only inches from her own. She could feel his presence, it made her spine tingle. She kept her eyes fixed firmly on the view from the window and forced herself to stand still.

'I held his arm,' she said carefully.

'But did he at any time stop and direct your attention to the view? Like this, perhaps.'

He rested his hands lightly on her shoulders. His touch was warm on her skin and it took all her will-power not to drop her head to one side and rub her cheek against his fingers. She was so tense she felt as brittle as glass. At any moment she might shatter. She had to struggle to answer him.

'No, he did not.'

'Then the man is most decidedly a fool,' murmured Daniel.

The vibration of his warm, deep voice was carried through his hands and into her bones. Her insides became an aching void, the ache spreading quickly into her thighs. Even her breasts felt taut. She knew she should make some flippant comment, slip out from under his hands and put distance between them, but she was no longer in control. She heard herself saying, 'Oh, and why is that?'

'Because from here it is the work of a moment to turn you, like this, and then...'

Gently he pulled her round to face him. Kitty turned, like one in a dream, and obedient to the pressure of his fingers beneath her chin she raised her head and found herself gazing up into his face. She watched the amused glint disappear from his dark eyes. They seemed to blaze, burning into her. The aching void was instantly filled with white-hot fire. Daniel swooped down, enveloping her. He crushed her against him, imprisoning her lips beneath his own, his arms binding her close. She was overwhelmed, confused, as if she was flying, drowning and burning all at the same time. Her knees felt weak, she clung to his coat, and all the while her senses were reeling under the onslaught of his kiss. It was as savage and wild as the Yorkshire moors and it drew from her a shuddering response. When Daniel loosened his hold and raised his head she gave a little cry and threw her arms about his neck, pulling him back to kiss her again.

Daniel found himself locked in a fierce, passionate embrace. Being alone in the candlelight with a beguiling young woman was certainly a temptation, and he had given in to it, but he had intended nothing more than a light kiss. However, when he had pulled her into his arms all conscious thought disappeared and a violent, uncontrollable desire ripped through him. That had surprised him, but what had completely thrown him off balance was that when he had tried to apologise for frightening her, Kitty had pulled him back and shown herself eager for his kisses. He found her inexpert but ardent response more arousing than the practised arts of any courtesan. She was so damned alluring. Dangerously so. He summoned every ounce of his will-power to break away. Gripping her arms, he pushed her gently but firmly back into the chair.

'Did, did I do something wrong?' She looked up at him, her eyes troubled.

'No, sweetheart.' He dropped to his knees in front of her and gave her what he hoped was a reassuring smile. 'I am at fault for taking advantage of you.' His hands slid down and he caught her fingers. 'I should never have allowed you to sup alone with me.' Shouts and the clatter of hooves in the yard made him look up at the unshuttered window. 'I only hope the stable lads were too busy with their work to notice what was going on in here. Thankfully it is brighter in the yard than in this parlour.' He glanced back at

Kitty, his heart turning over when he saw the anxious look on her face. He said bluntly, 'I am afraid I may have damaged your reputation, Miss Wythenshawe.'

'Because you kissed me?'

He squeezed her fingers.

'Just being alone here with me is enough to compromise you.'

She considered this for a moment. He was pleased to see the bemused look had gone and she was more in control of herself.

'I am sure Lord Leaconham and my godmother will not wish to talk about this evening.'

'But there is the landlord, and the servants.'

She shrugged.

'I am not known here, sir, neither are you. Who are they likely to tell?'

'A few judicious coins in the right hands might secure their silence. Are you willing to trust that no one will find out about our being here together?'

She gave him a little smile.

'What is the alternative, Mr Blackwood?'

He shrugged.

'That we marry, I suppose.'

Daniel cursed silently even as the words left his lips. Devil take it, what was he saying? He had surely imbibed more than he had intended tonight! He saw her eyes widen, felt the little hands tremble and a moment later she gently withdrew them from his grasp.

'Out of the question, sir,' she said crisply, leaving her chair and walking away from him. 'Why, we hardly know each other. And I am sure your family has no idea of your marrying a penniless bride.'

Daniel rose to his feet, not knowing if he was more relieved or disappointed at her response. Did she think so little of him that he was not even to be considered as a husband?

'No, of course not, but neither would they have me compromise a young lady.'

She was standing with her back to him but at this she turned. The lighted candles behind her framed her dark head with a golden halo, but the shadows concealed her expression.

'Then we must hope word does not get abroad,' she said quietly. 'Perhaps you would be good enough to—what is the term?— *grease a few palms* to ensure it does not. I shall retire now, and in the morning we may behave as if this evening never occurred.'

'If that is what you want.'

'It is.' She added lightly, 'Have I not told you that I intend to marry a lord?'

She gave him a little curtsy and went out, leaving Daniel staring at the empty space.

Chapter Six

Kitty entered the bedchamber quietly to find Lady Leaconham still sleeping soundly. She undressed quietly and slipped between the sheets, careful not to disturb her godmother.

The noise from the street had died away almost completely but despite this and the lateness of the hour, it was some time before Kitty fell asleep. Her body was still tingling with the excitement of being crushed in Daniel's arms, her lips still bruised from his kiss. It had been shocking, yes, but she had not been frightened. She had found it fiercely exhilarating. Even now she felt more alive than ever before. She did not want to sleep, she wanted to stay awake and relive that startling, earth-shaking embrace over and over again. The mere thought of it sent an aching excitement shooting through her. She turned on her side and curled up, hugging the feeling to her. She wanted to remember for ever those few short hours spent with Daniel, because they could never be repeated. It was not allowed for respectable young ladies to kiss gentlemen they were not going to marry, and Daniel had no intention of marrying her. He had suggested it, but only because he thought he had compromised her—had he not agreed that his family would not want him to take a penniless bride? And her own family, her mother, Aunt Jane, Godmama—they all expected her to make a very good match. She had been sent to London with the express intention of finding a husband, and she knew that in her mother's eyes at least, a mill-owner's son was not an eligible suitor. Kitty sighed and closed her eyes. Images of Daniel Blackwood filled her mind and another delicious tingle ran through her.

Stop this, she told herself fiercely. His actions were *not* those of a gentleman. No man of honour would have pounced on her in such a savage way. A man of honour, she decided, would have treated her with respect and even if he had been violently in love with her—which Daniel most definitely was not—he would have suppressed his feelings and done nothing more than plant a fervent kiss upon her fingers.

Kitty put her hand to her lips. There had been nothing suppressed about Daniel's embrace. He was clearly not an honourable gentleman. She had the daunting feeling that no honourable gentleman would ever be so exciting.

Despite the clatter of traffic from the street below their window, Lady Leaconham enjoyed a good night's sleep, waking refreshed and eager for news of her son. In contrast, Kitty's spirits were heavy and lethargic but she tried to conceal this as she helped her god-mother to dress and then followed her down to the private parlour, where they had been informed that Lord Leaconham was waiting for them.

They found Garston and Daniel seated at the table, which had been laid for breakfast. Although Garston replied breezily to his mother's anxious enquiries, Kitty thought he looked decidedly pale and drawn. By comparison, Daniel appeared full of vigour and vitality and it was with some trepidation that Kitty took her seat beside him. In the bright light of a summer's morning the parlour seemed a different world from the cosy, candlelit room she and Daniel has shared, but she was painfully aware of him beside her, his long fingers wrapped around a coffee cup where last night they had been warm on her shoulders. His very presence was like a magnet, tugging at her body. She wanted to lean towards him, to be touching him…

'Kitty, my love, you are shivering,' observed Lady Leaconham. 'Perhaps you should run upstairs and fetch your shawl.'

'I am quite warm enough, ma'am,' said Kitty hastily, aware of Daniel's keen eyes turned towards her. 'I am a little tired, that is all.'

'That is no wonder,' remarked Lady Leaconham, helping herself to a slice of bread and butter. 'I woke some time before midnight and you were not in your bed.'

Beneath the table Daniel's knee touched hers and Kitty jumped. Her whole body was a tingling, jangling mass of nerves. She stole a glance at Daniel. He had not looked up but his studied indifference made her wonder if the contact had been accidental. She struggled to concentrate upon her reply to Lady Leaconham.

'I came downstairs for a little supper, ma'am.'

'Oh? And what did you eat? After Garston's experience yesterday I am reluctant to break my fast here, but I cannot think there is any danger in taking a little bread and butter.' She cast a doubtful glance at her son's plate, piled with thick slices of ham and cold beef. 'You certainly seem to have regained your appetite, my love.'

Garston's mouth was too full to reply but Daniel said coolly, 'I believe a good breakfast will aid Lord Leaconham's recovery.'

Garston gave him a rather sheepish look and swallowed hard.

'Aye, it will indeed,' he agreed. 'Just what I need. I shall be well enough to travel back to Town with you today, Mama, never fear.'

'And I shall ride with you,' said Daniel. He turned to Kitty. 'May I pour you a little more coffee, Miss Wythenshawe? And perhaps you would like another bread roll?'

'Coffee, thank you, but no more to eat.'

'I hope your…supper did not prevent you from sleeping,' he remarked as he filled her cup.

Kitty felt the blood rushing to her cheeks.

'N-no.' His countenance was impassive but she observed the glint in his dark eyes and added firmly, 'I slept very well. I know of no reason why I should not do so.'

'Do you not?'

The blush on Kitty's cheeks deepened and she could only pray that the others were too intent upon their breakfast to notice her discomfiture. She shot Daniel an angry look.

'No,' she said in a tight voice. 'Nothing worthy of comment at all.'

With a smile, Daniel returned his attention to his breakfast. Was it cruel of him to tease her? Perhaps, but she looked so delightful when she was flustered. The touch of her leg against his had not been deliberate, she was far too respectable for that, but it had taken all his will-power not to react. That brief contact had sent a warm thrill rushing through him, reminding him again of the excitement he had felt when he kissed her. But he must be careful. He picked up his cup. There would be the devil to pay if last night's little encounter should be discovered. Doubtless he would be expected to marry the chit.

It was a sudden shock to realise that the idea rather appealed to him.

'Mr Blackwood, you have spilled your coffee!'

Lady Leaconham's voice recalled his wandering thoughts.

'I beg your pardon.' He looked down. The coffee had slopped on to his empty plate. 'That was very careless of me.' He shot a quick, apologetic glance at Kitty. 'Thankfully there is no harm done. This time.'

She met his eyes fleetingly.

'You must be careful to make sure it doesn't happen again.'

Her tone was cool but he was certain she was not talking about the spilling of his drink but of that blazing, explosive kiss they had shared last night. They had agreed the matter was best forgotten but after a night's reflection Daniel found he did not want to forget it. Kitty's reaction when he had kissed her convinced him that she was not indifferent to him, but could he be wrong? Was it possible that she had put the matter from her mind? He did not think so. He wanted to talk to her but she gave him no opportunity to do so, staying close to her godmother for the remainder of the morning and ignoring him when he tried to hand her into the carriage, turning instead to Leaconham to perform that duty. After that he could only ride beside the carriage, knowing Kitty was only feet away from him.

'I trust Lord Harworth will not be too put out with you for your absence last night, sir,' said Lady Leaconham when they arrived at Portman Square and she took her leave of him. Kitty, he noticed, said nothing, merely standing on the doorstep with her eyes downcast.

'I sent a messenger to him yesterday evening, to explain the situation.'

'Ah, of course. And I hope you will escort my son to his rooms—'

'Dash it all, Mama, I ain't in need of a nursemaid!' cried Garston, poking his head out of the carriage window. 'I am perfectly capable of getting myself home. Drive on, Dawkins!'

He dragged his hat from his fair head and waved it towards the coachman. Daniel nodded to Lady Leaconham.

'You need not worry, ma'am. I'll see him home safely.'

Then with a nod of his head he turned his horse and rode off. There would be no tête-à-tête with Miss Kitty Wythenshawe today. Perhaps that was for the best, he thought as he rode out of Portman Square, for the very unsettling idea was taking hold of him that where Miss Wythenshawe was concerned, he was standing on the edge of a precipice.

'Well, there is no doubt about it,' declared Lady Leaconham, leading the way into the house, 'Mr Blackwood is much more gentlemanly than I had at first thought. To be sure, he does not smile a great deal or go out of his way to make himself agreeable, but his stopping at the inn to look after Garston, and escorting us home was uncommon kind!' Her brows drew together. 'Do you think he has formed a *tendre* for you, my love?'

'F-for me?' said Kitty, forcing a laugh. 'What an absurd idea! He never speaks to me but to pick a quarrel!'

'Well, I am relieved to hear it,' said her godmother. 'Pleasant Mr Blackwood may be, but he is nothing compared to Lord Harworth. He is in trade and thus not to be considered at this stage. I think we had best concentrate on securing Bertram's interest in you. Ah, Meakin, there you are.' She turned to address her maid who was hurrying down the stairs and she continued in a much weaker voice, 'I need you to help me to my room. What with the anxiety over my son, and being obliged to remain overnight in a common coaching inn, my poor nerves are in shreds…'

She tottered to the stairs and into the arms of her waiting dresser. Realising that her assistance was not required, Kitty made her way to the servants' hall. She was far too tense to lie down in her room so she decided that she would take Titan for a walk and enjoy a little solitude in which to examine her own reaction to the previous evening.

The memory of Daniel's kiss kept jumping into her mind, bringing back that weakness in the knees and the feeling of her bones turning to water. She had no experience of being kissed before, and the thought that these sensations occurred every time a young lady allowed herself to be embraced by a gentleman alarmed her. No wonder anxious parents warned their daughters never to be alone with a man. It was also very daunting to think that not only had she allowed Daniel to kiss her, but she had responded in a most unladylike way. Indeed, she could not deny that she had enjoyed the sensation of being in his arms.

For the rest of the day guilt and shame raged within Kitty. She dare not tell anyone of her transgression, but she was determined that nothing like it should ever happen again. She would make sure in future that she was always suitably chaperoned. She would avoid the company of all men and especially, *especially* Daniel Blackwood!

Lady Leaconham was laid low with her nerves for a few days following the picnic and Kitty was glad of the excuse to remain indoors, even declining an invitation to drive out with Ann Harworth. However, the following week brought no hint that the events at the Rising Sun were known by more than those closely involved and Kitty was encouraged to hope that no one other than she and Daniel knew of their taking supper together.

She had not seen Daniel since that night and was nervous of meeting him again, so when Lady Leaconham informed her that her sister had invited them to the opera she was reluctant to accept.

'But, my dear, we must go!' cried Lady Leaconham. 'It is so near the end of the Season this may well be our last opportunity to visit the theatre. And Lord Harworth has hired a box for us all.'

'But I thought you were not a lover of opera, Godmama,' said Kitty, clutching at one last straw.

'Well, in general I am not, but this is a new working of *Dido,* and the review in the *Herald* says that there is to be a procession with an ostrich and an elephant! There, that will be something to see, will it not, my love?'

'Yes, it will indeed. Do you know who is to be in Lady Harworth's party, ma'am?' Kitty asked, trying to keep her voice casual.

'Well, Ann will be there, naturally.' Lady Leaconham gave a little chuckle. 'I have no doubt the two of you will have your heads together as soon as you meet.'

'And...and will any gentlemen be present?'

Kitty flushed as Lady Leaconham reacted to her question with a knowing smile.

'My sister does not say but I have no doubt that Lord Harworth will be escorting us. So we must make sure you are looking your best!'

Kitty did not reply. To ask more questions might make her god-mother suspicious. She could only hope that Daniel Blackwood was not musical, and would stay away.

Alas for her hopes, when they arrived at the King's Theatre, Kitty immediately spotted Daniel amongst the crowd. Catching her eye, he smiled at her but she immediately looked away, pretending she had not seen him. Lord Harworth was in good spirits and genially escorted them to the box, where he insisted upon directing his guests to their seats. His sister, however, immediately objected.

'I will not allow you to monopolise Kitty,' she cried. 'We shall sit together, at the front of the box where we may see everything.'

'And where you may be seen by all your beaux,' replied her brother, in high good humour. 'Very well, if that is what you want! Mama, you and my aunt should sit here, where you will have an excellent view of the stage. Blackwood and I will sit behind you. We can stand if we wish to see more.'

With everything arranged, the ladies made themselves comfort-able. Kitty knew Daniel was watching her but she avoided his gaze as she disposed her skirts carefully around her. Unfortunately her nervousness made her drop her fan and it was Daniel who imme-diately stooped to retrieve it. As he leaned over to return it he said quietly, 'I think you are avoiding me, Miss Wythenshawe.'

She tried to look at him to make her denial, but her eyes stopped at his mouth. She could not help admiring the beautiful, curving lines of his lips, remembering the feel of them pressed against her own. She found herself growing hot at the memory. A sudden fan-fare heralded the start of the performance and gave her the excuse to turn her attention to the stage, but she was all too aware of Daniel's warm breath on her cheek as he murmured, 'I hope you will oblige me by taking a stroll with me in the interval.'

The idea set Kitty's pulse racing, and she sat through the first part of the opera hardly taking in anything she was witnessing on the stage. She was conscious of Daniel sitting behind her and she resisted the temptation to turn and look at him. She longed to know if he was enjoying the performance or if he, too, was distracted. The thought that he might be studying her made Kitty feel a little light-headed. Despite her resolution to avoid him, she decided if he repeated his invitation to stroll out in the interval she would accept. After all, what danger could there be in walking together in a crowded foyer?

As soon as the front curtain was lowered a general buzz of conversation and movement ran through the audience. Kitty collected her fan and her reticule, anticipating Daniel's invitation.

'Miss Wythenshawe, will you walk outside with me?'

'Oh, that is very kind of you, sir,' said Lady Leaconham quickly, 'but I think Lord Harworth is before you…'

Kitty was dismayed at her godmother's interruption, but at that moment a number of visitors arrived in their box and it was clear that Lord Harworth would have to remain to talk to them. There was an added distraction as Lord Leaconham appeared, saying, 'I saw you from the pit, you know, and thought I should look in.'

'Garston, how delightful!' Ann waved an imperious hand towards him. 'Come and sit by me and tell me what you thought of the singing. Was it not dreadful?'

The small box was suddenly full of people, all talking at once.

'Shall we go, Miss Wythenshawe?' Daniel murmured in Kitty's ear.

She looked around. No one raised any objection when Daniel held out his arm to her and they slipped out to join the noisy crowd parading through the vestibule. It was so busy that Kitty was obliged to cling tightly to Daniel's arm, thankful for the strong, protective presence of her escort.

'I thought I might not get you away,' remarked Daniel. 'I haven't seen you since Barnet.'

She raised her hand in a small, defensive gesture.

'Please. We agreed not to mention it again.'

'Can you forget it so easily then?'

'Yes,' she lied. 'I have quite put it from my mind. It is an incident that could ruin my reputation.'

'Because you intend to marry a lord.'

'It would make *any* gentleman think twice about marrying me,' she responded frankly.

'Not if he really cared about you.'

'But I must not deter a suitor before he has a chance to care for me,' she reasoned.

'And must you have a title?'

'Yes, if I can.'

There. It was out, she was acknowledging her ambition. She wondered why she should feel so ashamed of it: after all, it was commonly expected that every young lady would make the best marriage she could.

Papa would not have liked such worldly ambition. The thought popped into her head unbidden, but almost immediately she imagined her mother's response: "Yes, and look where your father's lack of worldliness has landed us—in poverty!"

After a slight pause she said, 'Please, Mr Blackwood, do not think too badly of me: a good marriage is my mother's dearest wish and I must not disappoint her.'

She held her breath. There was no explosion, no angry retort.

After a moment he said coolly, 'If that is what you want then I wish you every success. There is the interval bell—shall we return to the box?'

Kitty awoke the next day to find the early morning sunshine flooding into her room, but she was conscious only of a dull depression. She sipped thoughtfully at her hot chocolate, trying to work out why there should be such a cloud over her spirits.

The visit to the opera had been a success: nothing had occurred to mar the good humour of the party. Lord Harworth had been an attentive host; the performance had been entertaining—the ostrich and the elephant most diverting—and her companions agreeable.

There had been no cross words or spiteful comments to spoil her enjoyment. She allowed her mind to dwell upon Daniel. He had said nothing out of the way, had been polite and gentlemanlike during their brief walk together and after that first mention of Barnet had assured her that the matter would not be mentioned again. His manner for the remainder of the evening had been no less gentlemanlike and he had taken his leave of her with his usual calm friendliness, but Kitty had the uncomfortable feeling that he had withdrawn from her. It did not matter, of course: despite what he had said at the Rising Sun they were not really friends—no more than mere acquaintances—but she was disturbed to find that she did not like the thought that somehow she had disappointed him.

The depression did not lift all day, but Kitty was able to push it to the back of her mind while she accompanied her godmother on a shopping expedition and later drove in the park with Ann, who was full of excitement over the forthcoming birthday celebrations her mother had arranged.

'Bertram is taking us north to Kirkleigh Hall the following week so this will be our last party of the Season,' Ann told her. 'I do hope the dry weather holds, for Mama is going to throw open the doors to the garden and hang coloured lamps from the trees. I think it will look magical, do not you? I cannot wait for you to see it. Bertram tells me that Mr Blackwood is engaged to dine out that evening so there will only be family sitting down to dinner beforehand. I am sure Mama can be persuaded to invite you and Aunt Leaconham...'

'That will not be necessary,' Kitty replied. 'Garston is taking me to Somerset House that afternoon and I doubt we would be back in time.'

'Garston?'

Kitty giggled.

'I am afraid I rather bludgeoned him into it. It is a lecture, or more properly a debate, on slavery and I knew that Godmama would not allow me to go unattended, so I persuaded Garston to accompany me.'

'But you will not miss our party?' cried Ann, alarmed.

'No, no,' said Kitty soothingly. 'Godmama and I will be there, I promise.'

She did not disclose to her friend that Lady Leaconham had almost collapsed in tears of despair and frustration when Kitty had told her of her determination to attend the debate.

They had been alone in the morning room when Kitty had mentioned the matter.

'I may as well wash my hands of you now, you unnatural girl,' Lady Leaconham had replied, falling back in her chair with her vinaigrette clutched in her hand. 'What is Garston thinking of to agree to such a thing?'

'He wishes to make up to me for his behaviour at the Rising Sun,' Kitty explained patiently.

'He would do better to make up to *me* by refusing to take you,' retorted her godmother, taking another sniff of her smelling salts. 'Oh, dear, what am I to do? Do you not realise the damage to your reputation if word of this gets out?'

'My dear ma'am, surely there can be no harm in my attending a lecture,' responded Kitty, amused. 'It is at Somerset House, and perfectly respectable.'

'On slavery!' declared Lady Leaconham. 'You have no business to be involving yourself in such matters.'

'My father would not have agreed with you, ma'am,' returned Kitty, a slight edge to her voice. 'He considered it every man's duty to reduce the suffering of others.' She dropped to her knees beside her godmother's chair. 'Dear Godmama, you have such a good, kind nature and you were happy that we should avoid buying sugar from the plantations, were you not? You would not have done that if you did not support the abolition.'

Lady Leaconham eyed her doubtfully.

'Far be it from me to see any poor creature suffer,' she said, 'but

with the situation in France, the poor rising up against their mas-
ters—it makes people nervous, Kitty. Support for the abolition is
fading. It is not so fashionable now.'

'I do not support it because it is *fashionable*,' retorted Kitty
through gritted teeth.

'No, of course not, my love,' said Lady Leaconham hastily. She
closed her eyes, took another sniff from the enamelled phial in her
hand then sat up, sighing. 'Well I suppose you will go, whatever I
say.'

'Yes, ma'am, unless you expressly forbid me to do so.'

Lady Leaconham softened immediately.

'Bless you, child, I will not do that. But Garston must bring you
straight back, and we will dine here quietly before going to the
party. And for heaven's sake, my love, when we are at Harworth
House, do *not* voice your opinions, or you will be quite cut out!'

Kitty had been too relieved to have her godmother's approval
to argue further and she had set out with Lord Leaconham for
Somerset House, promising to be back in good time for dinner.
The lecture was a lively one, and she returned to Portman Square,
her head ringing with arguments and ideas which she was eager to
share with her godmother. Garston was less enthusiastic.

'Can't say I took a lot in,' he said frankly as they sat down to their
dinner. 'Difficult to get worked up about something that is happening so many miles away. Besides,' he added, smiling at the ladies,
'it ain't as if I employ any slaves. No need, since I have no plantations, and I pay my servants to do everything that is required.'

'But you take snuff,' objected Kitty. 'Slaves are used to grow
the tobacco. And think of all the cakes and sweetmeats you like so
much. They are full of sugar, much of it grown by slaves.'

Lady Leaconham put up her hand.

'Now, Katherine, my love, you promised me if I allowed you to
go to Somerset House that would be an end to it. Let us have no
more discussion, if you please. And pray, if you have any feeling

for me at all, you will not refer to it again this evening. My sister would not appreciate you bringing such contentious issues to her party.' Kitty bit her lip and nodded, knowing she had stretched her godmother's good nature to the limit. 'Garston, your aunt assures me you are very welcome, if you wish to attend this evening.'

He gave his mother a pained look.

'Devil a bit, Mama, I am engaged to meet up with friends this evening—I am sure I told you of it.'

'You did, of course, but I wondered, since you have spent the afternoon with Kitty, that you might wish to escort her to Harworth House...'

Kitty hid a smile when she saw the look of horror on Lord Leaconham's chubby countenance. She was not at all offended: she had made shameless use of Garston to accompany her to the lecture that afternoon, but she was happy to admit that they had very little in common. Ann had confided to her cousin about their attendance at Mr Clarkson's meeting and Kitty knew Garston had been disapproving, regarding her ideas as dangerously liberal. Their exchange of views as they returned from Somerset House that afternoon had become quite heated.

'Don't know why you are botherin' your head with all this abolition business,' he had told her as he followed her into the coach. 'We have laws and preachers who deal with the rights and wrongs of the case.'

'Then they are woefully neglecting their duty!' she had retorted, frustrated by his refusal to discuss the matter. 'As a peer of the realm you could influence the government.'

'They know what they are about,' replied Garston, bored with the subject. 'I let Pitt and his cronies go about their business and I go about mine.'

'And just what *is* your business, Garston?' she asked him. 'Just what is it that you do every day?'

He regarded for a moment, uncomprehending.

'Do? I don't understand you.'

'You are a rich man, Garston—'

'Not that rich!' he put in quickly.

'Then let us say you have a comfortable fortune,' she amended. 'But what do you *do* for that fortune? How long each year do you spend on your estates, making sure everything is in order, looking after your land and your tenants?'

'But I have no need to do that, m'dear. I have an excellent steward who looks after everything. He would not thank me for interfering, I assure you.'

'So your days are spent in pleasure and idleness—'

'Pleasure, yes,' he retorted, sitting upright, 'but not idleness! I'll have you know there are some days when I barely have time to think! You can have no idea how long it takes me to get ready each morning—deciding what coat to wear, which invitations to accept.'

'Whether to attend a cockfight or a mill!' she threw at him.

'Well, yes, there is that,' he said defensively. 'When one has so many friends, it's impossible to spend time with 'em all.'

'I suppose today is the first time you have been called upon to give serious thought to anything for a long while.'

'Yes, it is,' he replied, eyeing her indignantly. 'And jolly poor sport I thought it, too. Why should I bother my head with matters I know naught of?'

'That was the point of attending, to learn more.'

'Well, that seems a pretty foolish notion. I have given up my whole day to you for this—'

'If it did not take you 'til noon to dress it would not have been your *whole* day!' she flashed.

Garston ignored that.

'I can't see that this outing has been of any use at all. Why should we make ourselves uncomfortable over it? It ain't our business. Let those who enjoy politics argue about these things!'

Kitty had realised that it was futile trying to persuade Garston. Her godmother had been a little more sympathetic but she was aware that her views filled Lady Leaconham with unease, especially when events in France were so disturbing. If the mob could rise in Paris and bring down the old order, who was to say the same thing might not happen in England?

Kitty understood Lady Leaconham's concerns and when, after dinner, she went off to change into her gown of white organdie with apricot sprigs and to drape her shawl of fine, apricot muslin about her arms, she determined that for the rest of the evening she would be the perfect goddaughter.

Chapter Seven

Ann was waiting for Kitty when they arrived at Harworth House and she was profuse in her thanks to Kitty for her birthday gift.

'Handkerchiefs!' she cried, tearing off the wrapping paper. 'Oh, how pretty, and you embroidered them yourself, did you not? How clever you are, Kitty! I do not have the patience for sewing, I rush my stitches too much, but these are exquisite, and just what I need. Thank you, my dear. Now, you must come and see the ballroom. Mama has lined it with ells and ells of blue silk draped across the ceiling to look like the summer sky. There.' Ann stopped in the doorway. 'What do you think of that?'

Kitty looked around her, amazed at the transformation of the elegant, rather austere ballroom with its pale walls and gilded plasterwork into a heavenly chamber. Candlelight from the chandeliers was reflected in the huge gilded mirrors that hung around the room and it glittered on the silver ribbons holding up the celestial blue silk. She glanced back at Ann, laughing.

'It will be like dancing in the sky. And your dress is an exact match for the silk! How clever of you. The colouring is perfect with your fair hair.'

'Thank you. Your own gown is very pretty, too.'

'It is one of the gowns I brought with me from Yorkshire,' explained Kitty. 'I thought it the height of fashion until I arrived in

Town and saw how high the waistlines had crept up, and how low the necklines had dropped!'

'It is still very fashionable,' Ann assured her. She put one hand to her bodice. 'You do not think my gown *too* low cut? I know Mama would much prefer me to be wearing a high neckline such as yours—although at one and twenty perhaps I should be wearing a cap and sitting with the dowagers.'

They giggled at the thought.

'No, your gown looks perfect on you,' said Kitty. 'I wish you enough partners to keep you dancing all night.'

'Thank you, but we will not only be dancing,' said Ann, leading her into the room. 'There will be music and singing, too—I have asked Martin Hamilton to join me in a duet and I shall be playing a new piece I have learned for the harp. Do you play or sing?'

'A little, but not well enough to perform here without practice. Pray do not suggest to anyone that I should do so!'

'No, of course not, if that is your wish.' Ann grabbed her hand again and dragged her across the room towards the tall windows. 'Let me show you the garden while the servants bring in chairs for the recital. Mama has had lamps strung between the trees and along the paths, and as darkness falls they will all be lighted so that the guests may step out of the room on to the terrace and even walk down into the cool garden. Aren't you glad the evening is so warm? It means that the windows can remain open: I do not know what we would have done if it had rained today.' Ann led the way on to the terrace and down the steps to the garden. 'I used to play here in the garden when I was a child. Look, my swing is still there, hanging from that tall beech tree. And come and look at the pretty little summer house. It is built in the style of a Roman temple.' She led Kitty through the trees. 'I wanted Mama to hang lamps in here, too,' said Ann, dancing between the pillars before sitting down on the wooden bench that ran along the back wall. 'Mama refused, saying she did not wish her guests to wander so far from the main path.'

'They should not need to,' observed Kitty, sitting down beside her friend. 'The flower gardens are delightful, and there are more than enough paths to accommodate everyone.'

Ann jumped up. 'I suppose we must go back. I have no doubt most of the guests will have arrived by now and Bertram will want to secure a dance with you.'

'Oh, I expect he is far too busy to think of that.'

Ann stopped.

'No, Kitty, he is very taken with you!' She caught Kitty's hand. 'Come along, let's find him.'

They hurried back to the house and were running up the steps to the terrace when a figure stepped out from one of the long windows and blocked their way.

'Miss Harworth.' Daniel bowed. 'I believe your brother is looking for you.' His dark, unsmiling gaze moved to Kitty. 'Miss Wythenshawe.'

Kitty inclined her head. She put one hand on the stone balustrade to steady herself. She could not deny the sudden bolt of pleasure at the sight of his tall, elegant figure but she was determined not to reveal how much his presence unsettled her. His athletic form was well suited to the tight-fitting black evening coat and satin knee-breeches and his hair, brushed until it glowed, glinted blue-black in the evening sunlight. She tried desperately to think of something witty to say, but her brain refused to work.

'Mr Blackwood!' Ann exclaimed. 'I was not expecting you to be here tonight. Bertram said you had other plans for this evening.'

'I changed them.' He looked at Kitty. 'I set off for Yorkshire tomorrow and Lady Harworth persuaded me to join you for one last evening.'

'I am very glad she did so,' replied Ann, voicing Kitty's thoughts, although with perhaps a little less intensity than Kitty was feeling. 'We are going to have such a jolly time, I know you will enjoy it.'

Kitty followed Ann back into the house, her spirits unaccountably lifted by the knowledge that Daniel was present. She found herself looking forward to the evening.

When Ann left to prepare for her harp recital, Kitty went off to find her godmother. As she stood wondering in which direction to go first, a passing waiter mistook her hesitation and held out his tray towards her. It was her custom at such parties to drink lemonade or orgeat but there was only wine in the glasses in front of her. Rather than refuse and wave him away, she picked up a glass and moved on. She was searching the crowd for the tall purple ostrich feathers adorning Lady Leaconham's turban but they were nowhere to be seen and she wandered through the reception rooms, which were growing more crowded by the minute. As Kitty eased herself past a particularly tall, rotund gentleman she found herself face to face with Daniel. He bowed and she was emboldened to stop.

'So you are going home, Mr Blackwood. Is your work here concluded?'

'It is.'

His response was curt but she pressed on, knowing it might be her last chance to talk to him.

'And are Lord Harworth's plans for a new spinning mill complete?'

'The mill? No, but I can do no more until I have seen the site.'

'You did not come to London solely to advise Lord Harworth, I think.' His brows drew together and she added quickly, 'You were staying at Greenwich when you first came to Town.'

'You remember that, do you?' His distant, shuttered expression softened into one of surprised amusement. 'My family has connections with several shipping families, and not only in Liverpool. With the unrest in France it is important we keep our shipping routes open.'

'But you use local wool in your mills, do you not, Mr Blackwood?'

'We spin worsted,' he corrected her. 'It is from the longer fibres of the wool: a fine, strong yarn suitable for greatcoats and pelisses but not the soft, fine cloth you would want to wear next to your skin.'

Something happened to Kitty's breathing. She had been listening to Daniel with interest but now, watching him, she had a sudden conviction that he was imagining her naked, draped only in a soft woollen shift. Perhaps it was the way his voice slowed and deepened as he finished his sentence, or the dangerously dark look in his eyes as they moved over her body. She was afraid to look down lest she discover that her fine, opaque muslin gown had disappeared. The air crackled around them, heavy and charged with an excitement. Daniel had brought his eyes back to her face and was staring at her with such intensity she thought she must burn up. It seemed a lifetime before Daniel looked away. He seemed to gather himself, giving a very slight shake of the head before he cleared his throat, saying brusquely,

'We...um...we export much of our cloth. And we have the cotton mills, too, that depend upon imports.'

'I beg your pardon,' said Kitty, trying to speak normally yet aware that her cheeks were aflame. 'I fear I am very ignorant of what you do.'

He shrugged.

'Manufacturing is not something often discussed in society's drawing rooms.'

'Very true, unlike politics!' declared Lord Harworth, coming up and overhearing this last remark. 'Although some like to keep silent on their true opinions.'

'I admit my views are more...reformist than yours, my lord,' said Daniel. He was smiling slightly and Kitty wondered if he, too, was glad that the conversation had moved on. 'But I would not be so ill-mannered as to quarrel with my host.'

'No, damn your impudence, but you didn't offer up the information when we first met, did you?'

'The subject did not arise,' was Daniel's mild reply.

Lord Harworth laughed heartily and clapped him on the shoulder.

'Very true, my boy! I suppose I was too keen to discuss building my mill to think of anything else!' He turned to Kitty. 'Miss Wythenshawe, did Blackwood tell you he was in favour of Grey's motion for electoral reform? Dashed poppycock. Wasn't best pleased when I found he had come to London to offer his support to Grey, but in the end it all came to nothing, so I didn't have to throw him out of the house.'

Lord Harworth threw back his head and laughed at his own joke. Daniel merely shrugged.

'I made no secret of it, nor of the fact that I would like to see the laws against Nonconformists and Catholics relaxed.'

'Whatever his faults, Pitt won't make a stand on that in the present climate,' returned Lord Harworth, shaking his head. 'He's too busy making sure we avoid a revolution like the one in France.'

'Do you think there is any risk of such a thing?' asked Kitty.

'Not if we contain the mob and keep the poor in their place,' replied Lord Harworth.

'Surely the poor should be encouraged to better themselves,' put in Kitty. 'We should educate them; teach the parents to read, perhaps, and open schools for the children...'

'Now, now, Miss Wythenshawe,' cried Lord Harworth genially, 'you are beginning to sound very like Blackwood here!'

'So I have found you at last, my love!' Lady Leaconham's exclamation forestalled Kitty's response. She addressed their host with a soft laugh. 'You must forgive my goddaughter, Bertram, she does not understand the complications of politics. You know what young ladies are, their kind hearts rule their heads and they are all too fond of expressing opinions on matters they know little about.' Kitty opened her mouth to protest but met with a warning glance from Lady Leaconham, who pinched her arm and began to pull her away. 'Come, Kitty, my love, we must find a seat in readiness for the recital. I believe Lady Celestine is to play for us upon the pianoforte, including something by Signor Clementi and I know you have been practising one of his pieces yourself...'

As she was almost dragged away, Kitty cast one last look back at Daniel. He met her eyes for an instant and nodded. Perhaps that earlier, incendiary moment between them had been in her imagination: certainly he gave no sign of it now, only reassurance that he understood what she had been trying to say and did not regard her as a foolish young girl, talking out of turn. The thought warmed her as she sat beside Lady Leaconham, listening to a series of musical performances including Ann's lively if not always accurate rendition on the harp of a piece by Mr Handel.

When at last everyone who wished to perform had done so, Lady Harworth announced that the room would be cleared for dancing. Ann was nowhere to be seen, so Kitty followed her godmother away to the supper room in search of refreshments. She saw Daniel standing alone and could not resist taking the opportunity to speak to him again. She refused to be intimidated by the rather severe cast of his countenance as he sipped at his wine: she was growing used to his sober mien and the fact that he was not scowling blackly she took as a good sign.

Daniel's heart sank as he saw Kitty coming towards him. Damnation. Surely his expression should tell her he did not want to speak to her—did the woman not know the effect she had upon him? His irritation passed. Of course not: she was such an innocent she did not realise how adorable she looked, gliding about the room in a cloud of pale gauze, curls tumbling artlessly about her head and her green eyes sparkling like emeralds. She attracted every man's eye, made every male pulse race. She had no idea that while he was trying to talk to her about serious subjects such as spinning and exports all he really wanted to do was to take her off somewhere and ravish her! She had told him herself that she was set on achieving a good marriage, possibly even ensnaring a lord, so he should not waste his time even thinking about such a woman. The problem was that he could not help himself. He squared his shoulders: he was no moth to perish at her flame—this would be the last time he spoke to her. After that he would make damned sure he kept away from Miss Kitty Wythenshawe.

Daniel schooled his features into what he hoped was a look of polite indifference as she came up to him, refusing to allow himself to respond to her shy smile.

'What time do you leave tomorrow, sir?'

'Directly after breakfast. I am travelling on horseback and expect to make good time.' He paused. 'And you, Miss Wythenshawe? Do you remain in Town?'

'I do not think my godmother has plans to leave just yet.'

'Perhaps she is remaining here in the hope that Harworth will offer for you.' He clipped off the words, angry that he had spoken of it. He had meant to remain aloof, to cut short this conversation and move away from her. Kitty did not appear to notice the bitterness of his tone and merely shook her head.

'I do not think that is likely.'

'But you would accept him, if he did propose to you?'

She hesitated.

'Yes. I do not think I have a choice.'

Daniel put his glass down with a snap; the tight rein on his temper had slipped a little further.

'We all have a choice, Miss Wythenshawe,' he said harshly.

Blinking, Kitty watched him walk away. She was confused by his anger: could it be that he did not wish her to marry Lord Harworth? Why should that be—did he not consider her good enough for his friend? Or—her mouth was suddenly very dry—could it be that he was jealous? Absently she took another glass of wine from a passing waiter. She must be mistaken: Daniel had never shown any sign of preferring her. In fact he went out of his way to quarrel with her every time they met—with the exception of that evening at the Rising Sun.

They had agreed the events of that evening meant nothing, but a tiny spark of excitement flickered within her as she accompanied Lady Leaconham back into the ballroom. *If* he liked her, *if* he wanted to talk to her, then surely he would ask her to dance with him.

Lady Harworth brought a young gentleman forwards to partner her for the first two country dances, then Lord Harworth claimed her hand for the next. From the corner of her eye she saw Daniel watching the dancing, and her spirits lifted when he led Ann on to the floor to join the next set. Kitty finished her last dance with Lord Harworth, who then asked his sister to be his partner. They went off, laughing, and Kitty waited expectantly. Daniel hovered for a moment then, his face set, he made his bow and walked away.

Disappointment and humiliation seared through Kitty. Tears threatened but she fought them down. She had been foolish to hope that he liked her. Daniel Blackwood had never given her reason to think it, save for one, fierce kiss that had shaken her to the core but obviously meant nothing to him. She put back her shoulders and pinned a smile in place as she walked across to join her godmother at the side of the room. If he did not wish to pursue the acquaintance, then neither did she.

'There you are, Kitty. I have someone here who is anxious to dance with you.' Ann came up, dragging a stocky young gentleman behind her. 'This is Mr Leonard Ashley, Kitty. You may remember he came to our picnic.'

'By Jove, yes!' declared the young man, making her a flourishing bow. 'I'd be honoured if you would stand up with me for the next set, Miss Wythenshawe.'

Kitty looked at the young man. She remembered him from Wormley Hall as the gentleman who had made such disparaging remarks about Mr Grant's poetry. Her impression then had been of a very square gentleman, for he was not above average height with a broad chest and a thick neck. That impression was reinforced now when she saw him in evening dress. He wore a bushy curled wig that made his head as wide as it was long. He was regarding her with blatant admiration in his rather small eyes. It was nearing midnight but Kitty was still smarting from Daniel's defection and she ignored the small voice within that urged caution. Mr Ashley's attentions were balm to her wounded spirits.

'Why, thank you, sir.' She gave him a wide smile. 'It would be my pleasure.'

Mr Ashley bowed again.

'Is it not the most wonderful party, Kitty?' cried Ann, clapping her hands. 'I vow I am quite out of breath with dancing so much, but I would not have it otherwise—oh, Bertram!' She looked up, smiling. 'What are you come for? If it is to ask Kitty to dance then you are too late, for you see that Mr Ashley has beaten you to it! Now, I have danced with Martin Hamilton, and George Camber— who else is there? Ah, yes, I must go and find Julian Grant: he is promised to me for the next dance.'

'If he can tear himself away from his poetry!' replied Mr Ashley with a loud snort of laughter.

Ann dashed away, leaving Kitty feeling quite breathless. She had time for a small, apologetic smile for Lord Harworth before Mr Ashley escorted her to the dance floor just as the musicians were striking up. Two energetic country dances followed and at the end of them Kitty was feeling flushed and very warm. She moved towards one of the open windows, fanning herself vigorously while her partner went off to fetch her a glass of lemonade. She could not see Daniel anywhere and wondered if he had gone out into the garden, where the coloured lamps shone brightly in the darkness. Not that she really cared where he might be. The sooner he took himself back to the north the happier she would be. A movement beside her made her turn and she found Mr Ashley had returned and was holding out a wine glass.

'Oh, but I wanted lemonade.'

'I know and I am very sorry for it but I could only find this.' Mr

Ashley pushed the glass towards her. 'It is champagne—have you tried it?'

'But of course.' Kitty raised her brows and tried to look as if she drank champagne every day. She took the glass from him and sipped it cautiously. The light, refreshing taste was very pleasant. She took another sip: the way the bubbles burst on her tongue was really quite delightful. She drank some more and gave a sigh of satisfaction.

'It really is frightfully hot in here,' remarked Mr Ashley. 'Would you care to take a stroll outside?'

He was smiling at her and holding out his arm. Kitty looked out of the window. Below the terrace she could see a number of couples wandering along the illuminated paths.

'I *should* like to see the lamps,' she admitted. She put down her glass, pulled her thin wrap over her shoulders and gave him a smile. 'So, yes, Mr Ashley, I would like to walk through the gardens.'

It was the work of an instant to step out on to the terrace, and another to descend into the gardens, where the night air was cool after the heat of the ballroom. For a moment Kitty felt quite dizzy.

'Steady, Miss Wythenshawe!' Mr Ashley laughed as she clung to his arm.

'I beg your pardon,' she muttered, breathing deeply as she tried to control her balance.

The gardens of Harworth House were extensive and the paths criss-crossed between the flowerbeds that filled the centre space. The area was bounded by the house on one side and the high walls on the other three sides were obscured by a belt of tall trees. It was from the branches of the innermost trees that the coloured lamps twinkled and shone. As they strolled along the outer path, Kitty could hear laughter and voices coming from the darkness. Peering through the gloom, she could just make out a ghostly figure moving gently back and forwards, a noisy group of gentlemen gathered around her.

'Ann is on the swing,' she remarked, pausing. 'Shall we join her?'

'Oh, I think not,' said her companion, gently drawing her on. 'I do not think she is in need of our company. Let us explore.' He led her away from the house until they reached a point where the main path turned to follow the edge of the flowerbeds, while a smaller track stretched off into the trees. 'I wonder where this leads?'

'To the summerhouse,' Kitty responded. 'I saw it earlier.'

'Splendid, just what we need.'

Kitty did not understand the remark but she accompanied him along the path and up the shallow steps. The light from the coloured lamps had not penetrated the trees and Kitty stopped between the tall pillars, loath to enter the shadows beyond.

'I do not think our hostess intended the guests to come here,' she said, trying to withdraw her hand from his arm. Mr Ashley gripped her fingers.

'Not all of them,' he replied. 'But now we are here, perhaps we should make the most of the solitude.'

He pulled her into his arms and with a jolt of surprise Kitty realised he was going to kiss her. She had experienced none of the awareness she had felt when alone with Daniel at the Rising Sun: there was no pleasant if guilty anticipation. Quite the opposite— she felt a definite aversion to the idea. She turned her head and tried to hold him off, but he was too strong and merely laughed at her struggles.

'Do not play the innocent now, Miss Wythenshawe. We both know this is why we came out into the dark!' He pushed her back against one of the pillars, trapping her with his body while his hand caught her face, turning it up so that he could kiss her.

Kitty shuddered and tried to pull away but she was powerless to move. She felt his knee pushing between her legs while his free hand began to pull up her skirts.

Thoroughly frightened, her hands pummelled ineffectually at his back. But her struggles only seemed to inflame him; his mouth moved savagely against hers and through the thin muslin of her gown she could feel his body hardening. Her knowledge of the coupling between a man and a woman was incomplete, gleaned from the books she had read and a few overheard conversations between Mama and Aunt Jane, but instinct told Kitty that Mr Ashley was beyond reason and meant to force himself upon her. In a panic she brought up her hand and raked her nails down his cheek. He gave a howl of fury and, gathering up all her strength, Kitty pushed him off enough to wriggle free. There was a ripping sound as his fingers caught the delicate lace of her bodice. She had barely reached the bottom of the steps when his hand grabbed her arm. 'Oh, no, you don't. I haven't finished with you yet.'

He tried to pull her back but Kitty's knees buckled and she sank to the earth, too exhausted to fight him again. She shrank from his loathsome touch.

'Take your hands off her!'

The words cracked like a whip through the darkness. The grasp on her arm loosened.

'Who the hell are—?'

The smack of a fist on his chin sent Mr Ashley crashing to the ground. Silence followed, then Kitty was aware of a pair of white-stockinged legs standing before her. Strong hands were helping her to her feet.

'Are you hurt?' Daniel's voice was full of concern. Kitty shook her head, unable to trust her voice. Behind her she heard her assailant grunting and she shrank against Daniel. He put his arms around her and spoke over her head, saying coldly, 'You will leave now, sir, if you know what's good for you.'

His tone was so menacing that Kitty trembled. From the corner of her eye she saw Mr Ashley dust himself off, glaring at them.

'She was willing enough,' he said sullenly. 'Why else would she come off the path with me—?'

With a growl Daniel released Kitty and lunged towards his opponent, but Kitty clung on to his coat, begging him not to fight. He stopped, saying savagely, 'I suggest you take yourself off immediately, before I forget there is a lady present and give you the thrashing you deserve.'

Mr Ashley hesitated, glaring pugnaciously at Daniel. 'Take her then, and welcome to her,' he snarled. 'Strumpet!'

Daniel moved so quickly that Kitty did not have time to protest. Again there was a sickening thud and again Ashley was stretched out on the ground. This time Daniel stood over him, his fists clenched.

'You will leave the house now, sir, and if I ever find that you have spoken a word about this, I swear I will call you out and cut you down like a dog.'

Daniel spoke quietly, but there was so much menace in his voice that his opponent made no attempt to rise. Instead he scrabbled away on all fours until he was out of reach of those punishing fists before clambering to his feet and hurrying away.

In the silence that followed Kitty did not move. Daniel turned back to her.

'He is gone now. You are safe.' He held out his hand. 'Shall I take you back?'

Kitty shook her head.

'N-no, not yet. I do not think I could face...' Her voice trailed away. With shaking fingers she lifted the shred of muslin that was hanging down from her gown and pulled it across the exposed linen of her under-bodice.

'Here, let me.' Daniel scooped her muslin shawl from the ground and wrapped it about her shoulders. 'If we cross it like this and tie the ends at the back, no one will know there is anything amiss.'

'Yes. Yes, of course, how...how sensible. Why did I not think of that?' She put a hand up to adjust the folds of the shawl but her fingers shook too much to be of use.

'You are trembling.' He took her arm. 'There is a bench in the summerhouse. You must sit down until you are feeling better.'

He led her into the little shelter and guided her to the seat. She clutched at his arm.

'Do not leave me!' Her voice shook pitifully and she was relieved when he sat down beside her.

'I am not about to leave you.'

'I d-did not know what he was going to do.' Kitty leaned against his shoulder, the soft, fine wool of his evening coat beneath her cheek. 'He s-seemed such a gentleman.'

She felt him take a long breath, as if controlling his anger.

'Have you not learned yet that it is dangerous to be alone with any man?'

'There were so many people in the gardens, I didn't think we *were* alone. I thought it would be quite safe...' She shuddered. 'It was horrible—'

'Hush now.' He put his arm around her. 'He is gone.'

She gave a sob and turned her face into his coat, one hand clutching at his jacket.

'I am so ashamed! To put myself into such a situation—I feel so foolish!'

'The fellow will say nothing, you may be sure of that. And no one else need know anything about it.'

'But *you* will know,' she said in a low voice. 'I did not w-want you to think ill of me.'

With a soft laugh he held her away from him and drew a handkerchief out of his pocket.

'I do not think ill of you,' he said, taking her chin between his fingers and turning her face up so he could wipe her cheeks. 'I think ill of that blackguard for his behaviour.'

He had turned her face to catch what little light there was and Kitty kept very still, gazing up into his shadowed countenance. Mr Ashley was forgotten. She was only aware of being very close to Daniel, of his thigh pressed against hers, his fingers holding her chin, the soft scented handkerchief sliding gently over her cheeks. She was tingling through the length of her body and her heart had begun to thud painfully against her ribs. Nervously she ran her tongue across her lips.

'Don't do that!' ordered Daniel.

Her eyes widened. Her tongue flickered again over her lips before she could speak.

'Do what? I do not understand you.'

He dropped the handkerchief and cupped her face in his hands, running his thumb gently along her bottom lip.

'Kitty, you little witch, stop it! You have no idea how adorable you are.' His voice had softened and the words wrapped themselves around her, deep and warm as he said, 'You do not know how much I want to kiss you.'

She might not have known the perils of stepping off the path with Mr Ashley, but Kitty was well aware of the danger Daniel posed to her. It was not safe to be alone with him. She should run back to the safety of the crowded salon, but the temptation to move even closer to Daniel was far, far too strong.

Torn between what she wanted to do and what she *should* do, Kitty did nothing. She remained very still, gazing up into Daniel's dark eyes, enjoying the feel of his hands on her face, aching for the touch of his lips against hers.

It never came. He gave a slight shake of his head; she heard a long exhalation as he gathered her in his arms and pulled her close.

'For me to take advantage of this moment would make me an even bigger scoundrel than the fool I found molesting you. We would both regret it, for I am going north tomorrow and you...' she felt his chest rise and fall on another sigh '...you are going to find a lord to marry.'

'You must think me very mercenary,' she whispered.

He laid his cheek briefly against her hair.

'No, you are doing the same as every other young lady in the Town; the difference is that you are honest about your goals. So I wish you well with your quest, Miss Katherine Wythenshawe.'

'You do?' Safe within his arms, Kitty turned her face up to look at him.

'Of course.' Daniel did not glance down but continued to gaze out through the trees towards the starry sky. 'Harworth is already showing an interest in you. With his fortune he has no need to marry money. He is a gentleman and I believe he will treat you well. What more could you want?'

A cloud had settled over Kitty's spirits. Perhaps everything she had hoped for was within her grasp but here, now, sitting in the little stone temple with Daniel, all she knew was that he was leaving in the morning and she would never see him again.

'You have been very kind to me, Mr Blackwood.'

'It is nothing.'

His dismissive tone was unsettling. She wanted to thank him, to make him know how much she would miss him. He was still gazing out at the night sky and suddenly Kitty was overwhelmed by the desire to kiss him. She lifted her head and strained to touch her mouth to the only bare flesh she could reach, the soft hinge where the column of his throat rose up from the folds of his snowy neckcloth and met the strong line of his jaw. A steady pulse was beating there and she felt it jump when her lips grazed his skin. He drew back and stared down at her, deep shadows concealing his expression.

'I beg your pardon,' she whispered. 'I know I should not—'

Her words were cut short as he bent his head and covered her mouth with his own. Like a spark in a tinderbox the white-hot flame of desire ignited within her. She clung to him as a drowning man might cling to a wooden spar. Indeed, she felt as if she was drowning in the pleasure of his kiss, which seemed to tug at her very soul. He teased her lips apart and began to explore her mouth with his tongue. The wild pleasure at her core intensified, pooling somewhere between her thighs. Her hips tilted restlessly towards him. His hold tightened and he pulled her on to his lap. He began to cover her face with kisses, then his mouth moved over the line of her jaw and trailed down the column of her neck, the feather-light touch of his lips making her moan with pleasure.

Gently he pushed aside the muslin shawl that he himself had tied over her shoulders. Little shivers of excitement coursed through Kitty as his fingers brushed her skin. The moonlight glinted on his hair as he bent his head to kiss the soft swell of her breast at the point where it emerged from the confining stays. She arched towards him, gasping. Every inch of her was alive and aching to be touched. If he had started to undress her there and then on the bench she would not have resisted him.

'Oh, Daniel!'

The words were little more than a breath. She ran her fingers through his silky hair, trailing them across his cheek as he raised his head.

'This has gone far enough,' he said, his voice cracking with strain. 'I came here to your rescue, not to ruin you.'

'Perhaps I do not wish to be rescued,' she whispered, her hand cupping his cheek, trying to draw him back down to her.

With a sigh Daniel slid her off his lap. The jolt of hitting the hard wooden bench was sobering. The thrilling tingle was replaced by the sudden, stark realisation of her situation. She put her hands to her mouth.

'Oh, heavens, what have I done?'

Daniel was adjusting his coat but he paused at her anguished cry.

'Why, you have done nothing, my dear. *Yet.* That is why I must get you back to the house before it is too late.'

Tears burned Kitty's eyes. She felt chilled, unwanted. Undesirable.

'Come.' He held out his hand to her. 'We will slip back on to the path and no one will be any the wiser. Your reputation will be secure.'

Kitty tried to stand. She was surprised to find her legs still obeyed her will. She put up a hand to straighten the folds of her shawl but Daniel reached out and grasped her fingers.

'It looks very well,' he assured her. 'Come now, we must get back to the house.'

He led her through the trees and they stepped out on to the deserted path. He pulled her arm through his just as another couple came into view. Raising his voice, he said loudly, 'The grounds were designed by Switzer some sixty years ago for the third Baron Harworth, you know. A little formal for our modern tastes, but delightful nevertheless.'

Kitty replied in kind, conscious of the chattering couples around them. The air was suddenly very heavy and oppressive, weighing down on her spirits. She was relieved to hear a low rumble of thunder in the distance.

'A storm.' She looked up. 'I am glad it is not my imagination. I thought perhaps this oppression was some terrible presentiment of my disgrace.'

He glanced down at her.

'It is no such thing. I am returning you to the house with your reputation—and your dreams—intact.'

Not my dreams!

The words echoed through Kitty's head. She realised with a bitter clarity that her duty and her dreams were two vastly different things.

As they approached the terrace the laughter and chatter from the ballroom spilled out towards them. Everyone sounded so happy, so different from the tumult of regret, misery and despair that warred within Kitty. She stopped at the bottom step and Daniel turned to look at her, his brows raised in enquiry.

'Pray, Dan—Mr Blackwood, let us take our leave of each other here.'

'If you wish.'

She put out her hand.

'Then, goodbye, sir. I wish you a safe journey tomorrow, and… and thank you.' She added, determined to be truthful, 'I am only sorry our first meetings were so…stormy.'

He carried her hand to his lips and pressed a kiss upon her fingers.

'We made a wretched beginning, did we not? For my part in that I humbly apologise, Miss Wythenshawe.'

'I should like to have known you better,' she confessed.

He gave her a wry smile.

'Nay, ma'am, how should that be? When tha'art a fine lady and meself but a manufacturer!'

'Will you never forgive me for that slight?'

'It is no slight,' he told her. 'I am proud of what I am.'

And I am ashamed I ever thought ill of you!

She wanted to utter the words but a sudden flurry of laughter told her that another couple was upon them, pushing past to ascend the steps. The moment for confession was gone.

Daniel took her arm and led her up to the terrace. Lady Leaconham and her sister were standing by one of the open windows, fanning themselves vigorously.

'So there you are, Kitty!' cried Lady Harworth, reaching out for her. 'The dancing finished some time ago and your godmother has been looking for you.'

'I beg your pardon, I—'

'The blame is mine,' Daniel interrupted her smoothly. 'I persuaded Miss Wythenshawe to give me the pleasure of her company in the gardens.' He gave Lady Harworth the benefit of his rare, charming smile. 'We have been admiring the decorative lamps, ma'am.'

'They are very pretty, are they not?' replied his hostess, beaming. 'I have been very pleased with the effect and will use them again, I think. Not this Season, of course, for the house will soon be shut up for the summer.'

'They were a splendid idea, my lady, and one I will take back to the Holme,' said Daniel. 'I think my mother will like the idea of being able to use the garden on warm summer nights. And I have no doubt my sister will consider it a splendid notion!'

'Sisters, hah!' chuckled Lord Harworth, coming up at that moment. 'They are always troublesome at parties, ain't that so, ma'am?'

Lady Harworth looked a little put out but she managed a smile.

'Alas, young people can get a little out of hand,' she admitted. Lady Leaconham's politely enquiring look obliged her to continue. 'I had to send Bertram out to fetch Ann away from the swing, Letitia. That little group was becoming far too raucous.'

Lady Leaconham smiled and tucked her hand through Kitty's arm.

'I am pleased to think my dear Kitty was not of their number.'

'No, she preferred to stroll in the gardens with a handsome young man, ain't that so, Miss Wythenshawe?' said Lord Harworth, clearly in the best of spirits. 'And I have no doubt that Blackwood, the young dog, was trying to cut me out!'

'No such thing, my lord, I assure you,' returned Daniel.

With another fat chuckle his host gave him a playful punch in the ribs.

'Oh, don't stiffen up so, my boy, I am roasting you—I know I have nothing to fear from *you!* I am delighted that you showed Miss Wythenshawe the gardens. As host I am afraid I did not have as much time to spare for my own pleasures as I would have liked.' He beamed at Kitty for a few moments. 'So you see, Blackwood, I am grateful to you, truly I am!'

'Thank you, my lord.'

Kitty watched as Daniel gave a stiff little bow to include them all and walked away. She felt very low. A cold chill had settled around her heart, like the mist that sometimes clung to the moors, blotting out the sun for days on end. He was leaving. They would not meet again and she must smile and say all that was proper as she followed her godmother through the crowded rooms to take their leave. They had reached the hall and were waiting for their wraps to be fetched before Lady Leaconham turned to give Kitty a long look.

'My child, I did not like to say anything before my sister, for I would not draw it to her attention, but what are you doing with your shawl crossed over your bosom in that fashion? It makes you look like a matron rather than a young lady in her first Season.'

Kitty had been expecting the question and had had time to work on her explanation, but she could not prevent the colour stealing into her cheeks.

'I spilled red wine on my bodice, Godmama. It looked very unsightly.'

'Oh, I see. Well, we must see if Meakin can wash it out when we get home—' She broke off as the footmen arrived with their cloaks and Kitty hoped she would say no more about it, but when they were shut up in the carriage and making the short journey back to Portman Square Lady Leaconham said suddenly, 'Just when did you spill the wine, my love? I hope you were not…carousing with Mr Blackwood.'

'No, ma'am. It was Mr Ashley.' Kitty was not sorry she could put some of the blame for the spoiled gown in its rightful place. 'He offered to fetch me some refreshment and I had asked for lemonade…'

Lady Leaconham gave a little huff of displeasure.

'My sister has only herself to blame if Ann and her friends grow a little wild at these parties,' she said severely. 'It is always a mistake to allow young people too much freedom. And the idea of *encouraging* guests to walk in the gardens! I cannot pretend that I am very happy about you going off with Mr Blackwood, but there were so many people strolling out of doors I am sure there was no harm in it.'

'No, Godmama. And you need not worry about Mr Blackwood. He is leaving for the north in the morning.'

'Yes, so I understand, and a very good thing, too. I know I am very much obliged to him for his services to us at Barnet, but I would not have him set himself up as a rival to Lord Harworth for your affections. I admit I was encouraged by the number of compliments I received upon your behalf this evening, my love, and several gentleman commented most favourably about you, but I have hinted them away, for the present. I will not say anything too final, of course, until we are sure of Harworth, but I am satisfied he is very interested in you.'

'Thank you, Godmama.'

'So you must be careful to keep gentlemen like Mr Blackwood at a distance in future, my love.'

'Since Mr Blackwood will be hundreds of miles away I think that is distance enough, Godmama, do not you?' replied Kitty, trying to make light of a fact that weighed on her spirits.

'Well, of course it is, for the next two weeks, until Lord Harworth goes north, but he is sure to come to Kirkleigh to discuss Bertram's schemes for his new mill.'

Kitty shrugged.

'That can have nothing to do with us, Godmama.'

'Heavens, child, if he would be confined to the steward's office I should not worry, but you have seen how Harworth treats him, almost as an equal! He lives too close to be invited to stay, so that's a mercy, but Bertram will ask him to dine with us, I am sure.' She paused, frowning at Kitty's look of bewilderment. Then her brow cleared. 'But of course, you do not know, for you were not with me when the invitation was issued. My sister has invited us to spend the summer with her at Kirkleigh! You look amazed and well you might! I have no doubt that it was Bertram that put her up to it and all because of you, you clever little puss! We are to go to Yorkshire.'

'No!'

'*Yes!* It is all arranged, we are to follow a fortnight after my sister. Garston, too, is coming with us and there is every reason to believe that Harworth means to propose to you!'

Chapter Eight

My dearest Kitty, how your aunt and I look forward to receiving your letters, with news of all the parties, routs and balls that you have attended! And now your godmother tells me you have been invited to Kirkleigh, as the guest of Lady Harworth no less! My dear child I am so proud *of you. Letitia has hinted of* An Alliance. *How wonderful that would be! And if the settlements could be drawn up before the winter, perhaps it might be possible to move out of our cottage here at Fallridge, for there is no doubt that the damp does not agree with your Aunt Jane. Her cough has returned and she is not in spirits. I fear another winter here may well prove too much for her, although she does not complain. Of course, we shall not try to influence you, my darling child, except to say that to see you* well established, *possibly as* a lady, *is the* dearest wish *of our hearts.*

But of course, my love, our greatest concern is for your happiness…

'How is your dear Mama, Kitty?'

Kitty looked up from her letter, forcing herself to smile.

'She is well, Godmama, although she says Aunt Jane is coughing again.' She looked down at the bread and butter on her breakfast plate, her appetite quite gone. There was such a weight of responsibility on her shoulders. Her godmother was so sure that Lord Harworth would offer for her and if he did, then it might be possible to find a new home for Mama and Aunt Jane before the winter. Perhaps they might even be allowed to live with her, but certainly she must do what she could to remove them from the cottage, which was cold in summer, draughty in winter and always damp. She glanced again at her letter. Mama insisted that she wanted Kitty to be happy, and by marrying Lord Harworth she *would* be happy, would she not, because she would be fulfilling the hopes of those she loved most…

'Now, we must finish packing today, my dear, because it is an early start tomorrow.' Lady Leaconham helped herself to another hot muffin. 'Garston has promised me he will be here at nine tomorrow and I must say I am not a great traveller, but I am looking forward to visiting Kirkleigh. I have not been there since my dear Leaconham died. My sister Harworth has her own circle of friends, you see, and I have mine. Since I have been widowed the time has never been right for her to invite me…' She paused for a moment to consider this, then looked up again, saying cheerfully, 'So I am convinced that this invitation is due to you, my love.'

Kitty glanced at her mother's letter again, her eyes drawn to one particular section.

It delights me to think that by the end of the month you will be less than fifty miles from us, my love. Not that we shall expect you to visit while you are with your noble friends at Kirkleigh. In fact, I expressly forbid it…

'Lord Harworth knows nothing of my family, does he, Godmama? More to the point, Lady Harworth thinks I come from a family of consequence.'

'Well, I have not gone into detail…'

Kitty waved an impatient hand.

'Have you told her I am rich, ma'am?'

'No, of course not!' Lady Leaconham concentrated on pouring herself another cup of coffee. 'I may not have told her *precisely* of your condition, but if my sister thinks you wealthy then she cannot claim that I told her so!'

'Perhaps I could visit Fallridge while we are there—'

'No!'

'My dear ma'am, I have nothing to hide. My birth is perfectly respectable, and if my mother has not the means now to live in the manner in which she was raised, that is not her fault...'

'No, of course not, my love, and you know I am excessively fond of your mama, but this visit is not the time to introduce her to Lord Harworth.'

'But, Godmama—'

'Once my nephew has made you an offer, then of course your circumstances must be explained,' said Lady Leaconham firmly. 'As a man of honour he will not consider your lack of fortune an impediment.'

'You mean once he has offered for me it will be too late for him to cry off.'

'My dear, how you do twist my words! That is not at all what I meant!'

'Then perhaps it would be best if I explained everything to him and to Lady Harworth before we travel north,' persisted Kitty.

Lady Leaconham put down her cup and bent a serious look upon her goddaughter.

'Now, Katherine, listen to me. My sister Harworth is naturally anxious for her only son to marry well. If she knew you to be penniless she would do everything in her power to prevent the match. I merely want her to—to give Bertram the opportunity to become acquainted with you. There is nothing so very wrong in that, is there? Especially when such a match would mean so much to your mama. She has only ever wanted one thing for you, my dear, and you have the chance now to make her dreams come true.' The look softened into one of entreaty. 'I know you abhor pretence, Kitty, and I would not have you *lie* to Lord Harworth, but, my dear child, pray *consider*. If you announce to the world that you are a pauper, you give up all hope of a good marriage.'

'Is that what I am, Godmama, a pauper?' asked Kitty in a small voice.

'Of course not, it was thoughtless of me to use the term. You are a gently born young woman who lacks a dowry. It is not a crime, and all I ask is that you hold back from explaining the true state of your finances until Bertram proposes to you. So—' Lady Leaconham beamed across the table '—that will not be so very bad, will it?'

Reluctantly Kitty gave her assurance to her godmother that she would say nothing and went off to finish her packing. She tried to console herself with the fact that Lord Harworth might not propose, but she was honest enough to admit that recently he had given her sufficient hints—drawing her aside for a few moments' private conversation whenever they met, squeezing her hand when taking his leave of her, and now this invitation to Kirkleigh, when Lady Leaconham freely admitted she was not in the habit of being invited to her sister's summer home. It seemed depressingly clear that Lord Harworth was singling her out. As she watched the coachmen carrying the heavy corded trunk out of her room she determined that if Lord Harworth made her an offer she would explain her situation. She would do so immediately, before any official announcements could be made, before he had time to tell his family. That way she could give him the opportunity to withdraw, if he so wished. She would not trap him into an unequal marriage.

These thoughts came back to her when, after three days of weary travel, Lady Leaconham's lumbering carriage arrived at the gates of Kirkleigh House. The entrance to Lord Harworth's main seat had been designed to impress. A long straight drive led off the road towards a high, battlemented stone wall where tall pillars topped with eagles flanked a pair of ornate iron gates. There was no lodge but a small gatehouse was built into one side of the wall and her godmother informed her that when the family was in residence a gatekeeper was on duty at all times. Even as she said this, a liveried servant dashed out to throw wide the gates and they entered the grounds. They drove through a good half-mile of landscaped parkland before passing through another set of gates and approaching the house itself. Kitty gasped, her eyes widening as she took her first look at Kirkleigh House.

It was a vast building in the Palladian style, the entrance front decorated by a series of columns built into the walls between the windows. A high-pitched roof extended behind a central pediment which proudly displayed the Harworth coat of arms.

'Well, Kitty, what do you think?'

Kitty did not know how to answer Lady Leaconham's question. The house was so large, so magnificent, that her heart sank within her. Could the owner of this vast pile really want her, little Kitty Wythenshawe, to be its mistress?

'It is very...grand,' she managed at last and drew a soft laugh from her companion.

'It is indeed, but you must not let that deter you. The house is run by an army of servants and there are housekeepers and stewards a-plenty to attend to everything.'

'If that is the case, ma'am, then what would there be for me to do?'

Lord Leaconham, sitting opposite, found the question highly amusing.

'Why, there will be nothing for you to do but to please your husband and enjoy yourself!'

The carriage drove past the first of two flights of steps leading up to the first-floor entrance and stopped at a wide doorway at ground level, where a series of liveried servants waited to hand them out of the coach. Kitty would have found their presence very daunting if at that moment Ann had not flown out of the house and enveloped her in a warm embrace.

'Oh, Kitty, I am so glad you are here! You are the first of our guests to arrive. It has been so very dull here with only Bertram and Mama to talk to! And Aunt Leaconham, too: welcome to you, dear Aunt! And Garston! I am delighted you could join us, Cousin. Now we shall be a merry crowd! Come in, come in, all of you! Bertram is out riding and Mama is resting in her room. She gave instructions that you were to be shown to your rooms first so that you might rest and change before we all met up at dinner, but I could not wait for that so I came out to meet you!'

Bemused by this enthusiastic but unconventional welcome Kitty was not sure how to react, but a glance at the butler's face showed her that that august personage was smiling benignly upon his young mistress, so she allowed herself to be marched off, leaving Lady Leaconham and Garston to follow at a much more dignified pace.

'Oh, I have missed you so,' declared Ann, leaning happily on Kitty's arm. 'I know it is only two weeks since we were in London but it feels so much longer than that! Tell me all that I have missed. Has everyone left Town now?'

'It is much quieter,' responded Kitty, adding with a twinkle, 'I think your departure signalled the beginning of the mass retreat!'

'No! Have all the gentlemen gone, then? I expected Mr Duffey to propose to that plain Jane he was courting, and Mr Ashley seemed determined to pay court to you at my party…'

Kitty did not wish to be reminded of Mr Ashley, but it was clear that she would need to give some sort of answer.

'He was interested only in a flirtation, which did not please me at all—'

'Oh, my poor little Kitty, did he try to make love to you?' Ann laughed. 'He is a rattle, but quite amusing.'

'Well, I did not find him amusing at all,' retorted Kitty, remembering her torn dress, and the lies she had told. 'I wish you had not introduced him to me.'

'Oh, dear, you are really upset. Pray do not be angry with me,

I thought he might amuse you. Did you send him away? I cannot recall seeing him at the house after the dancing.'

'I think he left early,' said Kitty, eager to change the subject. 'As for Mr Duffey, I believe he has gone into Devonshire, following his plain Jane.'

'Well, I wish him luck. He has been head over heels for her all Season, which made him very poor company, I can tell you. He was convinced everyone would think he was marrying her only for her fortune, because he has not a penny to fly with, but I told him no one cares for that any more! But enough of that—here is your room!'

It seemed to Kitty that they had walked miles up stairs, through elegant chambers and along echoing corridors to reach a large sunny bedroom.

'It is next to mine,' continued Ann, leading the way in. 'We are quite a distance from my Aunt Leaconham, but I hope you won't mind that, and I thought my maid could look after you, if you would not object. Then Meakin won't have to trail all the way up here from my aunt's chamber every time you change your dress.'

'You have thought of everything,' Kitty, responded, a laugh trembling in her voice. 'And, no, I have no objection at all to being here, if that is what you wish. As for a maid, I am very used to dressing myself, you know. I never had a maid until—' Even as the words spilled out, Kitty had a vision of her godmother's horrified countenance. With barely a pause she continued, 'I mean, I never had a maid of my own until very recently.'

'Norris will be more than sufficient for us both. And you know she is *very* discreet,' added Ann with a naughty twinkle.

She continued to chatter for a while longer until she saw Kitty trying to hide a yawn.

'Oh, dear, here I am talking non-stop and you will be wanting to rest before dinner!' She stepped up to give Kitty another hug. 'I shall leave you now, and I will send Norris to unpack your trunk while you sleep!'

* * *

If Kitty did not actually go to sleep before dinner she did at least rest, and when Ann came to collect her to take her down to the dining room she was feeling much refreshed and ready to see more of Kirkleigh.

Many of the windows had been opened and a cool breeze flowed through the house. Kitty might never have moved in such exalted circles, but she had grown up with the reminiscences and instructions from Mama and Aunt Jane, so the high rooms with their gilded ceilings and thick carpets, the bustling activity of the servants, even the call of the peacock coming in from the open window, seemed familiar. Ann had told her that several other guests had been invited to join them at Kirkleigh later that week, and she was relieved to think she would have a few days to become accustomed to the house and its ways before meeting new people.

Dinner was served in the small dining room, and although the mass of silver in the centre of the table resembled a small mountain range to Kitty, she knew this was an informal dinner. Everyone appeared to be in the best of spirits, even her godmother making light of the long journey north with its lame carriage horses and unaired sheets.

'It is even worse if one is travelling without a gentleman,' observed Lady Harworth. 'Bertram wanted me to bring Ann here on my own while he stopped off in Derbyshire, but I would not agree to it. I said if he could not come here directly with us then we would go with him.'

Lady Leaconham turned a smiling enquiry upon her nephew.

'And what was there in Derbyshire that required your presence, Bertram?'

'Mr Blackwood wanted him to visit Cromford and see Mr Arkwright's cotton-spinning mill,' put in Ann. 'Mama and I did not go into the mill, of course, but Bertram said it was a vast, noisy place, and everything is powered by water.'

'And you'll soon see we have plenty of that here,' declared Lord Harworth. 'Water and the hills make Kirkleigh ideal for a mill.'

'But you will not be building your mill anywhere near the house, my dear,' put in Lady Harworth. She turned to address her sister. 'I have never seen such a place as Cromford, Sister. The mill stands like a huge stone fortress, grey and forbidding.'

'It could well be the Castle of Otranto,' giggled Ann.

'And is Cromford itself a pretty village?'

Lady Harworth shook her head.

'Everywhere is dust and noise, because they are forever building. We were obliged to put up at the Greyhound. I have to admit it was very comfortable, nothing like the usual coaching inn. It is far more commodious: Mr Arkwright himself built it for his many visitors. I understand his mill attracts a great deal of interest, although I cannot see why that should be.'

'It is the future, Mama,' said Lord Harworth. 'With the new mills and machinery to spin cotton we can make cloth better and quicker than anywhere else in the world, and make a fortune to boot. Several fortunes!'

'I am not sure it is quite as easy as it sounds,' remarked Kitty.

Lord Harworth smiled at her.

'You are quite right, Miss Wythenshawe, which is why I have engaged Blackwood to help me! In fact, he will be riding over next week to look at the new plans my man is drawing up, so you will be able to renew your acquaintance with him—I shall ask him to stay for dinner!'

The news roused mixed feelings for Kitty. Much as she wanted to see Daniel again, was it wise, when he awoke such passion in her yet she knew nothing could come of it?

She had struggled with the problem throughout dinner, but when she carried a dish of tea across to Lady Leaconham later in the evening she discovered that her godmother was also unhappy.

'I cannot understand Bertram inviting that young man to eat

with the family,' she said, drawing Kitty down beside her on the sofa. 'He says himself he has engaged him, so he is in some ways an *employee*. And to have the man mixing with his own sister, who is at a very impressionable age!' She shook her head. 'I do not understand it,' she said again. 'And my sister, to allow it with never a word of reproach. She is usually such a stickler for propriety.'

Kitty listened to her in growing dismay. It seemed that as her godmother's hopes of a match between Kitty and her nephew had grown, so had her prejudice against Daniel Blackwood and despite her attempts to remain neutral, Kitty found herself more and more wanting to defend him.

'But the Blackwoods own several mills,' she said now. 'I believe they are a family of considerable standing in the north. And you said yourself he is quite eligible.'

'That was when I first met him, and I did not understand that he is still so involved in trade. Nor did I know Bertram was employing him. And as for his family—you knew nothing of him before you met in Town? Your mama never mentioned the Blackwood family?'

'Well, no, but we lived far to the west, and Mama...' Kitty paused for a moment '...Mama showed no interest in anyone except the very highest society. We had very few acquaintances.'

Lady Leaconham did not appear to notice the wistful note in Kitty's voice, too intent upon her own train of thought.

'But if the family is so well to do, then *why* is he working for Bertram?' she said. 'No, it does not make sense. But then, nothing makes sense any more in a world where the poor king and queen of France can be locked up by their own people. And now we must have tradesmen at our table!'

'But, ma'am, you were happy enough to recognise Mr Blackwood in Town.'

'But I never invited him to dinner, my dear. Oh, dear me, no. He may be an acquaintance of my nephew, and I do not deny that he behaved like a gentleman when he came to our assistance at Barnet, but that does not mean we should sit down to dinner together!'

The remainder of Lady Harworth's guests arrived the following day and soon Kitty found herself caught up in the busy routine of a Kirkleigh house party. With half-a-dozen young people in the house Ann was very happy, organising drives and picnics on fine days, theatricals and charades when the weather was inclement. The ladies would spend afternoons at their sketching and painting while the gentlemen took themselves off riding, mostly to inspect the woods and discuss the new coverts with Lord Harworth's gamekeeper, but the ladies knew that they sometimes went off to watch a cock-fight or a mill in a nearby village.

There were protracted breakfasts and noisy dinners and by the end of the week Kitty was relieved to slip away to spend a quiet hour alone with her books. She wrote long letters to her mother, describing life at Kirkleigh, but even as she wrote of the delights of having nothing to do all day but please oneself, Kitty knew she was not being quite truthful. She longed for an occupation; even helping the governess with the squire's children had made her feel more useful than idling away each day as she was doing now. However, she could tell her mama that she was learning one new accomplishment.

Many of the ladies went riding each morning, and when Ann discovered that Kitty had never learned the art, she was shocked.

'But everyone rides in the country! This must be remedied immediately: we shall teach you!'

'And how long with that take?' asked Kitty, torn between amusement at her friend's enthusiasm and alarm at the thought of joining Ann on one of her rides: she had heard Lord Harworth describe his sister as a bruising horsewoman, afraid of nothing.

'Not long. I shall have my old pony saddled up for you tomorrow morning. You need not look so anxious, Kitty: you will not be expected to jump fences or anything dangerous—at least, not for the first few weeks.' She twinkled mischievously. 'I shall have my groom lead you around the stable yard each morning until you are at home in the saddle.'

'That is very kind of you,' said Kitty. 'I confess I should like to ride with you in the mornings.'

'I am sure you will pick it up very quickly,' Ann reassured her. 'Dapple is very steady, you will find her as comfortable as sitting on a sofa.'

'Only considerably higher,' laughed Kitty.

Thus, on the very next fine morning, Kitty donned the riding habit that Ann insisted she should borrow and went off for her first lesson. She was quick to learn, and two days later they progressed to the park. The groom led Kitty around the perimeter, complimenting her on her improvement and suggesting that they could now dispense with the leading rein.

'Oh, not quite yet, if you please,' begged Kitty.

'Well, mebbe not, then, miss, seeing as someone is coming through the park. We don't want Dapple takin' off with 'ee.'

Kitty became aware of the sound of hoofbeats behind her and turned her head to see a rider cantering in the direction of the house. As he drew nearer she recognised Daniel Blackwood and her heart gave the now familiar little skip. He slowed and turned his horse towards them, raising his hat as he approached. She was a little disappointed that no flash of pleasure illuminated his countenance, nor did he look surprised to see her, but she thought it very likely that Lord Harworth had informed him that she was at Kirkleigh.

'Good morning to you, Miss Wythenshawe.'

She nodded, smiling as his eyes ranged over the pony. She felt compelled to explain. 'Miss Harworth tells me that everyone rides here so, as you see, I am learning!'

'A very useful accomplishment,' he said gravely.

Kitty continued to smile, inordinately pleased to see him again. She wanted to keep him with her, to begin a conversation, but he was smiling back at her now and her poor brain refused to work properly. Dapple shifted from one leg to another, unbalancing Kitty who clutched anxiously at the reins.

Daniel touched his hat.

'I will leave you to your lesson,' he said. 'Lord Harworth is expecting me: no doubt I will see you at the house later?'

'Yes, yes, I hope, I mean, I am sure—'

She broke off, covering her confusion by giving her attention to the mare who was objecting to having the reins twitched so nervously. With a nod, Daniel rode away.

'Oh, how embarrassing that he should see me thus!' she exclaimed, watching his retreating form.

'Nay, it ain't so bad,' said the groom, grinning. 'We all have to start like this. And if you'll forgive me, miss, I'd say that you will make a good horsewoman, given time. You have a good seat, and good hands, when you ain't distracted.'

'Thank you, Selby.' Kitty flushed, pleased with the compliment. 'I really would like to be able to ride well.'

'No reason why you shouldn't, miss. Now, shall we try going round the park without the leading rein?'

The groom's praise spurred Kitty to try even harder and she stayed so long in the park that breakfast was finished by the time she returned to the house and she was obliged to ask for a little bread and butter to be sent up to her room.

She found it difficult to settle to anything, knowing that Daniel was in the house.

'You may not see him,' she told herself. 'It is such a large, rambling building, and he is closeted with Lord Harworth in his office on the lower floor. There is not the least reason why you should meet.'

Despite this she found herself taking extra time over changing her gown, deciding upon her sprigged muslin decorated with ivy leaves embroidered around the neck and sleeves. Norris suggested dressing her hair in a new style, catching it back with a bandeau and leaving just a few dusky curls to escape and frame her face. Kitty allowed herself to be persuaded, and as soon as the maid had worked her magic Kitty hurried down to join the other guests.

The new look immediately found favour with Ann, whom she found in the garden where the younger members of the party were playing at bowls.

'I do wish my hair was fashionably dark and curled as yours does,' sighed Ann, tucking her hand in Kitty's arm and drawing her towards a table laden with lemonade, pastries and delicate little cakes. 'And you have a delicious colour in your cheeks—your morning riding lessons are agreeing with you! Selby tells me you are making good progress.'

'He thinks I will be good enough to ride out with you in the park soon.'

'That is excellent news, because Mr Hamilton has a plan to ride over to Titchwell and take luncheon at the Star next week.'

'That's right,' declared a lanky young man with a shock of yellow hair. 'I thought we should make up a party and ride out for the day, if the weather holds.'

'I can always follow in the barouche with Godmother and Lady Harworth,' offered Kitty.

'Oh, we are not intending to have Mama or Aunt Leaconham with us,' said Ann quickly. 'We shall have much more fun if we are on our own.'

'We?'

Ann began to count on her fingers.

'Well, me, you, and Garston of course. And Martin—that is, Mr Hamilton—plus Lizzie Camber and her brother George—those of us here now.'

'Will your mama allow us to go alone?' asked Miss Camber.

'Of course,' came the airy reply. 'Titchwell is part of our estate: Mama knows we shall come to no harm.'

Kitty glanced doubtfully at the little group. She knew Elizabeth Camber was barely sixteen and her brother little more than a year older, and although Mr Martin Hamilton was several years older than herself, Kitty thought him rather immature. She watched him now as he teased Lizzie Camber and laughed immoderately at something Garston was saying to him.

'You will of course be taking Selby?'

Ann wrinkled her nose.

'Oh, no, he is far worse than Bertram, always criticising! We should not have a minute's peace if we take him with us. No, this will be a party of *pleasure*. We shall be free to do as we wish for the day!'

'Well, I am not sure I shall be able to ride well enough...' began Kitty, but Ann stopped her.

'Of course you will. You must not worry about that. We will all look after you, won't we, Garston?'

'You may be sure of it,' declared Lord Leaconham, coming up. 'A gentle ride and a good lunch, it will be a splendid day.'

'Well, not too gentle a ride,' put in Mr Hamilton, grinning. 'George and I will want to try our horses over a few fences. But the ladies need not follow,' he added hastily, when Ann hissed at him and glanced in Kitty's direction. 'We shall all please ourselves!'

Kitty could not be easy. She had thought that Lady Harworth would not allow them to ride out unaccompanied, but when they all met in the drawing room before dinner she was surprised to find that Lady Harworth had already given her permission.

'Leaconham will be with them and I am sure the rest of us have no wish to drive out to Titchwell.' She smiled around at the assembled group. 'Young people have so much more energy, and they must be allowed to use it up. And after all, there are enough of them to look after each other.'

'I cannot like it,' opined Lady Leaconham. 'I am not at all sure that Kitty should go, not without a maid to give her countenance.'

'Oh, Aunt, none of the maids can ride,' cried Ann. 'And you know how tedious you would find it if you were obliged to come with us! We are only riding out to the Star. We will send ahead and have a luncheon prepared for us and when we have done we shall ride back.'

'And we will not be obliged to leave Harworth land at any time,' added Martin Hamilton. 'It will be *quite* unexceptional.'

'So you see, Letitia, there is nothing for us to worry ourselves over,' said Lady Harworth, smiling serenely at her sister.

Kitty had to admit that none of the older occupants of the room looked keen to join the young people on their outing. Most of the other guests were considerably older than their hostess and liked to spend their afternoons reading or dozing in the morning room until the dinner hour. She wondered if Lizzie and George's parents might object to their children riding off unattended, but when Kitty glanced in their direction she saw that they were both smiling and nodding benignly at Lady Harworth. Since they were both so corpulent that they took up a whole sofa each, Kitty had to stifle a giggle at the thought of either of them on horseback. She wondered if Lord Harworth might refuse his permission, but when their host did at last join them and Ann told him of the proposed expedition, he did no more than pat her arm and bid her enjoy herself.

'I would come with you myself, but I am meeting Reverend Miller and the churchwardens that day: we are to discuss a new church roof.'

'Poor Lord Harworth, he works so hard,' gushed Mrs Camber, beaming at her host. 'My dear sir, we have not seen you all day.'

'Business, ma'am,' returned Lord Harworth. 'Out riding on the estate for most of the day. But it's done now so I am free to enjoy myself. And we have an extra guest for dinner! I said I would ask him and Blackwood has agreed to join us. No need to trouble yourself, Mama, I saw Strutt on my way in and told him to lay another place at the table.'

Even as he finished speaking the door opened and Daniel entered. Lady Leaconham's countenance tightened with disapproval, but Kitty observed that Lady Harworth was showing no concern and her son was cheerfully introducing Daniel to his other guests. She had to admit that there could be no fault found in Daniel's appearance. His tight-fitting dark coat was beautifully made, not a wrinkle or a puckered seam in sight. His buff-coloured waistcoat and knee-breeches enhanced his athletic figure and the snowy froth of linen at his neck was immaculate. When he turned to greet her she could not resist asking him if he had been expecting the invitation to stay to dinner.

'Lord Harworth usually asks me so I always come prepared with a change of clothes.' He hesitated, as if he might move away, then he said, 'You are looking very well, Miss Wythenshawe. The country air agrees with you.'

'I think you are right, Blackwood,' said Lord Harworth, overhearing his comment and coming up. 'Plenty of fresh air and exercise, eh, miss? And m'sister tells me you are learning to ride, too!'

'Yes, sir. Ann has kindly loaned me one of her riding ponies.'

'Selby says she is an excellent student,' said Ann. 'We are making up a party to ride to Titchwell next Tuesday.'

'After only a week's tuition?' said Daniel. 'I am impressed.'

A smile tugged at Kitty's mouth, responding to the gleam in his eyes.

'Ann has promised me it will be a very easy ride. I shall not be expected to jump any fences.'

'I am sure you will manage very well,' he told her.

'And if you are at the Star around noon on Tuesday, Mr Blackwood,' put in Ann, 'you will be able to see for yourself, for we are taking luncheon there. You might even join us...'

Lady Leaconham stepped up.

'I have no doubt Mr Blackwood is far too busy to ride out on a whim.' She took Kitty's arm and led her away. 'Mrs Camber was complimenting me upon your gown, my love,' she murmured. 'She was most impressed with the embroidery. If she asks you about it pray do not tell her that your mama made it herself!'

This reminder of her humble state effectively robbed Kitty of all power of conversation and she was thankful when they went through to the dining room, where the elegant settings and superb food commanded everyone's admiration and attention.

Kitty found herself sitting between Mr Hamilton and Mr Camber. Since the former flirted with Ann for the duration of the meal and the latter devoted himself to his food, Kitty was left to enjoy her meal and her thoughts in peace. Daniel was too far away to converse with her, almost hidden from sight by a large silver epergne, but he seemed to be at ease. Whenever she looked at him he was engrossed in conversation with one or other of his neighbours. She was relieved. They, at least, did not seem to share her godmother's reservations about his suitability as a dinner guest.

Kitty heard her name and looked up to find Lady Harworth was asking a number of questions of her sister about Kitty's family and birth, all of which Lady Leaconham deftly turned aside. Kitty had to admire her tactics. She gave the impression that Kitty's parents were very rich but eccentric, refusing to give their daughter the lavish presentation she deserved and hinting that such a come-out was unnecessary for someone of Kitty's birth and fortune. It was subtly done and it satisfied her hostess, but it made Kitty uncomfortable, especially when she realised that Daniel was listening to the conversation, a sceptical look in his hard eyes.

What in hell's name am I doing here? Daniel was beginning to wish he had not accepted his host's invitation to stay for dinner. The knowledge that Kitty was at Kirkleigh had been gnawing away at him ever since Harworth had mentioned it. He had returned from London determined to forget Miss Kitty Wythenshawe. She had set her heart on marrying well, so let her get on with it. There were many girls far prettier: Miss Harworth, for example, with her generous figure and golden hair was generally acknowledged to be a beauty, but Daniel found his eyes drawn towards Kitty, with her dusky curls and expressive mouth and those deep green eyes that could darken and flash with anger.

When they had parted in London he had vowed he would never see her again: at the time it had seemed an easy promise to keep, since he was leaving Town. He had hoped that once he was home he would be able to forget her by throwing himself into his work, but he had not succeeded. She was always in his thoughts. It did not matter if he was surrounded by the deafening clatter of machinery in the mill, silently poring over the ledgers in the office or even riding over the moors, he found himself thinking of her, wondering what she was doing, if she was happy. Harworth had mentioned that she and Lady Leaconham were amongst his summer guests so he had not been surprised to see her in the park that morning, but he had been taken aback by his own soaring elation when he had ridden up and she had smiled at him with such obvious pleasure. She had looked very good sitting on the horse, too, the tight-fitting riding jacket accentuating her tiny waist and straight back. He smiled slightly, remembering her nervousness. That would go in time, of course. He had no doubt that she would be a good horsewoman. In his imagination he saw them riding out together over the moors in high summer, galloping along the paths lined with purple heather, the sky a vivid, unbroken expanse of blue…

Daniel caught himself up. What was he thinking of? That would only happen if she remained in the north—as Lady Harworth. He looked at his host, sitting at the head of the table. Harworth was sitting back in his chair, his eyes fixed on Kitty and a faint, satisfied smile on his face. A shiver rattled Daniel's spine. Had he offered for her already? No, he thought not: Lady Leaconham was still fending off her sister's questions about Miss Wythenshawe. If an offer had been made and accepted Daniel was certain Lady Leaconham would be looking much more complacent. But it was only a matter of time. He ground his teeth in frustration.

After dinner they gathered in the drawing room, where it was expected that the young ladies would each take their turn upon the pianoforte. He watched Ann drag Kitty forward, insisting that she should play. Daniel chose to stand at the edge of the room where he could watch her without being observed himself. As her fingers flew over the keys he was impressed. She played well, due no doubt to a good teacher and a willingness to apply herself—he was well aware of the tussles between his mother and Bella when it came to music lessons! All too soon the performance was over and Ann bounced up, declaring that they had been practising a duet. It was not yet dark enough for candles but the summer evening was drawing to a close, the setting sun casting a golden glow over the drawing room and adding an extra radiance to the two young ladies seated together at the pianoforte.

'Do they not make a beautiful picture?' murmured Lord Harworth, coming to stand beside him. 'Two fine girls, one so dark, the other fair: I would like to have their likeness captured, just as they are now. What do you say, Blackwood, they would look well hanging on the wall here, eh?'

'Very well, my lord.'

'Aye, I think so.' Lord Harworth turned towards him, saying confidentially, 'I am minded to offer for Miss Wythenshawe, you know.' Daniel clenched his jaw, not trusting himself to speak. 'I have been thinking for some time that I should settle down. There's the title to think of, I need an heir, you see. And Miss Wythenshawe is a pretty little thing. Besides, my mother likes her.'

'Does she?'

'Oh, yes. Well, she's her sister's godchild, so we know she comes from a good family. It's an anxious time,' continued Lord Harworth, shaking his head. 'Her godmother is very obliging, of course, but you said yourself the gel was above your touch: I only hope she doesn't turn her nose up at a mere baron! Oh, bravo, ladies, bravo!'

A smattering of applause told them that the duet was ended and Harworth walked away, clapping loudly. A bank of heavy cloud had blotted out the sun, and there was a break in the entertainments as servants hurried in to light the candles. Daniel remained in the shadows. He wished the evening was over so he could take his leave, but to set out before the moon had risen would cause comment. He must endure this torture a little longer.

The room was settling again. Over by the piano he could see Kitty shaking her head, politely declining to play more and she moved away as Miss Harworth prepared to display her expertise at the harp. Daniel drew a sharp breath: she was coming towards him.

'Do you play for us tonight, Mr Blackwood. Or sing, perhaps?'

'No, not tonight.' Thank heavens she had not asked him what he thought of her performance, he could not recall a note, only that he had been spellbound.

'I understand you have been out riding all day with Lord Harworth.'

He relaxed slightly. This was safer ground.

'Yes. We were looking at sites for his new mill. There are several that would be suitable.'

'It would require many men and women to work in such a place, would it not? Where would they come from?'

'From the surrounding farms and villages. Harworth is already improving the farming methods used on his estates so there is less work on the land. The people will make a better living in the mills.'

She nodded. Her eyes were fixed upon Ann, playing the harp, but he could tell that she was thinking of other things, and he watched her, entranced by the tiny crease in her brow, the slight quirk of her lips as some new thought came to her.

'Mr Blackwood, may I ask you a question?' She turned her disconcertingly clear gaze upon him and his heart skidded erratically within his chest. His brows snapped together: better that he should frown at her than she should know the effect she had upon him! She ran her tongue over her bottom lip in that nervous little habit of hers, rousing the demon desire in him. He had to steel himself not to reach out for her. She started to turn away. 'I beg your pardon. I can see you think it an impertinence...'

'No!' He put his hand on her arm. 'No,' he said again. 'Please. Ask me.'

His fingers seemed welded to her flesh. It took an immense effort to remove them when he saw the startled look in her eyes.

'Please,' he said again, giving her what he hoped was a reassuring smile. 'What is it you wish to ask me?'

'I wonder, sir, why you are working for Lord Harworth? From what I know of you…' She blushed a little. 'And I confess it is not very much! From what you have told me, you do not need this employment. And will not another mill be competition for you?'

'It will be competition, yes, but the industry is young, there is room for more manufactories. But if Harworth is determined to set up a mill, I am concerned that he should set about it in the right way. Soon he will need to bring in extra workers—whole families. I want to make sure they have proper housing, a school for the children, a doctor to look after them.'

He read approval in her face, but even as it made his heart soar he knew he must defend himself. He said curtly, 'Do not think of me as a saint, Miss Wythenshawe. This is not charity, it is good business sense. If men are sick, or ill fed, or worrying about their family, they do not work so well.'

There were more questions in her head, he knew it, and part of him wanted to draw her aside and continue their discussion, but that was madness: the longer he spent in her company the harder it was to tear himself away. A movement caught his eye and he looked up to see Miss Harworth approaching with her brother and Martin Hamilton at her side.

'Well, now, Blackwood, what did you think of that?' demanded Lord Harworth. 'Hamilton here says she plays like an angel, what?' He threw back his head and gave a loud laugh. 'Harps, angels—what a good joke.'

Ann tapped his arm with her fan and tried to frown.

'Martin meant it as a compliment, Bertram, and I shall take it as such.'

Kitty looked around, startled. Daniel wondered if she had even noticed that her friend's performance had ended.

'Having heard you perform on the pianoforte, Miss Wythenshawe, I know you are musical, too,' remarked Hamilton, in what Daniel considered to be far too familiar a fashion. 'What did *you* think of Miss Harworth's performance?'

Kitty stepped away a little before replying.

'It was delightful,' she said. 'I did not notice one wrong note.'

'And *you* are truly delightful to say so, Miss Wythenshawe,' chuckled Lord Harworth. 'Ann has only been learning the harp for a few months and I tell her she needs to practise more if she is to become really proficient.'

'But there are so many other things to do, Bertram, especially when we have company.'

'You cannot expect your sister to neglect her guests, my lord,' said Hamilton with a little laugh.

'Of course not, and I, too will now devote myself to our guests.' Lord Harworth bowed towards Kitty. There was no mistaking the warm, intimate smile he gave her. 'A task that will give me no small enjoyment, I assure you!'

Daniel thought it a clumsy compliment but it made Kitty blush rosily. She murmured, 'We must not take up all your time, my lord.'

'Nonsense! What are we here for if not to enjoy ourselves! In fact, I am thinking I should put off the meeting on Tuesday and ride with you to Titchwell.'

'Oh, no, my lord,' said Kitty faintly. 'If you are otherwise engaged...'

'I thought that meeting was arranged for some weeks,' put in Daniel, irritation sharpening his voice. 'Surely you will not rearrange it to accommodate an outing of pleasure?'

Lord Harworth blinked at him.

'I do not see... Well, perhaps not, I shall have to consider carefully, of course.' He bent another beaming smile at Kitty. 'I admit the temptation is very great!'

'We should of course be delighted to have you join us,' said Ann, not quite truthfully. She gazed up more hopefully at Daniel. 'Perhaps you, too, would like to ride over and join us, Mr Blackwood? It promises to be a very jolly party.'

Ann's smile awoke no response in Daniel. He scarcely heard her, his mind working out an excuse to get away before he said something he would regret.

'Alas, no,' he said shortly. 'I have engagements that day that cannot be put off. In fact, I have work tomorrow that requires an early start so I must take my leave of you now. If you will excuse me.'

Kitty's feelings were mixed as he gave a stiff bow and walked off. His presence unsettled her, but with his departure the room seemed a little less bright. Ann gave an uncertain laugh.

'Well, do you think I frightened him off, that he dashed away so suddenly? He looks so serious.'

'No, no, sister, Blackwood *always* looks serious!'

'He is a manufacturer,' said Mr Hamilton, raising his quizzing glass to watch Daniel's retreating figure. 'Such men would have us believe there is no time for anything but work.'

'I believe supervising the proper running of a mill does take a great deal of effort,' observed Kitty.

Ann pouted.

'Then I do not think you should build one, Bertram, if it leaves you no time for pleasure.'

'Pho, that is why we have managers and overseers,' declared her brother. 'Have no fear, Ann my love. Once the mill is up and running I do not expect it to take up much of my time at all. In fact, I mean to ask Blackwood to find me a good man to run the mill for me.'

'So you are serious about this mill business,' remarked Mr Hamilton.

'Yes, most certainly. The improvements I have made on my estates here mean that we no longer need so many people. Best to employ 'em to my benefit than to have them a burden to the parish. Blackwood's invited me to see his own mill over at Hestonroyd tomorrow. Perhaps you should come with me, Hamilton, to see for yourself how these new manufactories are run.'

'Not I, my lord!,' laughed Hamilton, throwing up his hands. 'I never had any head for business.'

Ann shook her head and laid a hand on her brother's arm.

'Oh, Bertram, surely you saw enough of mills and machinery at Cromford! How can you think anyone would be interested in such things?'

'I am,' said Kitty, greatly daring. Her spirit quailed as every eye turned in her direction. She swallowed. 'I would very much like to see a spinning mill, my lord.'

'Would you now, Miss Wythenshawe?' After his initial shock, Lord Harworth beamed at her.

'Yes, I would,' she declared bravely. 'Very much.'

'But, Kitty, we are going to take our sketchpads and easels into the park tomorrow and paint views of the house,' Ann reminded her.

'You can easily do that another day,' put in Lady Leaconham, coming up. 'I am sure Bertram would be delighted to have company tomorrow.'

'I would indeed,' declared her nephew. 'Perhaps we should make up a party...'

Kitty noted with wry amusement that this suggestion found little favour with the other guests, who all found reasons why they should remain in the luxurious surroundings of Kirkleigh Hall the following day.

'Well, if Kitty is determined to go then I shall go too,' declared Ann. 'You will not object to that, will you, Brother? And that way Kitty and I can chaperon each other. There will be no need for Mama or my aunt to come with us.'

Thus by the time the tea tray was carried in, the visit was arranged to everyone's satisfaction and the carriage was ordered for early the following morning.

'Well, what a clever little puss you are,' murmured Lady Leaconham, tucking her arm through Kitty's and taking her off to sit with her on a sofa by the window. 'I should never have thought of suggesting you go to the mill with Bertram, but it was very well done of you. He could not fail to be flattered by your interest.'

'I had no idea of flattering Lord Harworth,' Kitty protested. 'I truly want to see the mill.'

'Of course you do,' replied her godmother with a maddening smile. 'And nothing could make it plainer to my nephew that you are just the wife for him!' She patted Kitty's hands. 'Do not look so dismayed, my love. It was a little bold of you, to be sure, but it may be just the nudge Bertram needs to offer for you!'

Chapter Nine

After an early breakfast the next morning Kitty set off for Hestonroyd with Ann and Lord Harworth in an open carriage. As the miles sped by it occurred to her that they would not have to travel much further to reach Fallridge and her home, but she kept these thoughts to herself, remembering her promise to her godmother not to talk of her family. She longed to see Mama and Aunt Jane, imagining their pleasure at all she would be able to tell them, but it was not only Lady Leaconham's wish that she should not visit Fallridge while she was a guest at Kirkleigh. Mama too had expressly forbidden her to call.

Lord Harworth was addressing her and she looked up to respond. She was a little embarrassed in his company, conscious that by expressing her interest in visiting Hestonroyd everyone assumed she was determined to become Lady Harworth. Kitty thought of her mother's letters, the constant reminders that she should strive to find a suitable husband, but even the thought that Mama would approve of her actions brought her little comfort. Kitty sighed. Papa had always insisted that high rank and titles counted for very little, but it seemed that everyone else she knew, including Mama, thought they counted for a great deal. Her family would be very disappointed in her if she threw away her chance to marry a lord.

'Ah. We are nearly there now.'

Lord Harworth's words recalled her wandering thoughts. The carriage had slowed and now turned off the main highway to follow a well-made, winding road that led down into a thickly wooded valley. There was no opportunity to see very far ahead as the road twisted back and forth in its descent, but eventually they rounded the final bend and there before her was Hestonroyd Mill. She gasped, staring wide-eyed at the huge building that filled the narrow valley bottom. The stone walls were punctuated with dozens of windows on each of its four floors and the slate roof was surmounted by an elegant bell tower, not to call the faithful to worship, she knew, but to summon the workers to their posts.

The road descended to run alongside the mill, separated from it by a fast-flowing stream. They crossed the bridge and drove under the arch that led into a large courtyard, bustling with people and wagons. The clatter of hooves echoed against the stone walls, for the mill continued on three sides, while on the fourth was a series of smaller buildings. The carriage drew up outside the biggest of these, a square house that looked very much like a gentleman's residence but which Lord Harworth declared would be the offices. A sound like distant thunder reverberated through the yard and Ann looked around nervously.

'What is that noise?'

'The machinery,' said her brother. 'Water frames that turn dozens, even hundreds of spindles at a time, producing more yarn in a week than a woman could spin in a lifetime.'

As Kitty followed Ann down from the carriage, Daniel appeared. Lord Harworth hailed him, saying easily, 'Hope you don't object, Blackwood, but the ladies wanted to come with me. Miss Wythenshawe especially is eager to see inside your mill!'

Kitty's cheeks grew warm as Daniel's dark, unfathomable glance rested upon her.

'No,' he said at last. 'I have no objection at all, but I would warn you that the noise and bustle of a mill can be overwhelming.'

'You employ women here, do you not, Mr Blackwood?' asked

Kitty, brows raised. 'I am sure if they can live with it day after day then we can put up with the...*noise and bustle,* as you put it, for an hour or so.'

Daniel looked surprised, but she read approval in his hard eyes and felt a faint glow of satisfaction.

He nodded.

'Very well then. If you would like to come this way?'

They crossed the yard, keeping close to Daniel. Looking about her, Kitty saw that everyone was working busily, loading wagons or pushing handcarts across the cobbles, while all around them the mill rumbled and growled like some huge, sleeping monster. The noise of the machines grew louder as they stepped into the mill.

'We have spinning shops on all four floors,' said Daniel, leading them towards a heavy wooden door. 'No need to see them all, but I'll take you through a couple of them. Please be sure to stand clear of the mules—'

'Mules?' Ann repeated.

'The spinning mules—machines,' explained Daniel. 'They travel out over the floor and have moving parts that can snatch at your gown if you stand too close.'

He opened the door. As Kitty stepped into the spinning shop the deafening noise was like a physical assault. She glanced at Ann, who was clinging to her brother's arm, looking about her wide-eyed. The floor shook beneath their feet and the whole room seemed to be one seething, boiling mass of movement. It was very bright from the many windows on all sides. Banks of machines—the mules— ran the width of the building, each one carrying large spools of creamy-grey yarn.

Daniel was explaining the process to Lord Harworth and Kitty had to draw closer to hear anything at all. She heard him mention creels and bobbins, tops and roving and headstock, but it was difficult to concentrate with the incessant clatter of the machinery. She watched, fascinated, as the lower part of the mule moved out slowly. The thick yarns were paid out and twisted, then as the mule stopped and returned, the twisted thread was gathered up on the spindles.

She jumped when strong hands gripped her arms.

'You are too close.' Daniel's mouth was close to her ear. He was pulling her back away from the machines. 'Please, stand over here with the others, out of the way.'

Mortified, Kitty stood in one corner with Ann and Lord Harworth, watching the slow process of the spinning being repeated over and over again. She had not intended to draw attention to herself, but now she feared Daniel would think her troublesome. Another black mark against her. She allowed her eyes to shift to Daniel. He was walking between the machines, surveying the room, his keen eyes taking in everything. He stopped occasionally, exchanging a word here, issuing an instruction there. He stood tall, his black-coated figure conspicuous against the lighter, dust-covered clothes of the spinners. He was master here and it showed in the proud line of his bearing. She glanced at Lord Harworth, who was trying to hide a yawn behind his hand. She doubted he could ever be as at home in this noisy, busy place.

They moved on, taking the stairs to another spinning shop then on to the packing rooms. Daniel pointed out the joiners' and mechanics' workshops, and then took them off to see the huge water wheel that provided the power for the machines. His pride in the mill was evident. He was familiar with every process, every machine within his mill. He knew every man's name and it was apparent to Kitty that they esteemed him. There was no servile bowing and scraping when he was near, they were all too busy for that, but they responded with alacrity when he spoke to them, regarding him with respect.

'Well, I think we must have seen everything now,' declared Lord Harworth, taking out his watch. 'Do not forget we were going to discuss the returns I can expect on my investment, Blackwood. The wages you pay, working hours and the like.'

'We will go back to the office for that,' said Daniel. 'James

Stoodley is my mill manager and I think it would be useful for him to be present.'

'Very well, then. Lead on, sir!'

'I have instructed that refreshments should be brought to the office,' said Daniel as he took them back across the yard, stopping to allow a string of pack-ponies to pass. He pointed to the large bundles wrapped in oil-cloth strapped to each pony. 'That's the tops, the rough wool that we spin into yarn. It has been sorted and combed by families in the outlying villages, then my agents collect it up and bring it here for spinning.'

'It is my head that is spinning,' replied Ann, throwing a humorous glance up at Daniel. 'I vow I shall be glad to sit down for a little while.'

Kitty, too, was thankful when they reached the manager's office. It was a large panelled room overlooking the yard and it was mercifully cool and quiet. The large desk had been cleared and it now held a tray laden with decanters and glasses and a small plate of macaroons.

'I am afraid I only have wine, ratafia or water to offer you,' said Daniel. 'If I had known you were bringing ladies with you, my lord, I would have arranged for some lemonade to be prepared. I am sorry, too, that my father is not here to meet you. He has taken my mother and sister to Harrogate and will not be back until next week.'

Lord Harworth dismissed his apology with a wave of his hand.

'You know this was not intended as a social visit, Blackwood, but the ladies would insist upon coming!'

'I hope they have found it of interest.'

Daniel's eyes were upon Kitty. She felt obliged to respond.

'Yes, very much, sir, thank you. It was very informative.'

She accepted a glass of water and retired to a seat by the window, glad to have a few moments to think over all she had seen.

'But why worsted, Blackwood?' enquired Lord Harworth. 'Surely cotton is the thing now.'

'Our cotton mills are in Lancashire,' replied Daniel, handing him a glass of wine. 'We have been producing worsted here for generations—it makes sense when we are surrounded by sheep and we have the wool on our doorstep. Besides, I do not like to have all my eggs in one basket.'

'And your people here work only ten hours a day? They could do more, surely.'

Daniel shrugged.

'They could, but tired people do not work so well. And tiredness brings carelessness. That is when accidents happen.' He looked up as a stocky man in a brown coat entered. 'Ah, Stoodley, come in. This is James Stoodley, my mill manager.'

Once the introductions were complete Daniel moved away, leaving Lord Harworth deep in conversation with his manager.

'What were the buildings we passed on the way here?' asked Kitty. 'I thought I glimpsed a house and a garden, too—is that your own house, perhaps?'

'No, Miss Wythenshawe, I live a mile away on the edge of Hestonroyd village. The building you saw today houses the nursery and school. Perhaps, when you have rested a little you might like to see it?'

Kitty hesitated.

'I—I am sure you have other business to attend to, Mr Blackwood.'

'No, I was going to show Lord Harworth the ledgers and explain something of the costs involved in running a mill this size, but Stoodley can do that much better than I, if you ladies would like to walk to the nursery building?'

'I do not think I could walk another yard!' cried Ann, selecting a second macaroon from the plate on the desk. 'You go, Kitty, then you can tell me all about it later. I will wait here with Bertram.'

'Yes, off you go, my dear,' nodded Lord Harworth, sitting down at the desk and pushing the tray aside to make room for a large ledger. 'Stoodley can tell me anything I want to know here.'

Kitty was still undecided. Daniel held out his arm to her.

'Then shall we go, Miss Wythenshawe?'

After the briefest hesitation she placed her fingers on his sleeve and he led her out into the yard again.

'Do you wish me to summon the carriage to take us up the road?'

'No, no, it is not that far to walk, I think?'

She glanced up at him, looking quite enchanting with her dark curls peeping from under the straw bonnet that framed her face. He was struck again by her eyes; their colour reminded him of the vivid green of the moors after a summer rainstorm. It took a moment for him to realise she expected an answer.

'No—um—it will only take us ten minutes.'

He escorted her out of the yard and along the road. He had walked this way many times but rarely had the sun shone so brilliantly, nor had he noticed so many birds singing in the woods, or the merry babble of the stream. Kitty made some remark about the mill and he responded mechanically, but her interest was genuine, the questions she posed were thoughtful and soon he found himself telling her of his plans to expand, to develop and improve the spinning machines and add a loom shop—he even mentioned the idea of installing a steam engine, something he had not even discussed with his father.

'It all sounds very exciting,' she remarked. 'But some believe innovation is dangerous. Are there not risks involved in all these changes?'

'Of course. But there is even more danger in standing still. I hope that by the time the children in the nursery here are grown, not only will we be spinning but we will also have weaving sheds here at Hestonroyd.'

They had reached the path leading down to the square, white-washed building that housed the nursery and school. Daniel opened the gate for her to enter the neat gardens that surrounded it.

'This is much bigger than I thought,' she told him. 'I had imagined perhaps a small schoolroom…'

'I do not allow very young children in my mills,' Daniel explained. 'The parents leave their children here when they come to work. They are taught to read and write, and help in the garden, where they grow vegetables for their meals.'

'And when they are older?'

'Most of them come to work in the mill.' She did not reply but he knew she was thinking of the noisy, dusty spinning shops. He said, 'It is a harsh world, Miss Wythenshawe. They are free to find work elsewhere if they can. Those who master their letters might find work in the towns, but somehow they must earn their keep. If their parents did not work in my mill then these children would most likely be toiling in the fields now or helping in the home, rather than being schooled. I like to think that this way I am giving them a chance to better themselves.' He glanced down at her. 'You and I were fortunate, Miss Wythenshawe, we have never known poverty.'

'I am aware of that,' she responded quietly. 'And I am profoundly grateful.'

They had reached the house and the door to the schoolroom stood open. Inside the children were sitting at their benches, practising their letters. Daniel allowed the schoolteacher to show Kitty around. They disappeared briefly into the nursery where a nursemaid looked after the very young children before coming back to spend some time in the schoolroom. Kitty removed her bonnet and sat down with the children, talking to them and using her own dainty finger to draw letters in the sandtray on the bench before her. The afternoon sun was streaming through the window and as Kitty moved about the room the sunlight caught her hair. Strange that he had never noticed the hint of red in it before, an occasional glint of fire. He folded his arms and leaned back against the wall. She was so at ease here, coaxing even the shyest child to talk to her. He imagined her running just such a school as this, or even with a child of her own in her arms. She would want several, he thought idly, and he would wander into the nursery of an evening to find her there...

Hell and damnation, this was madness!

Daniel snapped himself upright. She was as good as promised to Harworth. Her coming here with him today was undoubtedly a declaration of intent. Daniel had been surprised when he had seen the ladies arrive with Harworth, but pleasantly so and he had enjoyed showing them around the mill. Ann Harworth had evinced little interest but Kitty had been eager to learn. He had noticed how she had moved closer when he was talking to Harworth and the questions she had posed today had been intelligent and apposite. If Harworth did marry her she would take an interest in his mill and its workers, he was sure. Daniel stifled the tiny voice in his heart whispering that Harworth didn't deserve her. He acknowledged his jealousy, but he would overcome it. He cleared his throat.

'I think we should be getting back, Miss Wythenshawe.'

Kitty looked up as Daniel's deep voice cut through the light chatter of the schoolroom. She had quite lost track of the time in talking with the teacher and the children. For the first time since coming to Kirkleigh she could see a purpose to her future life. Her concerns that as mistress of Kirkleigh she would have nothing to do were at an end. If Lord Harworth should offer for her then she would interest herself in his people. There were already his tenants and those who worked on his land to care for, but once his mill was working there would be even more families arriving, and many would have young children.

Kitty's head was buzzing with ideas as she walked back to the mill beside Daniel and they had gone more than halfway before she realised that her companion had not said one word to her since leaving the nursery building.

'Thank you for bringing me here,' she said earnestly. 'Is it very unusual to set up such a school as this one, Mr Blackwood?'

She was idly swinging her bonnet by its ribbons, too preoccupied to think of putting it on, or to consider the effect of the sun on her complexion.

'It is becoming more common,' he replied. 'Mill owners recognise the benefits of looking after their workers. This was my mother's idea. She visits frequently to assure herself the children are well cared for.'

'Yes, I can see that such a role might fall to the mistress,' murmured Kitty, frowning a little.

'Do you think men are so lacking in kindness?' he challenged her.

'I think they are more motivated by profit, and can forget the more civilised aspects of life,' she replied, thinking of Lord Harworth, poring over the ledgers in the office.

'It is not impossible for profit and philanthropy to go together, Miss Wythenshawe!'

Kitty stopped.

'I beg your pardon,' she said, her colour heightened. 'I did not mean to imply any slur upon you, Mr Blackwood.'

'I am well aware of what you think of me,' he muttered. 'I am hardly a gentleman in your eyes!'

He went to walk on but she caught his sleeve.

'Now what nonsense is this? I thought we had done with that misunderstanding. You know how much I regret ever thinking ill of you.'

He shook off her hand.

'That is not the point. Nothing can change the fact that I am a manufacturer.'

She was confused by his anger, and a little hurt, too.

'You told me you were proud of what you are,' she retorted. 'Do you think we came here out of idle curiosity, to look at your mill as one might look at a freak show? Lord Harworth wants to build a mill and has consulted you because your family knows more about the subject than anyone. *That* is why he came to Hestonroyd today.'

'And you insisted upon accompanying him,' he threw at her. 'Still toadying up to him, I don't doubt, showing him you are the perfect helpmate, entering into all his concerns!'

'No!' cried Kitty. What could she say? He was only repeating what everyone else thought of her. She moved a step closer, forcing herself to meet his eyes. 'That is not how it is. I wanted to come, I wished to see the mill. I wanted...I wanted to discover why it means so much to you, why you are so proud to be a manufacturer.'

The anger still smouldered in his eyes, his mouth fixed in a thin line.

'And are you satisfied?'

Kitty's anger melted. He looked so much like a sullen schoolboy that she wanted to reach out and brush the stray lock of hair from his forehead, to pull his face down to hers and kiss away his sulks. She dare not allow herself to do any of these things so she merely nodded.

'I think you should be very proud of what you have achieved here, Mr Blackwood.'

He continued to stare at her but she would not look away. She needed him to know she was sincere.

'You must think me a boorish fellow,' he said at last.

She smiled. 'I think you have a temper that is not always under control.'

His lips curved a little and the dangerous light faded from his eyes. The wind had whipped an errant curl across her face and he lifted one hand to catch it.

'You are right,' he said, tucking the curl carefully behind her ear. 'My mother despairs of me.' The touch of his fingers set Kitty's heart knocking painfully against her ribs, but when he dropped his hand the lack of contact was even more agonising. She forced herself to stand still while every nerve screamed to reach out for him. The world no longer existed, she was no longer aware of the rumble of the mill, the sound of the stream or the singing of the birds, there was only Daniel, standing so close, holding her eyes.

His face softened, he lifted his hand again. 'Miss Wythenshawe—Kitty—I...'

'There you are!'

Lord Harworth's jovial cry echoed over them. Daniel dropped his hand and Kitty was filled with an intense disappointment. As one they turned, schooling their features to smile as Lord Harworth approached with his sister hanging on his arm.

'You were gone such a time that we decided to walk out and meet you,' said Ann. 'What kept you so long? '

'I'm afraid I could not tear myself away from the children.' Kitty responded calmly, hoping the turmoil within her did not show in her face. To her relief Ann merely released her brother's arm and reached out her hand.

'Bertram thinks it is time we were going back to Kirkleigh, so I think we should walk ahead and let the gentlemen talk business. I know Bertram has one or two final questions he wishes to put to Mr Blackwood.'

Kitty dare not look at Daniel to see if he was happy with this suggestion. She allowed Ann to take her arm and walk with her back towards the mill entrance but all the time she was aware of Daniel and Bertram behind her and although they spoke of nothing but business her ears strained to catch every syllable that Daniel uttered, revelling in the sound of his deep mellow voice and knowing that she would forever wonder what he would have said to her, if they had not been interrupted.

Chapter Ten

Kitty did not know whether to be glad or sorry that the visit to Hestonroyd Mill attracted so little interest from Lord Harworth's guests. On the one hand she would have been glad to discuss all she had seen there, but she was aware that any such discussions must involve mention of Daniel Blackwood and she would much rather not talk about him. She did not even want to think about him, but the wretched man kept coming into her head and cutting up her peace quite dreadfully.

He had not spoken a word to her once Lord Harworth and Ann had joined them on the road outside the mill and when he escorted them back to their carriage she heard him tell Lord Harworth that he would be too busy to call at Kirkleigh again for several weeks.

Kitty was determined to put him out of her mind. She knew the best thing to do was to stay busy so she made great efforts to keep herself occupied. The dry sunny weather continued and the guests at Kirkleigh whiled away their time with pleasant diversions. The younger members of the party played bowls and amused themselves in the gardens while the gentlemen rode, fished and shot and the older ladies spent most of their time reclining in easy chairs, fanning themselves and complaining of the heat.

Ann was determined that nothing should spoil their ride to

Titchwell and resisted Lady Leaconham's suggestions that they should postpone the visit until the weather was cooler.

'Pho, Aunt, we are not such fragile creatures that we shall melt under a little sunshine. What say you, Kitty, are you not bored with sitting around the house? Do you not long to ride out in this glorious weather?

'No, I am not bored,' said Kitty, who was spending the long, lazy days at Kirkleigh practising upon the pianoforte, writing long letters to her mother or filling her sketchbook with scenes to show Mama and Aunt Jane when she returned home. 'I am a little nervous of riding out with you,' she confessed. 'Selby is very encouraging about my ability, but I am still very much a beginner...'

'You will be perfectly safe with us,' Ann assured her. 'We will enjoy the odd gallop but in the main we will keep to the lanes, so there will be no fences or ditches to cross.' She dropped her voice so that only Kitty could hear her. 'And think how wonderful not to have my aunt, or Mama or even Bertram telling us how to go on!'

Tuesday dawned fine and clear, and spirits were high when the young people gathered at the breakfast table. Lady Leaconham was still uneasy and pointed to the strong sunshine as a reason for deferring the ride.

'To be out of doors in the height of summer, exposed to the elements for hours on end,' she said. 'Just think of the damage to your complexions.'

Ann was quick to disclaim.

'We will have our bonnets, Aunt, and we can always stop under the trees if we need to rest.'

'But you cannot dismount,' objected Lady Leaconham. 'Who will look after your horses if you do not take your groom?'

'You may be easy, Mama,' put in Garston. 'Hamilton, Camber and I will be there to take care of the ladies.'

'Let them be, Letitia,' said Lady Harworth before her sister could speak again. 'Young people must be allowed a little freedom. And what harm can they come to as long as they are on our land?'

'But what if one of them should fall…?'

Kitty could see that her godmother was not reassured and she gave her a quick hug.

'Do not worry, ma'am, we will be riding directly to Titchwell and back again. I am not proficient enough for anything more than the gentlest of rides, is that not so, Ann?'

'We will proceed with great decorum, I promise,' said Ann, twinkling. 'You may expect to see us back here in very good time for dinner!'

In high good humour the riders gathered in the stable yard an hour later. There were several minutes of noisy confusion as the horses were brought out and everyone mounted up. Kitty looked askance at Selby as he walked up to her, leading a very pretty grey mare.

'Dapple has cast a shoe,' explained the groom. 'The mistress ordered Bianca to be saddled for you.'

Kitty eyed the mare doubtfully. She had grown used to the little pony and although the grey mare looked beautiful, she doubted she would be quite as docile as Dapple. She was obliged to take an extra step up on the mounting block to reach the saddle and she tried not to feel too nervous as she gathered up the reins.

'Just remember all I've taught you, miss,' said Selby as he adjusted the stirrup and checked the girth. 'She's a sturdy little mare, and will carry you all day without flagging, never fear.'

'I seem so much further from the ground,' said Kitty, trying a little laugh.

'You will be safe enough on Bianca,' said Ann soothingly. 'She has no vicious habits. And if we get separated,' she added, as she turned to lead the way out of the yard, 'just give Bianca her head: she knows her way home!'

It did not take Kitty long to settle on to her new mount and she soon felt very comfortable in the saddle. Ann suggested they should gallop through the park and Kitty found the mare's speed exhilarating. It was gratifying to be able to keep up with her friends and their compliments upon her ability helped her to relax and enjoy the long ride into Titchwell. The landlord of the Star was looking out for them and his stable lads were waiting to take charge of the horses as soon as they arrived.

Kitty allowed one of the diminutive stable boys to catch at the reins, holding the mare steady while Mr Hamilton ran over to help her dismount. Ann had already jumped nimbly to the ground and was gazing intently at a paper nailed to the doorpost as Kitty and her escort walked across the yard.

'Now what is that, Miss Ann?' demanded Mr Hamilton, laughing. 'What has caught your attention?'

Ann quickly tore down the paper handed it to Garston, who uttered a laugh.

'A little added entertainment,' he said, tucking the paper into his pocket as they all followed the landlord into the hostelry. Miss Camber and her brother immediately demanded to know what he meant, but Garston merely shook his head, and when they applied to Ann she would only smile mysteriously.

'Come now, tell us what is on that paper,' cried Mr Hamilton as they settled themselves around the table in their private dining room.

'Something very dear to Miss Wythenshawe's heart,' announced Ann.

Kitty looked up.

'I am sure I do not know what that might be.'

Garston pulled out the paper.

'An Abolition meeting,' he read. 'At Harper's Field, Chapeltown, this afternoon. Members of the Anti-Slavery Movement will address the meeting.' He looked up. 'These meetings are happening everywhere: I think it is time I attended one. Doesn't do to be behindhand, you know.'

'Chapeltown is not far from here,' said Ann. 'We could go there this afternoon.'

'But we promised Papa we would go directly back to Kirkleigh,' objected Miss Camber.

'It is only a little deviation from our route,' said Garston, studying the paper. 'The meeting is for two o'clock: no doubt it will be over by three and if we do not tarry, we will still be back in plenty of time for dinner.'

'Is Chapeltown part of Lord Harworth's estate?' enquired George Camber.

Ann waved one white hand.

'It is only a couple of miles outside the boundary.' She pouted. 'I should have thought that you of all people would want to go, Kitty. You were very keen to support the cause in London.'

'I am still a supporter, but this is not what we planned…'

'We planned to spend the day riding.' Mr Hamilton grinned. 'If we were to take a look at the meeting on our way home it can do no harm.'

'Perhaps Mr Clarkson will be there with his box.' Ann turned to Miss Camber, her eyes wide. 'You should have seen him, Lizzie, he pulled out thumbscrews and leg-shackles, all designed to subdue the poor slaves. I vow I almost fainted at the sight of such gruesome articles.'

'By Jove, I wish I had been there!' declared George Camber. 'By all means let us ride over after lunch and take a look.'

'We need not stay long,' added Garston, ' We do not want to be late for dinner.'

'And I should like to see what this Clarkson has to say,' added Mr Hamilton.

'Let us take a vote upon it!' cried Ann. 'Who would like to ride over to Chapeltown when we have finished our meal?'

Kitty remained silent, but the others were all in favour. She tried to hide her unease. She guessed that a large crowd meeting in the open air might not be quite so well behaved as those gathered in

Lombard Street. Something of her thoughts showed in her face, for Ann reached over and gripped her hand.

'Do cheer up, Kitty. You were doubtful about the meeting in London, were you not? And those fears were quite unfounded.'

'It did pass off very well,' Kitty admitted.

'And so will this one,' said Ann. 'Besides, this time we have three gentlemen to look after us.'

Mr Hamilton reached for the bottle of wine.

'Don't you worry, Miss Wythenshawe,' he said comfortably. 'We will take care of you all. And if we don't like the look of the meeting, we can always ride away.'

'Good notion, Hamilton.' Garston nodded. 'Is that the last of the bottle? Waiter, bring us more wine, and hurry!'

Because of their proposed detour the little party did not tarry over their lunch and they were soon on their way again, not riding back towards Kirkleigh but taking the road south to Chapeltown. It was a glorious day and the trilling song of a lark accompanied them as they rode between the thick green hedges that marked the lower valleys and provided a contrast with the dry stone walls of the hill farms. As they approached Chapeltown the road became noticeably busier.

'No need to fret about getting lost,' grinned Mr Hamilton, bringing his horse alongside Kitty's mare. 'I have just spoken to one of the men. He is a local, and says everyone is going to Harper's Field. All we need do is to follow the crowd.'

Ahead of them Kitty could see the people stepping off the road and into a field, where a number of carts and carriages were already drawn up close to a small copse, taking advantage of the shade. One farm cart had been stationed out in the open, and Kitty guessed it was to act as an improvised stage for the group of serious-looking gentlemen standing close by. She looked around. From her vantage point in the saddle she had a good view of the whole area. There were one or two better-dressed gentlemen sitting in the carriages under the trees, but the large crowd comprised mainly working men. Farm labourers, she guessed, with a few women amongst them and a noisy crowd of very young men in one corner that she thought could well be apprentices.

'You see,' said Ann, 'everyone is perfectly amiable.'

'They are also perfectly noisome,' giggled Lizzie Camber, holding a handkerchief to her nose. 'Let us move away from the crowd, shall we?'

'Aye,' agreed her brother. 'We could tether the horses in the shade. That fellow over there has a flagon of ale. I wonder if he would sell it to me. It's dashed hot here today.'

'Good idea, George. Let's get the ladies into the shade and we'll come back and ask him.'

They began to walk their horses towards the trees. Kitty noticed that more people were arriving, one or two on horseback but most were walking, including a large group of rough-looking men who strode purposefully into the field. Very quickly the festival atmosphere disappeared. The late-comers were carrying thick sticks that they brandished threateningly. The air was now full of menace and Kitty watched, horrified, as they began to force their way through the crowd, lashing out at anyone who got in their way. Angry roars replaced the laughter and chatter as fighting broke out amongst the men. Kitty looked towards the apprentices. With a loud halloo they charged into the crowd, fists flying. Behind her she heard Garston utter an oath.

'We should get out of here,' he said sharply. 'Camber, look to your sister. Ann, Kitty, come along.'

They turned towards the gate, but Kitty could see that their exit was blocked by even more people pouring into the field. Behind her, shouts and yells filled the air: men were grappling with each other, women screamed and people were running in all directions, trying to avoid the rough-looking men brandishing the cudgels.

'This way!' shouted George Camber, turning his horse about, but everywhere they looked there were groups of men, fighting. Lizzie Camber began to cry.

The crowd was spilling out around them. A man cannoned into Ann's mare, which reared and snorted nervously. Garston pushed his own horse closer and urged Ann to move away. Kitty fought down her nerves, trying not to snatch at the reins as Bianca sidled and fretted beneath her. A scream made her look round. A woman with a baby in her arms was being pursued by a black-jowled man in a leather waistcoat. The woman was turning, using her body to shield the child from the blows he was aiming at her with his short staff. The man was gaining on his victim; another few strides and his huge paw would close on her shoulder and she would be lost.

Without thinking Kitty kicked Bianca, forcing the horse between the woman and her attacker.

'No! Leave her alone, you fiend!'

The man pulled up quickly and narrowly avoided crashing into Bianca. He raised his head and glared at Kitty, his face contorted with rage. With a snarl he lifted his stick, whether to attack Kitty or Bianca she did not know, but even as she tried to move the mare out of the way, a huge black horse thundered up, its rider kicking out one booted foot to knock her assailant to the ground.

'Daniel!' Kitty gazed at her saviour, dizzy with relief.

He said nothing, merely grabbed at her reins and led her away from the immediate danger. Ann and the others trotted up. Kitty noticed that George Camber was riding very close to his sister, who was sobbing quietly.

'Blackwood, thank heaven—' began Mr Hamilton, but Daniel cut him short.

'We need to get out of here, immediately.'

Garston nodded, looking pale.

'I know,' he said, 'but the gateway is blocked with carriages and men fighting...'

'We will have to jump the hedge,' said Daniel shortly. 'The longer we delay the more chance that we will be attacked. Go on,' he ordered as George Camber began to protest. 'We must get the ladies out of here!' He held Bianca's rein to prevent her following as the others set off towards the far corner of the field. He turned to Kitty. 'You will have to jump, too. What practice have you had?'

She swallowed, her eyes fixed on Ann as she galloped up to the hedge and flew over it, skirts billowing around her.

'A few small jumps with Dapple, nothing at all with this horse...'

'This is Miss Harworth's mare, is it not? I cannot imagine her keeping a horse that could not clear a barn.' Daniel let go of the rein and rested his hand briefly over hers. 'You can do it, Kitty. Follow me, hold on tight and leave everything to the mare.' Kitty nodded and Daniel squeezed her fingers. His eyes crinkled as he gave her a quick smile. 'Good girl!'

Another shout told them the mêlée was closing in on them again. Daniel kicked his horse into a trot and Kitty followed. Soon they were cantering across the grass. They were obliged to swerve to avoid a running man, but Kitty kept her eyes fixed on Daniel riding ahead of her, trying not to think of the hedge looming like a solid green wall in the distance. It was not high; she could see the others gathered on the far side, waiting for them. She forced herself not to pull on the reins and instead tried to push down on to the saddle, tightening her leg firmly around the pommel and struggling to remember everything Selby had taught her.

Daniel's horse took the hedge with barely a break in its stride, then it was Kitty's turn. She felt Bianca check slightly and gave her a little flick with her whip, urging her forwards. Suddenly the mare pushed off from her haunches and they were flying through the air, clearing the hedge easily and landing gracefully on the far side. The jolt as they hit the ground almost unseated Kitty, but she clung on, aware of her friends' cheers as they applauded her. She realised she had been holding her breath and let out a huge sigh as she straightened in the saddle and pulled on the reins to bring Bianca to a walk.

Nothing happened.

Bianca continued to canter across the field with Kitty pulling ineffectually on the reins. She heard Lizzie Camber scream, her brother shouted in alarm, but Bianca's pace only quickened. They were galloping away from Harper's Field and Kitty could do nothing to stop the mare's headlong flight.

Kitty tried to relax her tense hands on the reins and commanded herself not to panic. She needed to concentrate upon keeping her balance and staying in the saddle. Bianca showed no inclination to swerve or buck but she had the bit between her teeth and was in no mood to slow down. Kitty managed a quick look behind and was relieved to see Daniel pursuing her. She settled into the saddle: his horse was so much bigger and faster, he could not fail to catch her very soon, she knew it.

By a cruel twist of fate the short turf was giving way to bracken and rough heathland with a narrow track through it, wide enough for a single horse. Kitty's heart sank a little: Daniel would only be able to follow her. She tried tugging on the reins again, but Bianca's neck was rigid, her ears flattened and she had no intention of stopping. There was nothing for it but to hang on.

'Very well,' muttered Kitty. 'Run if you must, you will tire eventually.'

On and on they went, the mare negotiating the twists and turns of the path with sure-footed ease. The others would follow her, she was sure, even though she dared not look around: she needed to keep her eyes on the path if she was not to be thrown off balance with any slight change of direction. The shouts and screams of the crowd had long ago disappeared and now the only sound was the thud of hooves and the creak of leather. The wind tugged at her bonnet, the ribbons came loose and she was unable to take a hand from the reins to prevent it being whipped away. As they rode further on to the moors she felt its chill seeping through her riding jacket. The path took a sudden upward turn and the mare's headlong pace began to slow. Kitty seized her chance. She pulled hard on the reins and felt the mare respond, slowing to a walk just as the track widened.

Almost immediately Daniel was beside her. He reached over and caught the mare's bridle, bringing both horses to a stand. Kitty realised she was shaking.

'I c-couldn't stop her.'

'You did very well not to fall off.'

She managed a small smile.

'Yes, I think so, too. Where are the others?'

'I sent them home. If none of you arrives in time for dinner there will be panic at Kirkleigh.'

She nodded, then frowned at him.

'But what were you doing in Harper's Field?'

'I know several members of the Anti-Slavery Society in this area. I had heard there was to be an open-air meeting at Chapeltown but it was only this morning that I realised how close you would be if you rode to Titchwell.'

'So you came to join us?'

'No! I came to get you away,' he retorted. 'These outdoor gatherings often end in rioting. I rode to the Star to tell you that you should avoid Chapeltown on your return journey, but I arrived too late. The landlord told me you had already set out for the meeting.'

'I did not realise.' Kitty shivered. 'Everything started so well...'

'Aye, that's the devil of it. The innocent and the curious find themselves caught up in violence. Those opposed to the movement often pay gangs of men to break up open meetings such as this one. There's more than one man in this area that would not be above such tricks.'

'Do—do you mean they c-came with the sole purpose of fighting?' Kitty shook her head, trying to clear her thoughts. 'I thought it was merely the heat, and too much ale...' She swayed in the saddle and Daniel quickly slipped from his horse.

'Come,' he said. 'You should rest a little.'

She kicked her foot free of the stirrup and slid down into his waiting arms.

'I d-do not think my legs will hold me.'

'They will not need to.' In one smooth movement he swept her up, just as everything went black.

When Kitty opened her eyes she could not at first remember what had happened. She was lying on a bed of soft bracken, the smell of peat and hum of insects filling her senses. She moved her head and saw Daniel standing beside the horses. He had removed his jacket and waistcoat and was wiping the sweat from Bianca with handfuls of dried grass, his arm sweeping over the mare's flanks in a smooth, graceful arc. As if aware of her eyes upon him he turned, and after giving the mare a final pat he threw away the makeshift brush and strode towards her.

'So you are awake.' He dropped down beside her. 'How do you feel now?'

She did not answer immediately and instead looked sleepily at the way the slight breeze rippled the fine linen of his shirt, outlining the muscled body beneath. She closed her eyes again as the pleasant image was marred by returning memory. She struggled to sit up and immediately his arm was around her shoulders, supporting her.

'Oh, dear,' she muttered, 'how…how *feeble* of me to faint off like that. I must get up…'

'Do not try to stand just yet. There is no hurry.'

'But there is! I must get back to Kirkleigh before dark.'

'Impossible.' Kitty stopped struggling. He said, 'It is at least two hours' ride and the sun is setting. We will ride as far as we can while it is still light, then we must take shelter until the moon rises. You are very pale,' he added quietly. 'I wish I had something for you to drink…'

She dragged up a smile.

'I will be very well again in a moment. You have done more than enough for me already, coming to my rescue.'

He shrugged. 'That was nothing; you had already regained control when I reached you.'

'No, not for following after me, although I am very grateful to you for doing so! I meant back at the meeting, when that man was about to attack...'

She shivered and as his arm tightened around her it seemed quite natural to shrink towards him and rest her head against his chest.

'I would not let anyone harm you.'

His words and the solid, steady thud of his heart beneath her cheek was very soothing. She closed her eyes, breathing in the familiar, reassuring scent of him, a mix of wool, soap and spices.

'You are a good friend to me, Daniel.'

He did not reply, merely squeezed her fingers and for several minutes they sat together in silence, staring out across the heath. It was so peaceful that Kitty was almost disappointed when Daniel suddenly jumped to his feet.

'We should move on, if you are able.'

He put on his waistcoat and shrugged himself into his jacket. His tone was brisk and Kitty felt a stab of guilt. No doubt he had made plans for this evening and they would now be ruined.

'Yes, of course,' she said quietly. 'I feel much better now.'

Silently she took the hand he held out to her and allowed him to pull her up. He walked her over to the grey mare and without ceremony he put his hands about her waist and threw her up lightly into the saddle. She looked down at him, a slight frown creasing her brow as he adjusted her stirrup. His face was stern, almost forbidding, but as if aware of her gaze he glanced up.

'Do not look so anxious,' he said gently. 'You will be back at Kirkleigh soon after midnight.'

'Yes, of course. It is very good of you to give up your time for me like this.'

His brows rose.

'Would you have preferred to find your way alone?'

'No, of course not, but the others…'

'They were all shaken by what they had witnessed. Miss Camber especially was very distressed. I thought it best they should return together. Besides, Marnie was by far the fastest horse, so it was logical for me to come after you.'

His answer was so matter of fact she felt quite daunted and did not venture to speak again. He scrambled into the saddle and led the way across the heath towards the road that could be seen snaking through the valley below them. As they rode Kitty watched a line of thick grey cloud bubbling up in the west. As soon as the path widened she brought Bianca alongside Daniel's black mare.

'When the sun drops behind that cloud it will very soon grow too dark to go on.'

He nodded. 'We have a little time yet: we will head for the road. It will be easier to find shelter down there. I doubt you had anticipated such an adventurous day's ride, Miss Wythenshawe.'

'Certainly not!' She tried to match his bantering tone. 'I expected the most exciting part of the day would be a short gallop.'

'Lord Harworth will take care not to let you go out alone in future.'

'Will he be very angry, do you think?'

'No, no. He will be anxious, of course, but you may have noticed that his sister can wind him around her finger.' A smile tugged at one corner of his mouth. 'My own sister is just such a minx!' He paused. 'Harworth is a good man at heart, and a responsible land-lord. However, there is a lot he has to learn about running a mill.'

'And can you teach him that?' she asked, turning her head to look at him.

'I shall try. It is something I have grown up with.'

'Has your family always been involved in spinning?'

'With cloth, certainly. My grandfather was a merchant. He was obliged to travel widely throughout the north, collecting pieces— woven sections of cloth—from the weavers who lived in the little

villages throughout the area. He traded in all sorts of cloth, cali-
mancoes, serges, camlets and so on. Grandfather encouraged his
younger sons to build a mill, just over the Pennines in Lancashire.
Using Arkwright's new cotton machines they soon had a thriv-
ing business. My uncle still owns that mill, but my father wanted
to return to Hestonroyd so he built his first mill there. I grew up
with the business. I have worked beside my father in each new
venture.'

'It must be very rewarding.'

'It is, but it is not to be undertaken lightly.'

Daniel began to explain to her about the responsibilities of a mill
owner and she listened, fascinated as he told her how his father had
built sturdy new cottages for the workers, schools for the children,
about the doctor he employed to make regular visits to his mills.
She put in questions occasionally, but they were hardly necessary:
he was eager to talk.

'Why are you telling me all this, Mr Blackwood?' she asked
him, when at last he fell silent. 'Do you explain your business to
everyone in such detail?'

He did not answer her immediately, but kept his eyes fixed on
the road ahead of them.

'Lord Harworth has excellent intentions,' he said at last. 'But I
fear that he may not understand that a mill requires constant su-
pervision. It is easy to be tempted into cutting costs and making
short-term profits at the expense of the workers. I believe that you
will be in a position to remind him of his duties, when other interests distract him.'

'I—I fear I do not understand,' she stammered.

'You will be able to look after the welfare of your people, when
you are Lady Harworth.'

The sudden disappearance of the sun made Kitty aware of the
chill breeze cutting through her riding jacket.

'I...I think you are mistaken,' she muttered. 'L-Lord Harworth
has not made me an offer.'

'Perhaps not, but it is his intention to do so.' He glanced at her, his face shuttered. 'It is what you want, is it not?'

'I—' Kitty swallowed. 'Why…yes, I suppose…'

'As Lady Harworth you will be in a position of influence,' he said. 'You will be able to ensure your mill-workers are treated well. Yours will be a very important role.'

Kitty was silent. So Daniel, too, thought Lord Harworth would offer for her. She bit her lip. Surely she should be happier than this at the prospect, but all she felt was confusion. The darkness that was enveloping them seemed to enter her very being, weighing her down.

'We will have to stop soon.' He pointed to a rocky outcrop looming over them. It had been quarried away to form a large semi-circular space beside the road. 'We could shelter there for an hour or so, or we could go on; there should be an inn somewhere along this road…'

'Let us stop here,' Kitty begged, exhausted as much by the tumult raging within as by her ordeal.

They moved into the shelter of the rocks and Daniel lifted Kitty from her horse. This time he released her almost before her feet touched the ground, increasing her feeling of desolation.

While Daniel saw to the horses she walked over to sit on a low ledge that formed a natural bench, the stone rising smooth and sheer at her back. Night fell rapidly. Bianca became a vague grey shape and she could not make out the black horse at all. When Daniel turned and walked towards her she could see only the pale blur of his face and his white neckcloth.

'What if the cloud moves in to cover the sky?' she asked him, a slight edge of panic in her voice. 'What if there is no moonlight?'

'There will be. The cloud is breaking up already.' He sat down beside her and they both leaned back against the hard stone. Kitty was very conscious of the gap between them. It was only a few inches but it was as if Daniel had put up a barrier between them.

He continued, 'The moon will rise in a couple of hours. As soon as it is high enough to light our way we will move on.'

'Until then we must sit here.'

'Yes.'

Kitty shivered.

'Are you cold?'

'A little.' She put out her hand, saying quickly, 'No, I would not take your jacket! If we could sit a little closer...'

He put his arms around her.

'Is that better?'

'Yes, thank you.'

She leaned into him, resting her head on his chest. Would any other man make her feel so comfortable? she wondered.

'You are always coming to my rescue, Daniel,' she said sleepily. 'In another life you would have been a knight, I think. A knight in armour. Rescuing damsels.'

There is only one damsel I would ever wish to rescue.

Daniel glanced down. He could see very little in the darkness but he felt her curls tickling his chin. Desire stirred within him and he cursed silently. Damnation, did she not realise the temptation she presented?

'I am not as chivalrous as you think me,' he muttered.

She raised her head.

'Why do you say that?'

Her face was very close, a pale blur in the darkness. He could feel her warm breath on his cheek.

'Because being here with you in my arms, I want to...'

He turned his head slightly and his mouth brushed her soft lips, as he had known it would. She trembled but did not recoil and he kissed her gently, savouring the taste of her, the scent of fresh flowers that clung to her skin. Her lips parted beneath his even as she melted against him, the movement slight but deliciously inviting. Slowly and with great care he lowered her down on to the ledge, half-hoping, half-dreading that she would protest and he would be obliged to draw back. Instead she gave a little moan and clutched at his coat, pulling him down with her. They were stretched out together and Daniel thought he would never want a more comfortable bed than this stone ledge with Kitty nestled against him. Passion threatened to consume him. By sheer force of will he contained it. With infinite tenderness he kissed her eyes, her cheek. He had no idea when she had removed her gloves but he felt her fingers driving through his hair, tormenting him with thoughts of how it would feel to have those same hands on his skin, stroking his chest, the fingers raking down his back. He sought her mouth again and while he kissed her he smoothed his hand over the tightly fitted riding jacket, following the curve of her waist up to the swell of her breast. Kitty shivered and arched towards his hand. His pulse leaping, Daniel unbuttoned the jacket. He gently pulled aside her neckcloth and opened the mannish shirt she wore beneath. It was too dark to see anything but shadows so he lowered his head and pressed his lips to the bare flesh of her neck. Kitty moaned as his fingers slipped beneath the shirt and found her breast. She shifted restlessly against his hand, her body arching when his mouth slid downwards, his tongue circling and teasing one erect nipple while his fingers caressed the other. Kitty gasped. Her hands clutched at his hair but she did not try to pull him away, rather she held him closer. She moaned and writhed beneath him, every movement an invitation for him to go further. If only she knew it.

Daniel's hand stilled. Her responses were instinctive; she had no idea how she inflamed him. Any man could be excused for taking this to its natural conclusion.

But he was not any man.

'Daniel?'

She whispered his name, her hand reaching out. He caught it and pressed a kiss into its palm, trying to control his ragged breathing.

'We must stop now, my dear, before we do something we will

regret.' It was too dark to read her face but he sensed her confusion. He leaned down to kiss her one last time. 'You are too, too alluring.' He spoke lightly, not wanting to embarrass her. 'I confess this is a delightful way to pass the time but it will not do. You are as good as promised to another man.'

He waited for her to contradict him. When she remained silent his disappointment was bitter as gall. She struggled to sit up.

'We—we are destined to bring out the worst in each other, are we not?' There was a catch in her voice, as if she was trying not to cry.

The worst? Is that what she thought of his love-making? He was aware of her every move as she sat beside him, re-tying her neck-cloth and fastening her jacket. His senses were heightened so much that when she touched his arm he flinched.

'Do you mind if we sit like this?' Her tone was hesitant, anxious. 'I am not comfortable, alone in the dark, but if it disturbs you...'

He put his hand over her fingers.

'There is nothing to be afraid of here.'

'You are not angry with me?'

'Angry with you? No, never.'

'Then you will let me sit here, beside you?'

He signalled his acquiescence by squeezing her hand.

'It will not be long now.' He stared up at the sky, a vast velvet curtain studded with diamonds. 'Look, the cloud has dispersed. As soon as the moon rises we will move on.'

Daniel settled back on the ledge and beside him Kitty made herself comfortable. When her head dropped to his shoulder he did not move away. Nothing stirred. The starlight was sufficient to see a faint line where the land ended and the sky began but little else. A few feet away the horses stood quietly, Kitty's grey mare a paler blur in the darkness.

Daniel did not sleep. His senses remained alert to the sounds of the night, the distant call of a night bird, the rustle of some animal in the bushes. A sigh escaped him. He could wish for nothing more than to be allowed to sit here for ever with this girl-woman beside him, but all too soon they would have to return to their worlds— very different worlds, for she was destined to be Lady Harworth. It was her wish, her dream, was it not? Sometimes he thought she cared for him and when she returned his kisses he was aware of the passion within her, but that was for her husband to awaken, not him. She snuggled closer and he had to grit his teeth to keep his desire for her under control, to sit perfectly still when he really wanted to pull her into his arms and cover her face with kisses.

Why did he not do just that? Why not keep her here all night? She would have given herself to him earlier this evening, so why did he not kiss her again, re-awaken her desire and make love to her? If they did not return to Kirkleigh until morning her reputation would be ruined—there could be no question of Harworth marrying her then. He gazed up at the stars but although they winked and twinkled at him they gave him no encouragement.

Daniel closed his eyes. If he took advantage of her, what future could there be for them? He would make her his wife, but would she always resent him for forcing her into marriage? With sudden, blinding clarity he knew what he wanted: he wanted Kitty to choose him and only him. But it had to be her free choice; he did not want to force the decision on her.

So he would ask her to marry him. Not now of course, when she might think he was only doing it to save her reputation, but once they were back at Kirkleigh. He would make her an offer; present himself as a suitor to rival Bertram Harworth. A silent laugh shook him. He had never made any great show of his family's wealth but perhaps it was time to puff himself off a little. Even without the land and mills he would inherit from his father, his own fortune was comparable with Harworth's. He would tell Kitty as much: she should choose her own future.

And his.

The decision made, Daniel was impatient to be moving. Beside him, Kitty's regular breathing told him she was sleeping and he turned his head to press a light kiss on her tumbled curls before settling back to watch the horizon for the first signs of the rising moon.

Kitty heard Daniel's voice calling her. As she awoke she realised her head was resting on his shoulder, the soft wool of his jacket pressing against her cheek. She was reluctant to open her eyes: it was so comfortable to be snuggled up beside Daniel, just the two of them alone together. She really did not want to think about anything else. He spoke her name again and reluctantly she sat up, yawning.

'Oh!' A fat, butter-yellow moon was resting on the rim of the far hills. 'Is it time to go?'

'Very soon. You have been asleep for some time: perhaps you would like to stretch your legs a little before we begin our long ride back?'

He stood up and held out his hand to her. She allowed him to pull her to her feet.

'Daniel, what happened here, earlier—I was too forward, I must apologise...'

He put a finger to her lips.

'Hush. There is no need to say anything.'

'But I want to—'

'Once we are back at Kirkleigh this will all be forgotten.'

She gazed up at him, trying to pierce the shadows that masked his face. Did he mean that *he* wanted to forget? She wanted to talk about it, to know if he too felt that irresistible tug of attraction whenever they were together. That he desired her she had no doubt, but Mr Ashley had desired her, and she knew that did not mean he really *liked* her. She wanted to ask him to explain himself but Daniel was already leading her across to Bianca. Silently she allowed him to throw her up into the saddle. Then, with the moon climbing in the night sky and turning the world from black to silver-blue, they set off along the road to Kirkleigh.

Kitty had never been on a horse for more than an hour before today and now her body ached, but that was nothing compared to the pain inside. When she thought of Daniel kissing her she found herself melting all over again. She could not deny that she had wanted him to kiss her. Once again she had offered herself to him and once again he had been the one to break away. She thought that he must indeed care for her to be so protective, but that was small consolation and the heavy cloud settled more firmly around her heart. He did not desire her sufficiently to declare the world well lost when she was in his arms. She glanced across at him as he rode beside her. There was no sign of fatigue in his upright figure; his face in the moonlight was unsmiling, as still and inscrutable as stone. He might have been hewn from the quarry where they had taken shelter.

'Is anything amiss, Miss Wythenshawe?' He looked across at her.

Kitty hesitated. Should she ask him why he had not taken advantage of her? Perhaps she had disgusted him. Her godmother had talked with contempt of the forward behaviour of some of the young ladies in Town, and had not Mama told her that on no account was she to allow a gentleman to go any further than kissing the tips of her fingers? She had allowed Daniel to do a lot more than that!

'I am very tired,' she managed at last. 'I have never ridden so far before.'

'And you have done very well. Look, there is Kirkleigh village ahead of us. Another half-hour and this nightmare will be over. You will be home.'

She nodded, too miserable to speak. So he thought of this whole episode with horror. For her, once the danger was past she had thought of it as a glorious adventure: the elation of successfully jumping the hedge, galloping headlong across the heath, kissing Daniel. Especially kissing Daniel.

I am undoubtedly a very wanton young woman, she told

herself miserably. *And after tonight I should not be surprised if Godmama sends me back to Mama and wishes to have nothing further to do with me!*

Chapter Eleven

Her unhappy thoughts kept Kitty occupied until at last they clattered into the stableyard at Kirkleigh. She was surprised to see so many torches burning. Selby came running out to meet them.

'Right glad I am to see you, Mr Blackwood, and you, miss! When t'others returned and said what had happened I was that put out. His lordship was all for setting out immediately but Lord Leaconham said as how you had gone after her, sir, so we decided we should wait 'til morning before getting up a search party. I should never have saddled up Bianca for you, miss, whatever the young mistress said. If that mare runs away with you then there's no stopping her. I was that afraid you had been thrown.'

'No, I am quite safe,' she said as he helped her to alight. 'Bianca carried me very well.'

'Miss Wythenshawe even took a hedge in her stride,' added Daniel, coming to collect her. 'You are a good teacher, Selby.'

'I allus said miss had the makings of a clipping rider,' responded the groom, grinning widely. 'Off you go indoors, now. You'll find her ladyship and all the others waiting up for you.'

'I wish I could just creep away to my room,' admitted Kitty as she accompanied Daniel into the house.

'Everyone will want to assure themselves that you are unharmed.' They stopped to allow the lackey to run ahead and open the door to the drawing room. 'Come, you have been very brave until now.' Daniel turned to her, encouragement glinting in his eyes. 'After you, Miss Wythenshawe.'

Their reception was rapturous. As soon as the door opened the room erupted in cries of relief. Ann flew out of her seat and enveloped Kitty in a tight hug before insisting that she come and sit down with her on the sofa. Everyone was talking at once, demanding to know what had happened. After the calm silence of their night ride Kitty found the cacophony of voices far too confusing. She was content to remain still and silent, sitting between Ann and Lady Leaconham while Daniel explained everything.

'Well, I am relieved that no harm has been done,' declared Lord Harworth, pouring brandy into a glass and handing it to Daniel.

'Except poor Lizzie,' put in Ann. 'She was so distraught that she took to her bed as soon as we got home.'

'I was obliged to give her a little laudanum,' added Mrs Camber, nodding. 'I am sure she will be fully recovered by the morning.'

'This would all have been avoided if they had stuck to their original plan and come straight home,' stated Mr Camber, frowning direfully at his son.

George Camber shrank down in his chair, looking sheepish.

'In Harworth's absence I should have taken responsibility,' put in Garston. 'I should never have agreed to it. It was a mistake, and I admit it.'

'You were not solely to blame, Cousin,' added Ann, 'we were all of us eager to go to Chapeltown, except Kitty.'

'Then she showed more good sense than the rest of you put together,' retorted Lord Harworth. 'I can only thank Providence that Blackwood was on hand.'

'If I had not been there I am sure Hamilton or Lord Leaconham would have gone after Miss Wythenshawe,' remarked Daniel.

'Aye, of course we would.' Martin Hamilton nodded. 'Not that we didn't have the devil's own job finding our way back to the road, even in daylight.'

'But we were only a little late for dinner.' Ann cast a soulful look at her brother.

'Aye, well, that was some relief, to have most of you home,' he agreed. 'And when it grew dark and the ladies began to fret about Miss Wythenshawe I told 'em not to worry. "Mark my words," I said, "Blackwood will look after her. And when darkness falls you may be sure he will take shelter at some inn or tavern until there's moonlight enough to see the way." And I was right, you see. But you'll not be riding back to Hestonroyd tonight, my boy? The least we can do is give you a bed for the night.'

'Thank you, my lord, I would like to stay,' replied Daniel. 'Very much.'

Kitty knew his eyes were upon her but she dared not meet his gaze.

'Did you dine on the road?' enquired Garston.

'No, we did not stop to eat,' said Daniel.

'Oh, how remiss of me!' declared Lady Harworth, tugging at the bell-rope. 'You must be quite famished! I will order something to be brought in immediately.' Kitty disclaimed, wanting only to go to her bed, but Lady Harworth insisted and when the servant came in she gave orders for soup to be prepared and sent up to Kitty's room. 'And for Mr Blackwood, too, but ask Cook to send up a plate of ham and some pickles as well for him. I am sure you must be very hungry, sir,' she added as the servant withdrew. 'But now it is very late, and I am sure we should all be in our beds…'

'Not quite yet, Mama, if you please, I would like to say something.' Lord Harworth moved to the centre of the room. 'In all the anxiety of this evening we have not been able to divert ourselves with charades, or billiards as is customary, and it has given me time to consider. I have made a decision and do not wish to put things off a moment longer. My mother and Aunt Leaconham are well aware of my intentions, and approve, so I think it is time to speak.'

Kitty was looking at her host, trying to appear attentive when all she wanted was to go to sleep. From the corner of her eye she saw

Garston lean down to whisper something to Ann, who giggled. She hoped Lord Harworth would hurry up and finish whatever it was he had to say so that she could retire to her bedchamber.

'Mama has been telling me for years that I should do this, and since I am assured by my aunt that there is no impediment I see no reason to wait. We'll have the lawyers discuss settlements and jointures and what-not later but I want to get this off my chest so I might as well do it now, while everyone is here, eh?' Bemused, Kitty watched as Lord Harworth crossed the room and lowered himself on to one knee before her. 'Miss Wythenshawe, will you do me the honour, very *great* honour, of accepting my hand in marriage?'

Kitty stared at him. Beside her, Ann was clapping and laughing, her godmother gave a gusty sigh and everyone else crowded round, eagerly awaiting her answer.

All except Daniel. Briefly raising her eyes from the figure kneeling before her, she looked across the room. Daniel remained by the door, his face pale and drawn with fatigue. Apart from a muscle twitching in his cheek he might well have been made from marble, so cold and indifferent was he. Lady Leaconham gave her a little nudge.

'Well, Kitty, answer his lordship.'

'I—um—I am honoured, my lord, and, and flattered that you should think me worthy...' She cudgelled her brain for the right words but it appeared she had said enough.

'Oh, my dear, I am so *pleased!*' cried Ann, enveloping her in another of her fierce hugs. 'Now I shall be able to call you sister!'

As soon as she emerged from Ann's embrace, Lady Leaconham pulled her close and kissed her cheek.

'Kitty, my love, how happy I am about this! And I cannot *wait* to tell your mama—you know how delighted she will be.'

Lord Harworth, having risen to his feet, held out his hand to her.

'Miss Wythenshawe—Katherine—*Kitty.*' He pulled her up to stand beside him. 'You have made me the happiest man on earth!'

He raised first one hand then the other to his lips before leaning forward to plant a kiss on her cheek.

'My lord, this is not—I mean—I must speak with you.'

He beamed at her.

'Of course, my love, of course, but everything else can wait until the morrow. We must let our guests go and get some rest now, eh?' He looked around. 'But where's Blackwood? Gone to bed already, has he? Young dog, not staying to congratulate me, but there, I suppose he is tired after all the adventures of the day!'

'I was concerned for a while today that he might cut you out,' remarked Lady Harworth, stepping forward to give Kitty a congratulatory peck on the cheek.

'Goodness, yes,' cried Ann, putting her hands to her mouth. 'Just think. If you had not returned until the morning then Mr Blackwood would have been obliged to offer for you!'

'Do not look so horrified at that, my dear,' said Lady Harworth drily. 'He would not be such a bad catch, rich as he is.'

Lady Leaconham bent an enquiring eye upon her sister.

'But, Clara, a manufacturer…'

'Not just a manufacturer, Letitia, although he has some very wealthy connections in the trade—one of his uncles is the richest wool merchant in Leeds and another owns several cotton mills in Lancashire, not to mention his father's interests in both wool and the cotton spinning. But not only that, he is to inherit a very sizeable property. Harworth tells me his father bought the Hartleydale estate last year.' She glanced speculatively at her daughter. 'Mr Daniel Blackwood stands to inherit a business worth in excess of forty thousand a year. To my mind that makes him a *very* eligible bachelor.' She added after a moment, 'He does not have a title, of course.'

'Well,' exclaimed Lady Leaconham, fanning herself briskly. 'I never would have thought it. He is extremely well presented, of course, but there is never anything ostentatious about the man.'

'But he is very much a gentleman, Aunt, do you not think so?'

said Ann, looking thoughtful. 'A few more fobs and seals, a little more time in Town...'

'Enough, enough!' cried Lord Harworth jovially. 'What care I how rich Blackwood may be? There is one prize he does not possess.'

He lifted Kitty's hands to his lips again, then stood beaming down at her. Realising she was expected to respond, Kitty could only think of one thing to say.

'Sir, I am very tired...'

'Oh, my poor child, of course you are!' Lady Leaconham was on her feet in an instant. 'Say goodnight, my love, and I will take you upstairs immediately. A betrothal, and after such a day of excitement, it is no wonder you are worn out.'

'Yes, I am, Godmama. If you will all excuse me...'

Lady Leaconham put one arm about Kitty and led her away and as she picked up a bedroom candle from the bottom of the stairs she gave a little chuckle of delight.

'Oh, my dear, was anything so fortunate? I was afraid at first that it was all up with you when Garston returned with the others and told me what had happened, but once it became clear that no blame was attached to you then Bertram was all concern. And to make you an offer here, in front of everyone—'

'He does not know my circumstances,' muttered Kitty. 'It must be explained to him how very poor I am—'

'Yes, of course, my dear, but what can that matter now?'

'It matters to *me,*' said Kitty, close to tears. 'I am sure he will not wish to marry me once he knows the truth.'

They had reached the door of her bedchamber and Lady Leaconham led the way inside.

'There can be no objection to your birth.' She went around the room, lighting all the candles from her own before coming to stand before Kitty once more. 'He has proposed to you most publicly, Kitty. Bertram would be a complete scoundrel to cry off now!'

* * *

Despite her exhaustion, Kitty's sleep was disturbed by dreams and she rose late the following morning. She was still pinning up her hair when Ann bounced into the room.

'Good morning, *sister!* You cannot know how happy I am to call you that. And I heard Bertram go downstairs this morning *singing,* so you have made him happy as well!'

'I am very glad of it,' said Kitty, forcing herself to smile.

'Shall we go down to breakfast together? There is so much to discuss. Mama says Bertram wants to hold a ball to announce the betrothal and Aunt Leaconham will be planning your trousseau already. We must make sure we have our say—'

'You go on,' Kitty broke in, 'I—um—I am not at all happy with this gown and will change it before I go downstairs.' Ann was looking very keenly at her and she added beseechingly, 'Pray go ahead of me and I will join you as soon as I am able.'

'My dear, you are very pale, are you sure you are not ill?'

'No, no, it is merely a headache.'

'Poor Kitty. After the exertions of yesterday it is no wonder you are looking hagged. I shall send Norris up to you with a tisane and you must go back to bed. And I shall have breakfast sent up to you, as well!'

Ann flew out of the room and Kitty dropped her head in her hands. She had been quite truthful when she had said she had a headache, but she did not think any tisane would cure it. Tears pricked her eyelids. All her life she had dreamed of becoming a lady, and now it was actually going to happen, but instead of elation Kitty only felt anxiety. She told herself that it was because she had not been honest with Lord Harworth. Once she had explained to him about her family and her lack of fortune she would feel much better. Stepping out of her dress, she lay down on her bed again and stayed there until the maid arrived with her tisane. She drank it, but she sent her breakfast away, saying she wanted to sleep again until her headache had eased.

* * *

Kitty was surprised to find that after another hour's sleep she did indeed feel better. She decided that her first task must be to find Lord Harworth and confess everything. She wandered over to the window and threw up the sash, leaning her head against the frame as she breathed in the fresh morning air. Of course there was always the possibility that once she had informed him of her true circumstances he would no longer wish to marry her, but she would face that problem when it arose.

A movement below caught her eye and she glanced down to see Daniel's tall figure striding through the garden, his dark coat a startling contrast to the colourful flowerbeds. She heard a faint call and saw Ann hurrying along one of the paths towards him. Daniel stopped to wait for her. He offered Ann his arm and they continued to stroll together, Daniel bending his dark head to catch something Ann was saying. With a sigh Kitty turned away from the window. Bertram's not wishing to marry her because she was poor was suddenly not the problem. It might be the solution.

'My lord, may I come in?'
Kitty peeped around the door of Lord Harworth's study and waited anxiously for his reply. He jumped up, smiling broadly.
'My dear Katherine, come in, come in! I was just writing out the notice for the newspapers. I cannot wait to tell everyone of my good fortune!'
'Before you do that, sir, I think there is something you should know.'

Twenty minutes later Kitty emerged from the study exhausted and depressed but still engaged. She had been at pains to explain to Lord Harworth how her father's misjudged investments had robbed the family of its income, how her mother and aunt now lived at Fallridge in their damp, cramped little cottage, and were obliged to take in sewing to make ends meet. Lord Harworth had indeed looked serious, but he was not inclined to call off the engagement.

'I cannot recall that you have ever told me anything of your family that was not true,' he said. 'You have not misled me, my dear. My mother will be disappointed, naturally, but if she was under the apprehension that your family were affluent then I am sure such a rumour did not come from you. What is not in doubt is that your birth is impeccable. Whatever hardships may have befallen your family you cannot be blamed for. It would not behove anyone who called himself a gentleman to think your lack of funds a reason to cry off from our engagement.'

So Kitty had retired, secure in the knowledge that Lord Harworth had no intention of casting her aside. She went in search of her godmother and found her in the morning room, engaged in writing letters. Kitty described her interview with Lord Harworth and watched the anxious look upon Lady Leaconham's countenance turn to delight when she told her of its conclusion.

'You see, my dear Kitty, I knew everything would turn out well in the end! I will pen a short letter to your mama today, and perhaps you would like to write a note to her yourself and enclose it inside mine; she will want to hear all the details. In fact, perhaps we could prevail upon Bertram to invite your mother and your aunt to Kirkleigh to join us. What do you say to that?'

Kitty mumbled some reply and Lady Leaconham shot her a frowning look.

'My dear Kitty, I do not know what is the matter with you! You have made a most excellent match and yet you look as if you had lost sixpence and found a groat!'

'I—I am sorry, Godmama, I am afraid I cannot quite believe it is happening to me.'

'I confess I have been pinching myself all morning, to make sure I am awake,' replied my lady, giving a very girlish giggle. 'Now go and write to your mother, Kitty: I cannot wait for her to hear the news—this is something she has dreamed of since you were a baby.'

Perhaps that was the truth of it. The thought shot through Kitty's head like a revelation. This had always been her mother's dream, much more than her own. She glanced up as Lady Harworth sailed into the room. Judging by the happy look upon her rather austere countenance Kitty did not think that Bertram had told her of his bride's impecunious state. Lady Harworth greeted her sister warmly, solicitously enquired if Kitty's headache had gone, then sank down on to a sofa.

'Well, this is turning out to be a most eventful morning!'

'What is it, Clara, what has happened?'

'My dear Letitia, you would never credit it! As if there was not enough to do organising next week's ball—Bertram is determined that we use the occasion to announce his betrothal and I am sure it is only right, and just what dear Katherine deserves, but I had barely left my room when—but here is Ann now. She must tell you herself!'

Ann came in, closely followed by Daniel. Kitty shrank back into one corner, wishing the ground would open and swallow her. She did not feel at all comfortable amongst so many happy people.

'Well, Mama, have you told them?' demanded Ann, giving a little skip.

'No, dear Niece, she has told us nothing,' cried Lady Leaconham impatiently. 'She is leaving that to you!'

Ann gave her beaming smile. 'Kitty is not the only one to find a husband, Aunt Leaconham, I am engaged!' She turned and held her hand out to Daniel. 'Mr Blackwood has proposed to me!' Her eyes fell upon Kitty standing in the shadows. 'Kitty, my love, I did not see you there! Is this not wonderful, will you not congratulate me?'

Kitty swallowed and forced her stiff lips into a smile. 'I am sure I w-wish you both very happy.' Her voice sounded strained, but

Ann did not appear to notice. She was already turning to receive her aunt's good wishes.

'Of course there will be no announcement until after the ball,' stated Lady Harworth. 'Bertram is adamant that nothing should detract from his own betrothal. He wants me to invite even more people to dine with us beforehand, which means a great deal more work, of course, for everyone must be told. Letitia, my dear, perhaps you would help me to write out the invitations.'

'By all means, Sister. Let us go now and I will collect your lists.'

'And you must let me see them,' said Ann. 'There are several of my particular friends that I want to come!' She turned to Daniel. 'You will not object if I disappear for a few minutes, will you, dearest? I will be back even before you have time to miss me!'

She swept out of the room behind her mother and her aunt, all three of them forcefully voicing their thoughts on the forthcoming ball. As the door closed behind them there was silence. Kitty and Daniel were left facing one another.

'I had no idea…' began Kitty.

Daniel cleared his throat.

'Nor I. At least, not until this morning, in the garden. Miss Harworth came to find me, she left me in no doubt of her sentiments… I confess I had not been aware…'

He did not look at her, but instead began to toy with a small vase on the side table. Strangely the confusion in Kitty's head had lessened. It did not matter what Daniel thought of her. There were no longer any half-acknowledged hopes. She felt very calm, but as fragile as the porcelain he was twisting between his restless fingers.

'Kitty—'

'No, please.' She put up her hand, holding herself together with an effort. She felt so brittle that one wrong word and she might shatter. 'Let us say nothing more now. I am sure you wish for my happiness, just as I wish for yours. If we understand that then there is no need to say anything more.' She put up her head. 'What a h-happy outcome after yesterday's horrid events. I am s-sure we could not have expected anything half so good to come of it. Now, if you will excuse me, I should go.'

He stood silently, his dark head bowed as she left the room. She would not cry, she told herself over and over as she made her way to her bedchamber. There was nothing to cry about. She had made a splendid match—how could she deny Daniel the same good fortune? His family had made their money by honest toil: marriage to the sister of Lord Harworth would be a splendid alliance for him. She slipped into her bedchamber and closed the door, leaning against it, as if to keep out the world.

'You see?' she said to the empty room. 'Everyone is happy.'

So why, then, did she feel as if something inside her had died?

Chapter Twelve

The succeeding days passed like a dream for Kitty. It was as if someone else inhabited her body and she was a mere spectator. She smiled and said all that was proper to the many visitors that came to Kirkleigh House, agreed with all her godmother's suggestions for which gowns she should wear and spent hours with her smile in place, listening to Ann chatter on about her own engagement.

She had not seen Daniel since the announcement. He had left that day for Hestonroyd and had no plans to return until the ball. She could not be sorry, for without his presence she found it much easier to pretend that she was happy. And she must *be* happy, a letter from Mama told her it was so. The news of her engagement had been greeted in Fallridge with much rejoicing, although the invitation to Mama and Aunt Jane to travel to Kirkleigh and attend the betrothal ball was regretfully declined: Mama had not yet recovered from a bout of influenza. Kitty thought that the decision not to travel might also be due to her mother thinking that she had nothing fine enough to wear on such a grand occasion. That would all change: Lord Harworth had told Kitty he would give her an allowance to buy her clothes for the wedding, and she had already determined to send a portion of it to her mother.

'So you see what a good thing your marriage will be,' she told her reflection, as she prepared for the ball that evening. 'Everyone will benefit, so you must look happy.'

She tried out a smile. The young lady smiling back at her from the mirror certainly looked well enough: Kitty's dusky curls had been brushed until they glowed and were caught up in a bandeau of gold ribbon to match the embroidery on her white muslin gown. Emeralds glittered around her neck and from her ears, a betrothal present from Lord Harworth, purchased at the same time as the large diamond that now flashed and twinkled on her finger.

'Are you ready, Kitty?' Ann appeared at the door. 'Shall we go downstairs together? Norris says that Daniel has arrived.'

With her eyes still on her reflection, Kitty saw her smile slip a little. She quickly pinned it back in place as she picked up her fan.

'Yes, I am ready now.'

The noise and chatter from the drawing room drifted up to them as they descended the stairs. Lord Harworth had told her there were only thirty sitting down to dinner, but the idea frightened Kitty more than the thought of the hundred or so guests who would be arriving later for the ball. The first person she saw as she walked into the room was Daniel, his tall figure commanding attention. He was deep in conversation with a group of gentlemen but the flurry of movement by the door caught his eye and he looked across the room. For a moment he looked towards Kitty, his gaze fixed somewhere above her head, his face showing neither pleasure nor pain, then his eyes shifted to Ann and he smiled a little as he came forwards to greet her.

'Well, my dear Katherine, you are looking magnificent, magnificent!' Lord Harworth was beside her, leading her away from Ann. 'Damn me if Blackwood wasn't right about emeralds being the stones for you.'

'M-Mr Blackwood suggested you buy these?' asked Kitty, surprised.

'Aye. He was with me in Leeds, you see, the day I bought 'em.

We had been visiting one of his business acquaintances and afterwards I told him I was going to get your ring and a little something to mark our engagement. "Emeralds," he said. "Buy her emeralds, to match her eyes." And for Gad he was right! Come along, m'dear, there's any number of people here you have to meet!'

Kitty accompanied him around the room, saying what was proper, smiling, always smiling, but Daniel dominated her thoughts. She wanted to look for him, she longed to hear his voice, but Bertram kept her by his side, presenting family and friends to her. Everyone wanted to congratulate the happy couple, the ladies wanted to gasp and sigh over the ring, the gentlemen winked at Lord Harworth and declared he was a lucky dog.

At dinner Kitty found herself sitting opposite Daniel. For once she was grateful for the mountains of silverware in the centre of the table. Much as she longed to look at Daniel she was afraid that thoughts she wanted to remain hidden might show in her eyes. So she kept her gaze averted, trying to concentrate upon what her neighbour was saying and to respond in kind. She had no idea what she ate, even less what was said during the protracted meal and she could only be thankful when at last they rose from the table.

Even then her ordeal was not over. Kitty stood beside Lady Harworth at the top of the stairs to receive the guests, then Bertram carried her off to dance with him. And all the time she was obliged to smile. She was grateful that Daniel did not ask her to dance: it was painful enough watching him across the room and when she saw him smile at Ann she felt sick at heart. Occasionally she was aware of Daniel's eyes upon her, but when she looked up he would quickly glance away. It was like some bizarre ritual: they circled the room, painfully aware but always avoiding each other. And smiling. Constantly smiling.

A steady stream of partners had kept Kitty on the dance floor until late into the night but at length she had had enough and as the music ended she slipped away before her godmother or Lady

Harworth could present her with another partner. She had been at Kirkleigh long enough to know the layout of the house and made her way to a small sitting room on the ground floor. It was used by the ladies of the house as a sewing parlour and, knowing it would not be occupied, she picked up one of the double candlesticks from a hall table and carried it into the room. The glow from the candles was not sufficient to light the room but it was enough for Kitty. She placed the candlestick on the mantelshelf and sat down in one of the worn armchairs beside the empty fireplace. As she clasped her hands together the diamond on her finger flashed, reminding her that she must not tarry long here or she would be missed.

A sudden flickering of the light made her look up. Daniel was standing in the doorway.

'I saw you leave,' he said, coming into the room and carefully closing the door behind him. 'I wanted to be sure you are not ill.'

'No, I am well. I needed to be quiet for a little while.' She rubbed her aching cheeks. 'I seem to have done nothing all evening but smile and exchange pleasantries.'

'I know.' He walked across the room to sit down opposite her.

She said, 'Ann is very happy tonight.'

'Yes.'

He sat forward, elbows resting on his knees and his hands clasped. He was so close she could have leaned over and touched him. Her knuckles gleamed white as she resisted the temptation.

'Your betrothal was very sudden.'

'Yes.' She thought he would not speak again and berated herself for her remark. It was no concern of hers what he did. Exhaling, he straightened, saying slowly, 'She came to me in the garden, the morning after you had announced your engagement to Harworth. She made it very plain that she would welcome an offer from me. I thought, why not? It would make Ann happy. You are going to marry Harworth. This way at least I shall know where you are, how you go on.'

Kitty's hands went to her mouth. The knife that had been twisting within her all evening now cut even deeper.

'You...you do not...love Ann.'

For the first time that evening he looked straight at her.

'No. I love you.'

His image blurred as tears filled her eyes. She tried to blink them away. If only she had known.

You did know! the voice screamed in her head. *You did know. Every act of kindness, every kiss...*

'Oh, Daniel.' She had to breathe very carefully to keep her unhappiness under control. 'Does it help to know that...that I love you, too? Only I did not realise it until it was too late.'

'No, that does not help at all.' His mouth twisted into a humourless smile. 'I thought you had achieved your dream.'

She shook her head.

'I realise now it was not really my dream, but my mother's: she had such hopes for me.'

'She is happy, then.'

She heard the bitter note in his voice and said quickly, 'Please do not blame her; Mama's life is very hard and she did not want that for me.'

The steady tick, tick of the clock reminded her that she must not stay away from the ballroom for too long.

'Soon we will be brother and sister,' she said carefully. 'How will we manage, meeting as if we mean nothing to each other?'

He rubbed a hand across his eyes.

'We must.'

A rogue tear escaped and she dashed it away.

'I am not sure I can,' she whispered.

With an oath Daniel was on his feet, dragging her up and into his arms.

'Then let us not even try!' he muttered, covering her face with kisses. 'We can both cry off. Surely it is better to tell the truth now than to make the four of us unhappy?'

He kissed her savagely and Kitty clung to him, responding with all the pent-up longing that had been slumbering within her.

'If you cannot face telling them then I'll carry you off now,' he muttered between kisses. 'We will go away; I'll write to Harworth and tell him what has happened...'

Steeling herself, Kitty put a hand to his mouth to silence him.

'You know we cannot do that.' She gave him a misty smile and reached up to brush back a lock of dark hair, her fingers trailing lovingly over his brow. 'You are too much of a gentleman, Daniel Blackwood. You cannot cry off.'

'Despite what she says I swear Ann Harworth doesn't love me—'

'That is not the point. You have promised to marry her. How could you live with your conscience if you broke off your engagement?'

'How can you live with *your* conscience,' he threw at her, 'knowing you married Harworth for his title and his money?'

She looked at him, saw the tortured anguish in his eyes. The confusion that had been banging around in her head for days suddenly resolved itself.

'I am not going to marry him,' she said quietly. 'Lord Harworth does not love me: when I told him I had no money of my own he decided the honourable course was to continue with the engagement, but I think he would be quite relieved if I were to withdraw.'

'But if you cry off, if you are free—'

'No!' She pushed away from him. 'I am nothing. If I cry off everyone will say Lord Harworth is well rid of me. His pride may suffer a little, and Lady Leaconham will be embarrassed, but that will pass, it will be forgotten. Society may want to punish me but that will not be possible, for I am not really a part of that world. I can retire to Fallridge and obscurity. I shall be no worse off than when I began. For you to jilt Ann Harworth would bring shame and embarrassment upon her and social ruin upon you and your family.'

'But I love you!'

'And I love you too much to bring disgrace to you.'

'But it needn't be like that.' He reached out for her again. 'Ann could cry off—'

'You would make yourself so unpleasant to her that she no longer wants to marry you?' Kitty shook her head. 'You must not hurt her, Daniel, she is my friend. I could not bear you to do anything so dishonourable.'

'No! Listen to me—!'

She put out her hands, stepping back to put a distance between them. She said slowly, 'I will make you this promise, Daniel. If you or Ann do anything to break this engagement, I will *never* marry you.'

'And that is your final word?'

'It is.'

She kept her eyes on his face. He must not be in any doubt that she spoke with deadly sincerity. The silence stretched until she thought she might scream with the pain of it. At last Daniel spoke.

'Then there can be no hope for us.'

'None.' She added quietly, 'You told me once that we all have choices. When those choices are made we must live with them.'

He stared at her, such passion in his eyes that for a moment she feared he might drag her into his arms again and if he did that Kitty did not know if she had the strength left to resist him. Instead he reached out and caught her fingers, carrying them to his lips. Kitty blinked rapidly. She must not cry now. There would be plenty of time for tears later. Gently she disengaged her hands.

'Goodbye, my love,' she whispered as she turned and walked out of the room.

Chapter Thirteen

Three days later Kitty was back at Fallridge, where her mother's silence was harder to bear than the tears and recriminations she had anticipated. The announcement that she was not going to marry Lord Harworth had been met with bewilderment and outrage at Kirkleigh. Lady Leaconham had pleaded and Ann had begged her to reconsider: Bertram adopted the role of martyr but in Lady Harworth Kitty found an ally. The lady had never reconciled herself to the idea of her son taking a penniless bride and she showed more kindness than Kitty thought she deserved.

Lady Harworth arranged for her own carriage to take Kitty back to Fallridge, together with the trunks full of clothes that she had accumulated in London and a purse full of coins. To Kitty it felt as if Lady Harworth was buying her off, but she did not refuse the money, knowing that it would bring some relief to her family, from whom she had so cruelly ripped the possibility of comfort and riches.

A letter from Lady Leaconham followed her, detailing how badly she had been deceived and stating that she would do no more for her goddaughter, to which Mama insisted that Kitty should reply with a very civil apology and an assurance that she would not call upon her for any further assistance.

'Your godmother has been very good but we must now think of what we are going to do with you,' said Mama, sealing up the letter and with it all her hopes. 'Mrs Midgley has put some work my way, so there is a little sewing you can help me with until you have stopped crying all the time.'

'Mama, I do not cry all the time!'

'Do not tell me that you do not water your pillow every night, my love, because the walls are very thin and even Aunt Jane can hear you, and as you know she is very deaf!'

'Very well, I confess that my spirits are a little low.'

'It is my belief that you are nursing a broken heart,' said Mama. 'But I will not ask you to tell me anything about that if you do not wish to do so.'

Kitty bowed her head.

'Oh, Mama, I am such a disappointment to you.'

'Nonsense, you are a credit to me! Why, look at you, so pretty as you are, and with an excellent education, too. I was always afraid Letitia Leaconham was aiming a little too high, hoping to catch a baron for you. I could wish that the squire had not seen the announcement of your betrothal, because it is very hard to hold one's head up knowing that everyone is wondering just what occurred to make you break off the engagement. And of course there are some ill-natured enough to gloat at your misfortune. But we shall take no notice of them.' She looked closely at Kitty. 'Are you sure there were no other gentleman dangling after you, not even one who might be keen enough to seek you out and come courting you?'

An image of Daniel rose before Kitty and the tears that were never far away clogged her throat. She shook her head, unable to trust her voice.

'Well, then, we must think of an occupation for you,' Mama said briskly. 'I had it from Mrs Hobbs that the squire's governess has given notice. Now I suggest you put on your bonnet and take yourself off to the squire's house this minute and put your name forward. You have always been a favourite with the older girls, so I think you have a good chance of securing the position.'

'Really, Mama?'

'Of course! I don't say I wouldn't prefer to see you married, but if it isn't to be then we must find you some other way to support yourself.'

The weeks dragged by and Kitty fell into a regular routine at Fallridge. The squire and his lady agreed to take Kitty on as governess, but she was not required until the end of November, when the present governess was leaving to live with her sister. In the meantime Kitty worked at home and took over many of the household tasks, leaving Aunt Jane and her mother free to concentrate on their sewing. Aunt Jane might tut and bemoan the fact that Kitty's hands were growing rough from the hard work but Kitty preferred the activity, because she found sewing left her mind far too free to think about Daniel.

Even when her hands were red and sore from washing clothes, or her eyes smarting from dust as she swept out the cottage, she could not regret calling off her engagement. It was not just the idea of marriage to a man she didn't love: that might have been bearable. Given time they might even have grown quite fond of one another, but her heart recoiled from the thought of watching Daniel with another woman. Also, knowing that Daniel loved her, it would not have been fair to Ann for Kitty to remain. This way she could at least give them a chance of happiness. This thought was her only consolation as she dragged herself to bed every night, afraid her dreams would be filled with painful visions of Daniel, but disappointed if they were not.

She refused to discuss what had happened at Kirkleigh with her mother, and when Mrs Wythenshawe read for herself in the London newspaper the brief announcement that the betrothal was terminated, she immediately went off to visit the squire and to beg him not to pass on any further newspapers since her interest in London society was now completely at an end. Thus Kitty was spared any news of Daniel and Ann's betrothal. That part of her life was over. She must now look to the future.

* * *

August was almost over when the quiet of the village was disturbed by the arrival of a large travelling carriage. Kitty had been gathering fruit from the hedgerows and was making her way home as the elegant vehicle swept past her. She saw it stop at the green and the driver leaned down to address one of the lads tending the pigs there before setting off again, only to pull up a few yards on, outside of her mother's cottage.

Kitty stopped, her skin prickling with a presentiment of danger. As she watched she saw two ladies descend from the carriage and after a moment they disappeared into the cottage. Kitty breathed again. For a dreadful moment she thought it was Daniel come to find her. Settling her basket more comfortably on her arm, she began to walk towards her home. It must be someone with a commission for Mama. She quickened her step. It might even be a very lucrative order, since the lady could afford to travel in a coach and four.

The cottage was very dark after the bright sunshine and Kitty paused in the doorway, waiting for her eyes to adjust.

'Ah, here is my niece now!' Aunt Jane's greeting was preceded by her hacking cough. 'Come in, Kitty, come in and meet our visitors!'

Kitty stepped in, dropping a slight curtsy towards the two ladies. They were mother and daughter, she guessed, because despite the difference in their ages they were both black-haired and dark-eyed, and both had the same direct gaze that they now turned upon her. Kitty gave them her shy smile, wondering if she had met them before.

'Goodness, you have been busy, my love,' said Aunt Jane, taking the basket from Kitty. 'Wimberries, lovely—and elderberries, too!'

'Yes,' said Kitty. 'I thought it might be a little early for the elderberries, but I found some, not enough for cordial, of course, but we can put them into a pie, I thought...'

'Excellent! I shall take them through to the back. Your mama is gone to fetch down her pattern books but she will be back directly. Oh, but where are my manners? Mrs Blackwood, may I present to you my niece, Katherine. Mrs Midgley recommended us to Mrs Blackwood, Kitty, and she is come to have a gown made up for her daughter—'

Blackwood! Kitty's heart lurched. No wonder they looked so familiar. She shifted uneasily from one foot to the other, painfully aware of her old gown and fruit-stained hands. She welcomed the sound of Mama's footsteps on the stairs.

'Now, I have a number of patterns here that might be suitable, as well as a number of magazines that you might like to look at. My daughter was in London recently and brought them back for me... Oh, Kitty, there you are! I hope Jane has introduced you...'

'Yes, she has,' put in Mrs Blackwood, smiling and looking so like Daniel that Kitty wanted to cry. 'I wonder, Miss Wythenshawe, if you are not too tired from your berry-picking, if you might take a turn around the green with me? There are such a number of books and pictures for Bella to go through that it will take her quite some time, I think. I am sure I can rely upon your mother's judgement to guide her towards a suitable selection from which to make our final choice.'

'Yes, do pray leave me, Mama,' said Miss Blackwood, bending her own mischievous smile upon Kitty. 'I am sure I shall decide much quicker without you sighing over me and growing impatient!'

'You see, Miss Wythenshawe, we are quite *de trop*,' chuckled Mrs Blackwood. 'Let us walk.'

Silently Kitty stepped back out into the sunshine. This matron could only be Daniel's mother—and he had mentioned to her that he had a sister—*a minx* had been his words, and recalling the mischievous twinkle in the girl's dark eyes Kitty could well believe this was she. How unfortunate that Mrs Midgley should recommend Mama as a seamstress for them. However, it was highly unlikely that she would come into contact with Daniel. It was rare for gentlemen to accompany their womenfolk on such errands so there really was no reason to think it would ever be discovered that they had been acquainted.

Mrs Blackwood set out for the green at a brisk pace and Kitty fell into step beside her.

'Well, Miss Wythenshawe, it has been quite a task to track you down.'

Kitty started.

'Our cottage is a little out of the way…'

'That is not what I meant, my dear. I was referring to the way you disappeared after jilting Lord Harworth.'

'Oh.' Kitty swallowed. 'It…it was not deliberate. I merely came home.'

'As any loving daughter would.' Mrs Blackwood nodded approvingly. 'I am sure I cannot blame you, for you could hardly remain at Kirkleigh, could you? And I understand Lady Leaconham has washed her hands of you.' She gave a little tut of disapproval. 'I find it hard to understand why people should object to a broken engagement, when one or other party realises they have made a mistake. It is surely better they discover the sad truth before the knot is irrevocably tied.'

'It would have been a very advantageous match for me,' put in Kitty, determined to be honest. 'I have disappointed so many people by my action. I only hope that Lord Harworth can forgive me, in time.' She added, 'I do not believe his affections were engaged.'

'No, I think you are right. My son tells me he is even now turning his attentions to Miss Leyton-Smythe, a wealthy heiress who has recently arrived in the area.'

Kitty hesitated a little before asking the question that was uppermost in her mind. 'Is—does Mr Blackwood spend a great deal of time at Kirkleigh?'

'Whenever his work can spare him, yes. But that is only to be expected. He is still advising Lord Harworth on his building project, and of course he must visit Miss Harworth.'

Kitty nodded, wondering miserably why it had been so important to ask the question, since the answer only brought her more pain.

Mrs Blackwood continued thoughtfully, 'But I do not believe he is happy.'

Kitty's eyes flew to her face and found herself subjected to a piercing scrutiny.

'I think something occurred at Kirkleigh, something that my son will not divulge, but I hope that you can help me.'

'Oh, no, no,' stammered Kitty. 'I am sure I do not know...'

Mrs Blackwood continued as if she had not spoken.

'You see, when Daniel returned from London he made several references to you, Miss Wythenshawe.'

'He—he did?'

'Yes. He wanted to know if I had heard of the family. I am afraid I could not help him, but I thought perhaps he had formed an attachment, for he was quite preoccupied, you see. Oh, he did not neglect his duties, but I found him not quite so...attentive as he had been. My daughter Bella noticed it as well, and she also noted that Daniel's behaviour changed markedly when Lord Harworth brought a party to Kirkleigh.' A little smile tugged at the corners of her mouth. 'It did not take long to discover that the mysterious Miss Wythenshawe was one of Lord Harworth's guests.'

'But there was nothing—' cried Kitty. 'We hardly saw each other—I mean—'

Mrs Blackwood patted her arm.

'Oh, do not distress yourself, child. Daniel said nothing, I assure you. It was all conjecture on my part, but I think I know my son pretty well: it was very plain to me that Daniel had fallen head over heels in love.'

Kitty wrung her hands. 'No!' she whispered.

'You may imagine my surprise when Daniel came home to tell me he was engaged to Miss Harworth. Of course, he also informed me that you were to marry her brother and I began to see that something had gone terribly wrong.' She stopped, turning to look at Kitty, a mixture of sympathy and enquiry in her dark eyes. 'Am I right to think you did not know of my son's feelings for you?' Miserably Kitty shook her head and heard her companion give an exasperated sigh. 'Oh, the foolish boy.'

'Pray do not blame him, ma'am! He…he believed I wanted to marry Lord Harworth. And…and I thought so, too, for a while.' She fixed her eyes upon Mrs Blackwood, willing her to understand. 'I did not know he l-loved me, until it was too late, until he was engaged to Ann. If I had married her brother then we would have been constantly thrown together. The idea of seeing him every day and not being able to…' She pulled out her handkerchief and resolutely blew her nose. 'Once I knew he…he loved me I was sure I must not stay. If it had been only my feelings that had to be suppressed, every look, every gesture designed to conceal what was in my heart, that would have been painful enough, but to know Daniel was suffering, too—I thought it best to leave. Without me there to remind him, I thought he would soon become accustomed to his new life. Miss Harworth is a splendid young woman: she will make him a good wife.'

'But he loves you.'

Kitty closed her eyes. She said quietly, 'It is an excellent match, ma'am. I believe in the highest circles many married couples begin with mere liking but soon develop a sincere affection. I can only pray that that will happen.'

'I hope so, Miss Wythenshawe, since I can see no way out of the betrothal.'

'I am so sorry.'

'So, too, am I. You have been very foolish, the pair of you, but what's done is done and we must look to the future. Tell me your plans, Miss Wythenshawe.'

'Me? Well, I must earn my living,' said Kitty. 'I am to become a governess in November.'

'And is that what you want?'

Kitty spread her hands.

'It is a good situation; the present governess is only leaving because she is obliged to return to the family home. She has told me the squire and his lady are very considerate employers.'

'And you turned down marriage to Lord Harworth for this?' There was a note of wonder in Mrs Blackwood's voice. Silently Kitty spread her hands again, too miserable to speak. 'Well, you must let me do something for your family.'

'Oh, no, please! That is not necessary—'

'It is in some part my son's fault that you are reduced to this.'

'It was my decision,' replied Kitty, raising her head. 'I could not accept charity, especially from you, madam.'

'You must accept it for your mother and your aunt,' came the firm reply. 'They will not be able to continue with their sewing for many more years, and if they remain in that damp little house their health will soon fail. I shall set up a fund of some sort to provide them with a small income. My lawyer will arrange everything. It shall be anonymous—your mother will believe it is some benevolent acquaintance of your father's. Will that do?'

After a moment Kitty nodded.

'I want nothing for myself, but I will accept your offer for my mother's sake, Mrs Blackwood, and thank you for it.'

'Good. Then it is settled. Now let us return to the house and see what unsuitable designs Bella has chosen for her new gown!'

'…what say you, my dear?'

'Hmm? Yes, if you wish, Mama.'

Daniel had no idea what his mother had asked him. His thoughts had been far away, as they were so often these days. He knew his mother's eyes were upon him and gave her an apologetic smile across the breakfast table.

'I am sorry, Mama, what did you say to me?'

'It hardly matters, my dear. I was only saying that Cook has procured a couple of rabbits and I wondered if we should add them to the dinner tonight. Your father is bringing your uncle back to dine with us and he is very partial to rabbit.'

'Then by all means have them,' he replied. 'I regret I shall not be here; I am promised to dine at Kirkleigh.'

'Oh. I had thought that now your work on Lord Harworth's mill was complete you would have a little more time for yourself. You are looking tired, my son: I am well aware that you have spent two hours at the mill already this morning. I wish you would stay home and rest today. I am sure you are eager to hear from your uncle how Barrowford Mill is faring.'

He said quietly, 'Miss Harworth expects me.'

There was a heartbeat's hesitation.

'Of course,' nodded Mrs Blackwood. 'You must not disappoint her.'

After breakfast Daniel excused himself and went off to the study. There were letters to be answered before he could set off for Kirkleigh. He yawned. Perhaps it was not strictly necessary for him to visit the mill every morning, but when his father was away he liked to assure himself that everything was in order for the day.

He sat down at the desk and pulled the pile of letters towards him. There was nothing urgent but he wanted to deal with them all before setting off for Kirkleigh. A tiny voice in his head whispered that he was putting off the journey. It was true. He was reluctant to spend more time at Kirkleigh than was necessary. There were too many memories. With something like a growl he forced himself to concentrate on his correspondence, working his way doggedly through the pile of letters until each one had been answered. The official documents that had arrived from London received no more than a cursory glance before being put aside to discuss with his father.

The chiming of the church clock reminded him that it was getting late. Reluctantly he sent a message to the stables to have Marnie saddled up.

* * *

The ride across the moors toward Kirkleigh usually provided him with some relief from the deadly depression that dogged him, but today he could not seem to shake it off. It was a beautiful day, the sun blazing down from a cloudless sky on the purple heather, which was fading now that summer was ending. He told himself he should be enjoying the freedom of the journey, the refreshing breeze on his face and the skylark trilling above him, but it was no good. After a brief gallop he allowed Marnie to slow down and pick her own way along the well-worn path while he gave himself up to thinking about Kitty. He rarely allowed himself the agonising luxury of wondering what she was doing, if she was happy, but that did not mean she was not constantly in his thoughts. Every waking moment conjured a picture of her: when he poured himself a cup of coffee in the morning the dark liquid was the colour of her hair; when he was surrounded by the roar and clatter of the spinning shop he could hear her asking questions about the mill and its workers. At Kirkleigh it was even worse, for everywhere he looked there were reminders of Kitty—taking her riding lesson in the park, drinking tea in the drawing room. When he sat down to dinner he expected at any moment to see her peeping at him between the epergne and the candlesticks. There was no escape from her—even at night the sky reminded him of the time he had brought her back from Chapeltown. Sometimes she was so real to him he thought that if only he looked around quickly enough he would see her at his shoulder.

Angrily he shook his head. It did no good to dwell on the past. Ann was waiting for him at Kirkleigh and not for the world would he have her know how bitterly he regretted asking her to marry him. As Kitty had said to him, the very last time he had seen her, they had to live by their choices.

He straightened his shoulders. This maudlin behaviour would help no one. Neither would being late for dinner. With a flick of his whip and a word of encouragement to his horse he settled himself in the saddle and cantered on towards Kirkleigh.

He rode Marnie to the stables and entered the house by a side door, where he was surprised to find himself accosted by one of the footmen, who informed him that Lord Harworth and his sister were awaiting him in the study.

'I thought you might be sitting in the garden on such a lovely day,' he said, tossing his hat and gloves on to a chair. 'Is there some business to discuss, my lord? I thought we had covered everything on the mill.'

'We have, Blackwood, and the building work is progressing smoothly.' Lord Harworth replied. 'This has nothing to do with the mill.'

Daniel looked from Ann to her brother, his brow contracting a little.

'Is something amiss?'

Lord Harworth picked up a newspaper from the desk.

'I need you to explain this.' He held out the paper. 'I have just read a report of the petition presented to Parliament by the West Riding Anti-Slavery Society—you did not tell me you were a member of the committee.'

Daniel's brows rose fractionally.

'The subject never arose.'

'I thought I made my views on this matter perfectly clear.'

'You did,' agreed Daniel. 'They are not *my* views, however, and I have never made any secret of that. The sooner we stop trading in slaves the better.'

'You do not know what you are saying, Blackwood. That way lies anarchy! You have seen what is happening in France. If we show weakness now...'

'It is not weakness to object to these poor souls being bought and sold and then worked to death for profit.'

'This is dangerous nonsense,' retorted his lordship. 'Who knows where it would end? Such radical views must not be encouraged. I would be obliged if you would send a note to the newspaper immediately, declaring that you have withdrawn your support.'

'I cannot do that, my lord.'

Ann rose from her seat, her manner unusually serious.

'You see, Brother, I told you he was a man of principle.' She turned to Daniel. 'Perhaps you do not understand: Bertram has explained it all to me. We have plantations in the West Indies and depend upon the slaves there to work the land. I admit I was shocked when I learned of the horrific conditions endured by some of these poor wretches, but we could work towards improving their lot.'

'I am very sorry but that is not good enough. The trade must be ended. England will not become bankrupt, as some predict. We will find a way around the problems...'

'And what of your mills?' Lord Harworth challenged him. 'There are many who say your workers are little better than slaves.'

Daniel drew himself up.

'You have seen for yourself the conditions in my mill: I pay an honest wage and look to the welfare of my workers and their families. One does not have to be a Quaker to run a mill well.'

'Very well, very well,' said Lord Harworth testily. 'I admit that your mills are exemplary, but what of this slavery petition? My name cannot be connected to that.'

Daniel said with great deliberation, 'I will not withdraw, my lord.'

A long silence ensued, broken only by the ticking of the clock on the mantelpiece.

'Very well, Blackwood,' Lord Harworth said at last. 'I may have to accept your views and deal with you on matters of business, but this is not something I can allow in my own family. I have already discussed this with Ann and explained to her that if you will not change your mind, then the engagement between you must end. I will forbid the banns!'

He waited expectantly but Daniel made no reply. He glanced

at Ann. Her eyes were fixed upon him but he could not read her thoughts.

He said quietly, 'If that is the case then I am very sorry for it, but I cannot in conscience withdraw my support for this cause.'

'Very well, if that is your final word.' Lord Harworth turned to his sister. 'Ann?'

She rose, drawing the diamond ring from her finger and holding it out to him.

'Do not feel too sorry for me, Daniel,' she said. 'Being engaged to you was not half as much fun as I expected it to be.'

He nodded, relieved. 'Perhaps that is because I am not the right man for you.'

'Perhaps not. I have thought for some time now that Garston might suit me better. He is family, you see. He understands our position.'

'Then I wish you every happiness, Miss Harworth.' Daniel picked up his hat and gloves. 'In the circumstances I think it would be best if I did not stay for dinner. Please convey my apologies to Lady Harworth.'

'I will.' Lord Harworth gave a dismissive nod. 'I bid you good day, Blackwood.'

As Daniel reached the door Ann called to him. He turned.

'When you find Kitty will you give her my love?' she said, smiling a little. 'And tell her there is no ill will in this house towards her. Is there, Bertram?'

Lord Harworth shifted uncomfortably and gazed down at the carpet, tracing the pattern with the toe of one beautifully polished boot.

'No, none,' he muttered. 'Pray tell Miss Wythenshawe I realise now that our marriage would have been a grave mistake.' He looked up. 'Tell her she is welcome at Kirkleigh at any time. As are you, sir, as long as you leave your opinions at the gate!'

Chapter Fourteen

'Oh, dear, I cannot make head nor tail of this letter.'

Mrs Wythenshawe passed the paper to her sister. 'Jane, dear, you must read it and tell me what you think of it.'

Aunt Jane coughed and put the letter in her lap.

'Well, it is from a London lawyer.' She cleaned her spectacles and settled them back more firmly on her nose. 'I do not claim to understand every word of it, but it says there is an annuity due to the widow of Mr Walter Charles Wythenshawe.' She looked up, her mouth open in astonishment. 'Three hundred pounds a year!'

Kitty gave a little gasp. Mrs Blackwood had kept her word, but Kitty had not expected her to be so generous.

'And you have no idea who is our mysterious benefactor?' Aunt Jane handed the letter back. 'My dear sister, can you recall no acquaintance of Walter's who would do this, and after all this time, too?'

'No, I can think of no one.' She looked up, her eyes shining. 'We shall be very comfortable now! We shall be able to rent a better house. Kitty will not need to become a governess! And we will not need to take in any more sewing!' Mama gave a little skip as she crossed to the little table beneath the window. 'I shall reply to this immediately, for the lawyer asks me to advise him of the bank I wish to use to receive the money. Oh, dear, how exciting! I am sure I shall not be able to set a stitch today!'

'Then do not, Mama,' Kitty urged her, smiling. 'You should take a holiday.'

'And so I shall, my love, but first we have Miss Blackwood's two gowns to finish. They are promised for tomorrow morning, and no matter how rich we may become, I will not go back on my word!'

It was Kitty's intention to be at home the following day. She wanted to meet Mrs Blackwood and thank her for her generosity, but a sleepless night sapped her courage. To see Daniel's mother again, or his sister, would only reinforce the feelings of desolation and loss that constantly dragged at her spirits. She rose from her bed, determined not to meet them. She would pen a letter to Mrs Blackwood. A much better idea, she decided, since she would be able to choose her words carefully and ensure that her gratitude was properly expressed.

Having made her decision, Kitty dressed quickly and announced that she was going out.

'I am going to see…going to see…' Kitty searched around in her mind for a name. If only her mother had not kept her quite so confined she might have comfortably spent the day with someone in the village, but her mother had never mixed with their neighbours and there was no one Kitty knew well enough to call upon unannounced. She thought with regret of Ann Harworth: by giving up the chance to marry Ann's brother, she had lost her only real friend. The pain of that disappointment gave her an even greater desire to escape. 'I am going to walk over the moors to Coldclough Valley. To collect elderberries.'

'But that is such a long way,' declared her mother. 'It will take you the best part of the day!'

'I know, but all the ripe berries around the village have been picked and the valley is particularly well stocked with elders.'

'But Mrs Blackwood is coming this morning,' protested Aunt Jane. 'Will you not stay to see her? Upon her last visit she showed you such a flattering amount of attention…'

'Then please, make my apologies, Aunt,' said Kitty hastily. 'I am sure you do not need me—indeed, it will be very cramped in here if we all stay. Besides, I fear the weather is going to break and if I don't collect the berries today they may all be ruined.' She picked up her basket. 'Do not be anxious for me, I shall be back before dark!' And with that she whisked herself out of the house.

Kitty hurried out of the village and was soon following the path across the moors. It was such a warm day that she tucked her shawl into her basket. The sun burned through the thin muslin of her gown, warming her shoulders. She loved the empty moors on days such as this when the late August sunshine seemed to acquire an added brilliance, a sudden, flaring reminder that autumn would soon arrive.

By the time Coldclough Valley was in sight she was hot and flushed with her exertion, but her spirits had risen considerably. Perhaps the future was not quite so bleak after all, and although her spirit balked at taking charity from Mrs Blackwood, she could not deny that the annuity settled upon her mother would make life considerably easier.

'And Mrs Blackwood was very right,' she told herself, coming to a halt on the path. 'We would not have been in this situation if I had never met her son. Horrid, horrid man!'

As she tilted her face up to catch the sun a sudden movement attracted her eye and she looked back the way she had come. There in the distance was the small black shape of a horse and rider. Kitty gasped.

'It could be anyone,' she muttered, trying to calm her racing heart.

She blinked and rubbed her hand across her eyes. The figure was too far away to pick out any detail, but instinct told her it was

Daniel. The big black horse, the upright figure—it *had* to be Daniel. As she stared, the rider changed course and began to move more quickly. He was heading in her direction.

'Oh, heavens!'

She picked up her skirts and ran towards the clough. He was such a long way behind her, she only had to reach the wooded valley and she might be able to evade him. She reached the ridge and hurried down the path into the valley, allowing her pace to slow a little once she was sure Daniel could no longer see her. She was dismayed to see how far she would have to walk before she reached the woods, but there was no choice: the river cutting through the valley bottom might be small but it was very deep and it effectively blocked her path. She must go either up or downstream. She chose to head towards the woods. She half-ran, half-scrambled down the bank, thankful that the ground beside the tumbling waters was covered with a short, springy turf that allowed her to make good progress.

But not good enough. All too soon she saw Daniel on the ridge above her. She began to run, but he urged his horse to descend the shallow bank diagonally to cut her off. She heard the jingle of harness and the thud of hooves. Speed was useless. Kitty slowed again to a walk, turning to glare at Daniel.

'How did you find me?' she called out.

'Your mother described to me the path you had taken. You have her eyes, you know: a beautiful moss green. She is a most delightful woman: I left her taking tea with Bella and my own mother. I think they will get on very well.'

Kitty refused to be pleased.

'I do not want to talk to you. Pray go away.'

'But I want to talk to *you*.'

'There is nothing to say!'

'But there is. Kitty, listen to me—'

'Go away!' she cried. 'How dare you come here and—and torture me like this! I told you I would have nothing more to do with you.'

'But I am a free man—Ann and I are no longer engaged.'

'So you have broken her heart, too!'

'No, it was—! Kitty, hell and damnation, *will* you stand still for a moment!' He jumped down from his horse and came towards her.

'No!' Kitty stopped, putting up her hand as if to hold him off. 'Do not come any nearer. If you do I will...I will jump in the beck!'

His lips twitched. It pierced her heart to remember how much she loved his smile.

'That would be a little extreme, don't you think?'

'No!' she retorted angrily. 'You have b-brought me nothing but pain: I would walk through *fire* rather than talk to you again!'

That wiped the smile from his face, but his consternation cut even deeper into her heart.

'I did not cry off, Kitty, you have my word on it. You see—'

She said quickly, 'I made a solemn vow that I was done with you for ever, so whatever tricks you used to force Ann to jilt you they are wasted! I will not have anything more to do with you!'

She began to move again, hurrying along the riverbank. For a short while she thought Daniel had stopped following her, but a quick glance behind showed that he had merely paused to remove his coat and throw it over the saddle.

'Do you know, it is far too hot for so much exertion. I wish you would slow down.'

He spoke in a conversational tone, as if they were enjoying a gentle stroll together. Anger was warring with frustration in Kitty. How dare he torment her in this way? Ahead she could see a bridge across the stream, a series of flat stone slabs supported on boulders in the stream bed. If she could cross that, the path wound up past a small cottage where a wisp of smoke trailed from the chimney. Perhaps the owner would allow her to rest inside and shut the door upon Daniel.

'Kitty, will you please stop and allow me to explain!' He reached for her and she sprinted away from him.

'Go away, Daniel. Go away and leave me in peace!'

She had reached the bridge. Gingerly she stepped on to the first slab. It wobbled slightly beneath her. A few more steps took her to the centre, but Daniel had caught up with her. His hand shot out and gripped her arm, stopping her in her tracks. She tried to shake him off.

'How dare you touch me? Let me go this instant, you...you fiend!'

'I will let you go, if you promise to listen to me and to stop acting like some angry fishwife!' Kitty froze, furious at his insult. He was scowling down at her, his chest heaving. 'Well,' he said at last. 'If I let you go will you promise not to run away?'

'Yes.' The word forced itself out between her clenched teeth.

He nodded and released her arm. Kitty glared at him as he stood beside her on the narrow bridge. Every slight, every insult she had suffered at his hands returning to her mind, magnified tenfold. Deliberately, she put her hands against his chest and pushed.

If Daniel had not been about to step away from her it would never have happened, but he was momentarily distracted and Kitty's push caught him off balance. He twisted, his arms thrown wide as he toppled into the river. Kitty watched in a mixture of horror and fascination as he disappeared beneath the water, only to surface a few moments' later, coughing and spluttering. He rose to his feet, standing thigh-deep in the fast-flowing water.

Kitty's hands flew to her mouth. A fleeting, sickening dread that he might have been seriously hurt on the stony river bed was replaced with fear for her own safety as he stood braced against the current, glaring up at her through the heavy curtain of wet black hair that clung to his forehead. She swallowed, transported back to their very first meeting, when she had addressed him as a servant and he had scowled at her so blackly that she had been afraid he would drag her from the gig and strangle her. That fear of reprisals returned to her now. Then, to her astonishment, she saw the gleam of amusement in his eyes. He threw back his head and laughed. A deep, rich sound that drew a reluctant smile from her in response.

'*Touché,* madam! No doubt you think that a sweet justice.' He grinned up at her. 'Do you consider yourself revenged now for my dropping you in that muddy ford?'

'Well, yes,' she replied frankly. 'I do!'

She reached down her hand to him, but as soon as his fingers curled around hers he gave a tug and she toppled off the bridge, landing with a splash in the water beside him.

'Oh! Oh, you…you…!' She spluttered and coughed as he pulled her to her feet beside him.

'You did not think I would let you get away with that, did you?'

Kitty put up her hands to wipe the wet hair from her eyes, a furious retort rising to her lips, but it died when she saw him laughing down at her. A gurgle of laughter bubbled up inside her and instead of pushing Daniel away she found herself clinging to his arm, giggling helplessly.

Still laughing, they struggled to the bank and dragged themselves out, lying side by side on the short grass. Daniel reached for her hand.

'I did not cry off from my engagement,' he said, suddenly serious. 'Neither did Ann. It was her brother who withdrew his consent.'

She sat up.

'Lord Harworth? Why should he do that—oh, poor Ann!'

'He objected to my liberal views. And you must not think Ann was heartbroken, I suspect she was as relieved as I was to be released from the engagement. She is thinking of marrying Leaconham.'

'Garston!' Kitty stared at him, astounded. 'How could she prefer Garston to…?'

'I am only too thankful that she does prefer him,' retorted Daniel, pulling her down to him. 'But that is not important now. What is important is that I am free.' He reached up a hand and cupped her face, her wet hair clinging around his fingers. 'Since neither Ann nor I cried off, you are not bound to refuse me.' He gently pulled her face down and kissed her. 'I love you, Kitty,' he whispered. 'Say yes. Say you will marry me.'

'Oh, Daniel!' Kitty stopped, unable to say more because of the constriction in her throat. Silently she nodded and with an exultant gasp Daniel pulled her back into his arms, rolling her beneath him as he covered her face with hot kisses.

'Kitty, you are crying.' He broke away. 'Dearest, what is it?

She sat up, shaking her head.

'N-nothing,' she managed, smiling mistily through her tears. 'It is j-just that I am s-so happy!' The salty tears on her cheeks were hot and made her aware of her wet gown, which was rapidly cooling. 'We must move, and quickly,' she said, struggling to get up. 'It will not do to grow chilled.'

'We will call at the cottage,' said Daniel, scrambling to his feet and nodding towards the little house at the top of the bank.

'Your horse is still on the other side,' she remarked.

Daniel gave a long whistle.

'Marnie, come on, girl! Come!' With a toss of her fine head the black mare stepped up to the bridge and daintily trotted across. 'Horses are like women,' he said, mischief glinting in his eyes. 'Better when they are well trained.'

With a laugh he dodged the blow she aimed at him. Then, as she began to pummel him he caught her wrists and whipped her hands behind her back, pulling her against him and kissing her soundly.

'How on earth am I to quarrel with you,' she said severely, when at last she could speak again, 'when you take such advantage of me?'

'I do not want us to quarrel,' he said, lightly kissing the end of her nose. 'I want only to make you happy for ever more.' He put his arm about her waist. 'Shall you walk up the bank or would you like me to put you up on Marnie?'

'Walk, I think. The exertion will warm us.'

With Daniel's arm around her they started up the bank. An old woman in a grey dress hurried down towards them, trailing a large shawl from one hand.

'Oh, my goodness, whatever has happened to you?' She demanded as she drew closer. 'Oh, my poor dears, took a tumble in the beck, did you? You must come in and dry yourselves. Quickly now.' She wrapped the shawl around Kitty's shoulders and took her arm to hurry her towards the cottage.

'Thank you, mother,' said Daniel, falling into step beside them. 'We saw the smoke from your chimney and were going to ask if we could warm ourselves by your fire.'

'Aye, of course. And you're very lucky that I have kept it in, only I fancied a drop o' soup before settin' off for t'village. It won't take a minute to get it blazing again.' When they reached the small gate in the wall that bounded her garden the old woman turned to Daniel. 'You can tie that great brute of a horse to the gate. No one will take him while you and your lady are indoors, and I don't want 'im eatin' my herbs!'

Meekly Daniel did as he was bid while the old woman led Kitty into the house. After the bright sunshine the room seemed very dark at first, but Kitty's eyes soon grew accustomed and she saw that they were standing in a small but very tidy chamber, most of the space being taken up by a large spinning wheel. The room was bare of comforts save for a small cushioned settle and a colourful rag rug before the fire. The old woman immediately set to work stirring up the coals before taking a few small logs from the basket to place on the top.

'Please, mother, do not use all your fuel for us,' said Daniel quickly.

The old woman waved aside his protest.

'Lord love ye, sir, if ye don't get warm you'll be catching your death, right enough. Besides, my son Jack brought me over a sack o' coal only last week, so we're not short o' fuel.' She pointed to a door behind them. 'Beyond there is my bedroom, sir. If you and your lady will remove thy wet things I'll hang 'em out to dry. An hour or so in the sun and with this breeze they'll be good as new. And don't you be afraid to give me your shirt and britches, young man: I have sons of my own, so you've nowt I haven't seen before!'

Kitty was aware of Daniel's eyes upon her, but she said nothing. She walked into the bedchamber and began to struggle out of her sodden gown.

'She thinks we are man and wife,' muttered Daniel, following her into the room.

'I know.'

He pulled a ring from his little finger and held it out to her.

'Here, wear this. I would not embarrass the woman by having her guess the truth.' He picked up Kitty's hand and slipped the ring on to her wedding finger. 'I hope you will allow me to replace it with the real thing soon enough.'

Kitty's cheeks burned and she turned away, giving her attention to removing her wet clothes. She stripped down to her shift and looked round for the woman's shawl to put over her shoulders but Daniel had already appropriated it to wrap around his waist, his clothes lying in a wet puddle on the stone floor. She held her breath, unable to tear her eyes from his naked torso. He seemed to fill the little room; his broad shoulders and muscled arms still glistened with damp and she was shocked by her desire to put out her hand and touch the black curling hair on his chest.

'We, um…' She swallowed, not meeting his eyes. 'We should ask our hostess if she has a towel we may use to finish drying ourselves.'

'Just a moment.' He picked up a thin coverlet from the bed, folded it diagonally and threw it over her shoulders. 'There. Do you feel more comfortable now?'

Daniel was smiling at her, and Kitty wondered if he knew that it was not standing before him in her shift that was unsettling her but her desire to feast her eyes upon his body. Quickly she scooped up their clothes and carried them into the other room. The old woman took them from her.

'You leave these to me, my dear, and sit yerself down in front o'fire until you are dry again.' She gave a little chuckle when Daniel walked in and she saw the use he had made of her shawl but she said nothing and hurried away to hang out their clothes.

'You have not yet given me an answer,' said Daniel, sitting down beside Kitty on the narrow settle beside the fire.

'An...an answer?'

'You have not said that you will marry me.'

'After this I do not think we have a choice, sir,' she said, trying to speak lightly.

'No!' Angrily he gripped her arms, turning her to face him. 'I do not want you forced by circumstances to become my wife. I want you to choose me—*me,* Kitty, do you understand? For better or worse, richer or poorer. It must be your decision, freely made. If you are not sure then I will remove myself from your presence until we are fit to return to Fallridge—'

'That will not be necessary,' she said quickly. 'I w-want nothing better than to be your wife, Daniel.' She added quietly, 'For no other reason than that I love you, with all my heart.'

She smiled, her spirits soaring when she saw the glow of delight in his eyes.

His hands tightened and he was about to drag her into his arms when the old lady came bustling in again.

'An hour, two at the most, and your clothes will be dry.' She hesitated, took a couple of steps towards the fire, then stopped again.

'Thank you, mother, but do not let us keep you from your work, if you have spinning to do...'

'Ah, well, you see I hadn't finished my spinning when Mr Jobbins called first thing this morning.' She pointed to a large cloth bag beside the door. 'I said I would take 'em on t'village as soon as they was done. I get paid by the hank, you see—in a good week I can make five shillings or more, but what with Jack comin' round yesterday, and bringin' the bairns to see me—well, they're bonny children, to be sure, but I got behind...'

'Oh, please, if you have to go out then we will leave,' said Kitty rising.

The old woman waved her back into her seat.

'That you won't. You are quite welcome to stay here while I go out. I was planning to spend the night with our Jack, so you can stay here as long as you wish.'

'Thank you, mother,' said Daniel. 'You may be sure we will lock up behind us.'

The old woman gave a cackle of laughter.

'Bless you, sir, there's no need for that.' She held out her hands and looked around. 'There's nothing here worth the trouble o' stealing. And besides it's rare that anyone passes this way. No, my dears, you sit there as long as you want, there'll be no one to bother ye. You'll find a bit o' broth in the kettle by the fire: you're welcome to that and if you want water the pump is just outside the door,' She gave another toothless cackle. 'Although I'd say you'd both had enough water today! Well, I'll bid you good day then.'

She picked up her bundle.

'Goodbye, mistress, and thank you!' called Kitty.

The woman gave them a final wave and went out, closing the door behind her.

Silence settled around them. Daniel looked down at his bare feet, suddenly feeling awkward. What was he doing here, sitting near-naked in a spinster's cottage? A glance at Kitty showed him that she, too, was uneasy.

'What a good soul,' she said with forced brightness. 'And trusting, to leave us here alone.'

'She saw the quality of our clothes. She knows we are not vagabonds.' Eager for a distraction, Daniel moved over to the fire and poked at the logs until they were blazing merrily. He glanced back at Kitty. 'Your hair is still wet. Will you sit a little closer to the fire?'

'Yes, please.' Kitty rose and rubbed her arms as Daniel tried to move the settle, which creaked alarmingly. She laughed. 'I think we should leave it where it is. I am afraid if we move it from the wall it will fall apart. But I have an idea!'

Daniel watched her pull the cushions from the settle and put them on the rug in front of the fire. Then she knelt down with her back to the fire, shaking her hair loose. His breath caught in his throat as he watched it ripple down her back like a dark waterfall. Daniel quickly turned away, knowing the shawl wrapped around his hips would not conceal his desire from her.

'Daniel, will you not sit beside me?'

She spoke softly but he heard the wistfulness in her voice. He dropped down on to the rug behind her and put his hand to her hair, allowing the dark tresses to flow through his fingers like silk. With a sigh she tilted back her head and rested against him, her eyes closed. It was irresistible: Daniel leaned forward to place a gentle kiss on the slim column of her neck. Her hand came up to his cheek. She twisted round to face him, her mouth seeking his. Daniel had intended nothing more than a tender kiss but as soon as their lips met she trembled against him and a ripple of excitement flowed between them as her lips parted and their tongues engaged in a sensuous, silent conversation. He wrapped her in his arms and eased her down on to the rug. She clung to him. The firm swell of her breasts pressed against his chest, only the thin fabric of her shift between them. He raised his head, trying to contain his excitement, then he began to kiss her again, his lips caressing her eyes, her cheeks. He trailed his tongue along her jaw and lightly over her neck. His fingers clenched on the folds of the shift. He wanted to remove it, since it was the last barrier between his body and Kitty's soft white skin. She struggled beneath him and immediately he pushed himself away from her, determined that he would in no way force his will upon her.

Kitty sat up. The cottage was silent save for the fire crackling behind her and Daniel's ragged breathing. Keeping her eyes fixed on his face, she crossed her arms in front of her and took hold of the shift, lifting it cleanly away and upwards in one smooth movement. As she raised her arms above her head Daniel reached out for her. She gasped. Her arms and head were temporarily imprisoned in the fine linen, leaving Daniel free to plunder her breasts, cupping them in his hands, burying his face between them before fastening his mouth on one tender bud and causing a shaft of white-hot desire to drive through her. She threw off the offending material and reached for him, driving her fingers through his hair, clasping him to her as she fell back against the cushions. She had no control over her body. It arched and moved against him, inviting his hands to caress her. She moaned with pleasure as his fingers traced a line from the inside of her knee and along her thigh, gasping as those same fingers moved into her and roused her to even higher realms of delight. His fingers caressed effortlessly, she was slick with desire, opening for him, raising her hips in blatant invitation. In one swift move he rolled over her and she felt his aroused body pressed against her. His hands slid under her hips, lifting her up to receive him. Kitty clung to him, her fingers digging into his back as he entered her. A tiny gasp, a tiny pain, then the joy and exhilaration of their union overwhelmed her. She tried to follow his lead, moving with him, a fierce excitement coursing through every part of her body. She was flying, soaring, her senses on fire as they moved together. She was vaguely aware that Daniel was holding himself in check, moving for her pleasure rather than his own, but she could do nothing about it, for he was lifting her to such a height of pleasure that she was helpless beneath him, crying out as her body exploded. Deep within her, muscles were clenching in spasm and with an almost painful pleasure. She clung to Daniel, whispering his name, knowing they were still joined. He held her safe in his arms as her body relaxed against his, a perfect fit. She was filled with a pleasant torpor with Daniel's hands gently caressing her body. Then he was kissing her, feather-light touches along her neck, fanning the flames of desire until her body began to pulse again. This time she pushed against him, revelling in her power to make him gasp and moan with delight. She quivered as he took her once more to the peak of excitement and this time he was with her, pushing, tensing and crying out as they soared together before falling back to earth, clinging to one another.

They lay before the fire, wrapped in each other's arms, while the sun moved across the sky.

'We must get back,' murmured Kitty.

'Soon.' Daniel nibbled at her ear.

Kitty gave a little gasp and struggled to sit up.

'We will be missed,' she said urgently. 'Your mother will be waiting…'

'No, we agreed she would take Bella home. I told her it might take me some time to…persuade you.'

Kitty turned to look at him. He was lying naked beside her, re- minding her of the statues displayed in many of the grand houses she had visited with her godmother, although there was nothing cold or lifeless about Daniel. She reached out to touch him, her fingers splaying through the crisp black hair of his chest.

'And…was I difficult to persuade?'

'Very.' With a growl Daniel pulled her back into his arms. 'I am not convinced I have yet succeeded.'

They made love again and this time it was even more delight- ful as they explored new ways to please each other as their naked bodies tangled together. Later they took great pleasure in dressing each other, with much laughter and fevered kisses until at last they were ready to leave the little cottage. Daniel dropped a handful of coins in a cup on the hearth.

'I would give her ten times as much if I had it on me,' he de- clared, grinning. 'The old mother has secured a wife for me.' He caught Kitty up in his arms and kissed her. 'You must marry me now, you shameless wench!'

She wound her arms about his neck and kissed him back fiercely until with a groan he put his hands on her waist and put her away from him.

'If you do not behave I will have to take you again,' he muttered. 'Come along, we'll walk to the top of the clough, then Marnie will carry us both home.'

'I fear we will be very late,' remarked Kitty. 'And I was supposed to be collecting elderberries. What shall I tell Mama?'

'We will tell her the truth, that you lost your basket in the beck.'

'And my shawl, too! Oh dear, she will be so vexed with me!'

With a low laugh Daniel turned her to face him, catching her face between her hands.

'I doubt she will give your shawl a thought when we tell her that you are going to be married!'

It was growing dark as they rode over the moor, Kitty sitting across the saddle in front of Daniel, enveloped in his arms. The sun had disappeared below the horizon and the first stars twinkled in the sky. Daniel lowered his head to rest his cheek briefly on her curls.

'Happy?' he murmured.

'Mmmm.'

He reached for her left hand and raised it to his lips, kissing the finger that bore the little ring he had given her.

'Tomorrow I shall buy you a diamond ring. The best I can find.'

'Not too big,' she protested. 'I should be afraid of losing it, and I want to wear it, always.'

'If you lose it I shall buy you another,' he said grandly. 'And you must have emeralds to replace the ones you left behind at Kirkleigh.'

Kitty shook her head. 'Those jewels were never mine. They were intended for the next Lady Harworth.' She wrapped her arms around him and snuggled closer. 'I am so relieved it will not be me.'

'You are not sorry, then, to be marrying a mere tradesman?'

She chuckled.

'I am not, but I fear Mama might be disappointed.'

'I have news that may be of some consolation to her.'

She sat up.

'News?'

He grinned at her.

'My father is to become a baronet. He will be Sir Samuel Blackwood.'

'Oh, Daniel, how wonderful! How long have you known of this?'

'Since I left London. I had several meetings in Whitehall while I was there, you see. My father has been helping Pitt with, ah, shall we say, financial support. The baronetcy is by way of a reward. And as it is hereditary, you will become a lady after all!'

She hugged him.

'You are right. Mama will be delighted.'

'And you are not?'

'It does not matter to me at all. I only want to be your wife, Daniel.'

He brought Marnie to a halt.

'Are you sure, Kitty?'

'Perfectly sure.'

He cupped her face and kissed her.

'I love you, Kitty Wythenshawe.'

'To think we almost lost each other.' She put her arms around him, resting her head on his shoulder, gazing up at the darkening sky.

'I am afraid if it had not been for me you could have married your baron,' he said ruefully. 'I will do my best to make sure you never regret it.'

She looked up at him, her eyes shining softly.

'You told me once I was trying to catch the moon, do you remember? What I have now is so much better, Daniel. I have your love: I have the stars.'

* * * * *

HISTORICAL

Novels coming in August 2011

MARRIED TO A STRANGER
Louise Allen

When Sophia Langley learns of her estranged fiancé's death, the
last thing she expects is a shock proposal from his twin brother!
A marriage of convenience it may be, but Sophie cannot fight
the desire she feels for her reluctant husband…

A DARK AND BROODING GENTLEMAN
Margaret McPhee

Sebastian Hunter's nights, once spent carousing, are now spent in the
shadows of Blackloch Hall—that is until Phoebe Allardyce interrupts
his brooding. After catching her thieving, Sebastian resolves to keep
an eye on this provocative little temptress!

SEDUCING MISS LOCKWOOD
Helen Dickson

Against all advice, Juliet Lockwood begins working for the
notorious Lord Dominic Lansdowne. Juliet's addition to his staff
is pure temptation for Dominic, but honour binds him from
seduction…*unless, of course, he makes her his wife!*

THE HIGHLANDER'S RETURN
Marguerite Kaye

Alasdhair Ross was banished for courting the laird's daughter,
Ailsa. Six years later, toils and troubles have shaped him into a
man set on returning to claim what's rightfully his. When Ailsa
sees him, she knows a reckoning is irresistibly inevitable…